DEATH TAKES A SUBLET

"It would be great to have a space to work out." Nick stepped to the doorway. "What do you think, Maggie?"

She was down the hall, looking into the little front room, the one that sported the oriel window over the main door. For a moment she remained there, still, not answering.

"Do you like the place?" Len prompted.

She turned back to them slowly, and Nick, suddenly concerned, took a step toward her. But it was Len she answered.

"Yes," she said, "it's a great place. There's only one problem.

"There's a corpse in it."

MURDER UNRENOVATED

(Maggie Ryan 1972)

P. M. CARLSON

BANTAM BOOKS
NEW YORK • TORONTO • LONDON • SYDNEY • AUCKLAND

MURDER UNRENOVATED

A Bantam Book / January 1988

*Grateful acknowledgment for use of lines of verse by
Dorothy Parker is made to the Property of the Estate of
Dorothy Parker and the NAACP. Permission granted by
Joyce H. Knox, Associate General Counsel, of the NAACP.*

ISBN 0-553-18522-5

Published simultaneously in the United States and Canada

---

*Bantam Books are published by Bantam Books, a division of Bantam
Doubleday Dell Publishing Group, Inc. Its trademark, consisting of the
words "Bantam Books" and the portrayal of a rooster, is Registered in U.S.
Patent and Trademark Office and in other countries. Marca Registrada.
Bantam Books, 666 Fifth Avenue, New York, New York 10103.*

PRINTED IN THE UNITED STATES OF AMERICA

OPM   12 11 10 9 8 7 6 5 4 3

How shall your houseless heads and unfed sides,
Your looped and windowed raggedness, defend you
From seasons such as these?

—King Lear, *act III, scene iv*

1

Naked, delicate, lovely, Nancy Selden came back into the bedroom. The pale early sunlight slanting across her fair hair and skin made her look fragile, almost evanescent. She noticed Len's rapt eyes on her and smiled hesitantly. "Len," she said, "I'm pregnant."

"You're what?" Len Trager sat up abruptly in the bed. She didn't answer, just reached for her hairbrush, watching him. He swallowed. "You're going to have a baby?"

She bent over to brush her misty blond hair down away from her head. "I said I was pregnant."

"Oh." It was too early; he couldn't think yet. He ran a hand through his own rumpled hair and said, "But we were careful."

"Yeah. Doctor said it was ninety-six-percent effective."

"Yeah. Okay." He tried to think what he should say. It was so early. He stood up and went over to the bureau to pull out his clothes. Pregnant. Nancy pregnant. Her small body swelling, filling. Because of him, because of their joy in each other. A baby. Goddamn. Len felt ridiculously virile, powerful, helpless, tender. And frightened. He didn't know how to be a father. What the hell was a father, anyway? Not Len Trager.

The shirt he was holding was not the one he wanted. He

1

dropped it back into the drawer and began digging for the right one.

Maybe not a baby. Maybe an abortion. Probably an abortion. Nancy was just beginning to get some good assignments at work. She'd been given the graphics for the MacIntyre fall catalog. Eyes shining as she told him the news a few weeks ago. And now, somehow, pregnant.

"What are you thinking?" she asked.

He shrugged. He was proud, astonished, depressed, intensely confused. What would this mean to them? But it was her decision. He said, "I guess someone has to be in the four percent. We hit the jackpot."

"I guess so." Coolly, she was pulling on pantyhose, blouse, skirt.

"You're sure about it?"

"They gave me the test results yesterday. I've been trying to think how to tell you."

"Nance." He stepped around the bed and hugged her. She rested a moment in his arms, then pulled away.

"What do you think, Len?"

"I don't know. What are you going to do?"

"What am I going to do?"

"I just wondered," he said humbly. Her career, her body, her life.

"You think *I* should do something?"

"No. I don't know. I mean, it's not up to me."

"It wasn't spontaneous generation, buddy." She turned away, wriggled her feet into her pumps, and brusquely picked up her shoulder bag.

He followed her into the little entryway. "Nance, I'm sorry. What do you want me to do?"

"How the hell should I know?" She was jerking her coat from the front closet.

"Wait, Nance, you haven't even had your coffee."

"It's late. I'll get something on the way to work. Maybe."

"I just want to help."

She paused in the doorway, fretfully. "Well, I'll see you at dinner."

The door closed. Damn. But he couldn't blame her for being upset. His own mind was staggering, and it wasn't even his decision. Len shaved, pulled on his clothes, and poured himself some orange juice. She was right, it was getting late. He made some instant coffee, gulped it while

he tried to tie his necktie, and hurried out into the chilly
April day.

Automatically, he bought a *Times*, drove the twenty
blocks to the office. Nancy was pregnant. Goddamn. What
should they do?

It was her decision, of course.

Joyce Banks Real Estate occupied the first floor of a
converted brownstone near Flatbush, in one of Gordon
Banks's buildings in Brooklyn. Inside, it was clean and
understated, earth tones and white walls and plants. Small,
but with desks for all of them and a separate office for
Joyce that could serve as a conference room. Renata was
already there, wearing a mauve granny dress and platform
shoes, her round face in the hornrims bent over her
typing. "Hi, Len. What's happening?"

He wished he could tell her this amazing thing, that
somehow, against all odds, he and Nancy had created a
life. Instead he put down his unread paper and said,
"Nothing much. The city's still skidding into bankruptcy.
And Muskie's quitting the Presidential race."

"Didn't think he'd last long."

"How's your brother?"

Renata grimaced. "Grouchy. It's a bad trip." Her sixteen-
year-old brother, Tony, never the steadiest of young men,
had managed to get into a high school brawl last week and
had suffered a broken leg.

"Did you find out who did it?"

Renata had been voluble in the past about the vicious
hoods who had attacked Tony and how she would leave no
stone unturned to find them. But now she shrugged
vaguely, "Oh, we're still asking around."

"I thought the insurance people wanted to know."

"They want to know your whole life history. God, I wish
spring would come."

"So do I," agreed Joyce Banks fervently, closing the
door as she entered, elegant, as always, removing her
fur-trimmed camel coat to reveal a navy-blue suit with a
gold stickpin on the lapel. She was a tall woman in her
forties, a onetime swimming champion and Olympic med-
alist, with blond hair swirled professionally around an
intelligent, dimpled face. Gordon Banks, her husband,
reputedly picked up six figures a year from various invest-
ments. But Joyce was energetic and ambitious in her own

right, and had used her Brooklyn roots effectively to build her real-estate business into one of the leaders. Today, though, she added, "It's hard to sell when it's cold and gloomy." Edgy for Joyce.

Len said lightly, "Go into the space-heater business."

"We'd do volume," Joyce agreed absently. "Well, at least it's not rainy. Maybe it'll warm up enough so I can have the party outdoors Sunday."

"You're an optimist," said Renata, tugging the sheet from her typewriter and squinting at it.

"That's one of the tricks of the trade, being an optimist," said Joyce. "You and Nancy are coming, right, Len?"

"Sure." Joyce's parties for clients and business associates, at her penthouse or the Bankses' Westchester estate, were not to be missed, and this one was also an unofficial celebration of her fifteenth wedding anniversary. "By the way, Joyce, I had a thought about the Marshall corporation."

"Yes?"

"Yesterday morning you mentioned that they were after that Fifth Avenue parcel Chet's group put together. But yesterday I was showing that laundry on Seventh, and the tenant there mentioned that the next four buildings all belong to Rosenzweig."

"Really! And he's talking about getting out of real estate! Len, you dear, I'll get right on it." She smiled her dimpled Esther Williams smile and disappeared into her own office.

Len sat down at his desk. God, he hoped she'd make the sale. Joyce was fair; she'd give him a small percentage. He could use it, if there was a baby. And maybe Joyce would trust him with a few of the more expensive properties in the future.

The other agents arrived: Pete Cronin, who handled most of the rentals; Karen Weld, gloriously copper-colored from two weeks in Florida; and Fred Stein, a thin graying man with the quick nervous air of a squirrel. He left almost immediately to meet a client. As he went out he held the door open an extra moment to admit a chunky middle-aged couple. The man had thinning dark hair and a blue blazer. The woman, with a puffy hairstyle that made her look taller than the man, wore a fifties-style cashmere wrap coat.

"Hi, Mrs. Lund, Mr. Lund," said Renata.

"Renata, old kid! Have you sold my place yet?"

Len stood up and reached across to shake Lund's hand. "We're working on it."

"But the card's not even in the window!"

"We have to rotate the cards. Give everyone a chance."

"It's been eight damn months! And only one offer!"

"Loretta, dear!" Joyce sailed from her office and leaned down to kiss both Lunds on the cheek. "How are you, Arthur?"

"Hurting, Joyce, hurting. We need our cash. I've got to unload that place! These short-term loans are eating me alive."

"I know, I know," Joyce soothed. "But I've told you, we just can't get your price with the old lady there."

"God, that old witch!" Lund's rosy nose twitched with rage. "If it wasn't for her—see, the place is in good shape! Well, sort of shabby, maybe, but I fixed the plumbing Monday."

"I know, I know."

"And cutting the water supply didn't get rid of her anyway. She just hauled water from her church while the pipe was out. That old hag's impossible!"

"Absolutely impossible," echoed Mrs. Lund.

Joyce said smoothly, "Well, I hope you've learned never to get involved with rent-controlled tenants again, Arthur."

"How was I supposed to know her son was a lawyer?"

"Arthur, dear, you just aren't ruthless enough. You've got to stick with it till she leaves."

"She'll die first. Look, I don't want to face a lawyer, Joyce. It's a good solid place. Other places are selling that are a lot shabbier."

"Arthur, Loretta, just look." Joyce scooped up Len's newspaper and opened to the real-estate ads. "We started your ad again. Here. 'Park Slope, four-story brownstone, fireplaces, details.' Last time it got calls. They asked, is it in good condition? We said, sound and solid, needs a little cosmetic work. They asked, is it delivered vacant? All but the garden apartment, we said. Rent-controlled? Well, we said, um, yes. That's when most of them hang up. A few looked. And you know what she's like, Arthur. She's ragged and she smells, and the first thing she says is, 'I'm never moving out. My son is a lawyer.'"

"God. How could someone like her raise a lawyer?" Lund, mollified by the sight of the ad, was more morose than angry now. "Damn old biddy. She used to be so nice."

"She was always a little strange. But sharp," his wife reminded him.

"Well, we'll keep trying." Joyce folded the paper and handed it back to Len. "But I have to tell you the truth, Arthur. Get her out, or drop your price fifteen percent."

"We can't afford to drop it that much. Listen, she pays the rent on time. Do you tell them that?"

"Yes. But they're savvy, they know what that means. She's not giving you any excuse to evict her. Listen, I was wondering. Have you called the health department? You might be able to hassle her on the garbage."

"Joyce, honey, I've tried that. Got the inspector, didn't even tell her we were coming."

"Not wise, Arthur, if her son is a lawyer."

"Made no difference," he said glumly, prodding at the tray of paper clips on Len's desk with a stubby finger. "When we got there it was like *Better Homes and Gardens*. Neat as a pin, her in her Sunday best, smiling and nodding and offering the inspector a cup of tea. I could have throttled her."

Joyce wisely changed the subject. "How's your new place?"

Loretta brightened. "Oh, it's wonderful! Thanks so much for finding it for us! It's just that we really need to renovate the kitchen, and we can't..."

"I know, I know, Loretta. We'll bring you any offer we get."

Lund shook his head. "Damn old biddy. I've offered her a thousand bucks to move. A thousand!" They went out into the chilly April sunshine.

"He'll never get rid of that one," said Len.

"Oh, don't give up. She's declined a lot already, if she used to be as sharp as he claims. That lawyer son of hers will put her in a home soon, I imagine."

"Lucky you ran the ad again. Quieted them down."

"Actually, I figured if anyone called, we could show them the St. John's building too. I promised Abernethy I'd push harder. It'll look like a bargain after they meet Mrs. Northrup." She went back into her office.

Len turned back to the paper, skimming it for news that might lead to prospects, to deals, to financing. But his mind kept shifting back to Nancy and her astounding news.

The cruellest month. Especially this year, when the damp and cold had lingered on for weeks. Early for his appointment, Nick O'Connor thrust his hands into his pockets and sauntered across Central Park. He was a burly, balding man in a turtleneck, with clear brown eyes that were a little melancholy today. Despite the thin sun, it was chilly. Not many people in the park now. And why should they be? By now there should be magnolia and dogwood and cherry blossoms. Instead there was only a pale green haze on the bushes, a faint promise of foliage to come. Proud-pied April, dressed in all his trim, was passing them by this year.

Footsteps sounded behind him. He glanced sideways as a lanky young woman in a trench coat drew even, blue eyes vivid under a red beret, a red scarf bright at her throat. She waved a cigarette at him and asked in a husky voice, *"Haben Sie Feuer?"*

"Ja." He glanced around. There was an old man pottering along the next path; a young couple disappeared around the bend ahead. He decided to risk it. He pulled out his lighter and said, "Agent Forty-two, I presume?"

A curt nod as she exhaled a cloud of smoke. "Come wit' me, pleess, Twenty-nine." She plunged down one of the tangle of paths that wound toward Olmsted's lake, briskly leading him among rocks and woods to the footbridge. His melancholy evaporated in the energy of those lively eyes. The right Promethean fire.

"Silence!" she warned abruptly, grinding out the cigarette on the asphalt walk across the slatted wooden bridge. She stepped closer, seized his upper arms, and suddenly tucked a leg behind his knee, jerking him off balance. As he stumbled back she pressed the heel of her hand to his jaw and fell onto him, guiding his fall. Grappling, they tumbled together down the rocky bank in a flurry of twigs and last year's dry brown leaves. They ended in the sheltered shadow under the bridge, hidden now from anyone on the forsaken paths.

Nick found that somehow, on the trip down, he had been expertly unbuckled and unzipped. Now, with a wriggle, Forty-two straddled him, flipping her trench coat into more appropriate folds. The warm thighs were naked already. She smiled at his surprise and murmured, "An agent should be ready for anyt'ing, Twenty-nine."

"I'm ready." Nick's voice was husky too.

"Mmm. So you are."

A little later, relaxed now and almost demure, she leaned against his shoulder. Nick smoothed back a black curl from her forehead. The beret had long since fallen off.

"What brings you here, Forty-two?"

"You mean other than lust?"

"Well, you don't usually spend your coffee breaks tricked out like a flasher, accosting innocent spies in the park."

She grinned. "I saw you starting across the park looking blue, and had a sudden uncontrollable urge to stalk you through the paths of darkest Berlin." She bounced to her feet, clapped the beret back on, then dodged further under the bridge and turned her back, suddenly engagingly modest, to pull on her pantyhose. Nick found himself grinning foolishly at her back. Her quick glance caught him. "My maidenly blushes amuse you?"

"Under the circumstances."

"The circumstances now include two old couples and a golden retriever that have all fixed you in their beady glares, longing for a reportable incident."

"Golden retrievers don't have beady glares," he objected gently. He offered her his arm and they climbed decorously up to the path again. "Now, Maggie, tell me why you were stalking me."

She pulled a scrap of newspaper from her pocket. "There's a new Park Slope ad."

"Aha. Nesting instinct again. Your raging hormones."

"Right. I'm out of control. Ready to rape and pillage for a bigger place. This time I'm doing it right."

"Well, I'll be finished at George's by noon. Why don't you get us an appointment to see it during your lunch hour?"

"*D'accord.* One o'clock, unless I call. I'll meet you at the realtor's. Joyce Banks. Seventh Avenue, remember?"

"Okay. But even if it's a great place I won't be interested unless you promise me one thing."

"What?"

"Don't give up raping and pillaging. You do it so well."

Her wide smile was lively as spring. "I promise, Twenty-nine." Late, she sprinted away across the park again.

Len was having an irritating lunch with Fred Stein. It wasn't Stein's fault. He'd been generous with helpful tips when Len first started in real estate and Len usually liked him.

"Listen," said Fred, with a nervous nip at his burger, "you remember Dr. Carr and his buddies? Joyce sold him the Eighth Avenue apartments."

"Yeah?" said Len listlessly. If Fred would only shut up, he could think what to do about Nancy.

"Well, I've been managing it for them," said Fred. "And they want to invest in residential property again, it's doing so well. I mean, office space is slumping right now, but it's like Joyce says—now's the time to buy. They're thinking the Grand Army Plaza area will hot up. Asked me to manage it again."

"Congratulations. Joyce will be pleased."

"Well, not really. See, they want a place they can reno-vate. And you know that sketch you did for Eighth Ave-nue? The lobby?"

"Right." In the fifties, the owner of that building had tried to spruce up the lobby with paneling. The results had not been happy. Joyce had sent Len over with instruc-tions to think of a couple of suggestions so potential buyers would see the possibilities, and he had realized immediately that the scuffed paneling hid some interest-ing Art Deco detail. Seeing a sketch of his guess about what the old lobby might have looked like, the doctors had purchased the place and taken his advice, discovering, beneath the encrustations of plywood and linoleum, dra-matic polished marble and modeled arches. The restored apartment building had become popular with young pro-fessionals, with a hundred-percent occupancy.

Fred nibbled at his burger and said, "They want you to design their new project too. And they weren't really happy with the contractor last time. I wondered if you and I together could work with them."

"Mm, I don't know. Joyce wouldn't like it." Joyce and Gordon Banks had interests in development firms, which were kept strictly separate from the sales and rentals of the real-estate office.

"Right," Fred agreed with a little squirrel smile. "But do we want to be stuck with her all our lives, forking over to her a percentage of all we earn? God, Len, I've dreamed of developing a building. I'd buy one myself but I can't these days, with my nephew off to college."

"Well, you deal with the doctors then." Len jabbed at his dill pickle. He couldn't do a damn thing for Nancy, one way or the other, he knew that; and yet her news obsessed him.

"I would, but—hell, Len, you know I've got no eye for design. But the two of us together—I mean, you're like a son to me. Think about it, okay?" Fred's thin gray face was anxious.

"Okay," Len agreed, as though he didn't have enough to think about already.

Joyce was donning her coat as they came back in. "Oh, Len, good, I want you to take care of this note. Someone just called about the Lund place. They want to see it at one o'clock, but everyone's at lunch and I have to see Rosenzweig."

"Sure." He made a note in his book. "Um, did you call Mrs. Northrup?"

Joyce grimaced. "Yes, I had poor Renata set it up. Listen, leave time to show the Abernethy place afterward. They said it was more than they wanted to pay, but they'll probably change their minds if you show them the old lady first. Oh, and if I'm not back by three-thirty, get the info on the Flatbush listing." She hurried out.

The man arrived a couple of minutes before one, a big broad guy, friendly brown eyes, jeans and turtleneck. He was getting bald.

"Hello, Mr.—is it Ryan?" Len asked, glancing at Joyce's scrawled note.

"Nick O'Connor. Ryan is my wife."

"Oh, right, sorry, Mr. O'Connor. I'm Len Trager."

"Call me Nick." They shook hands.

"I'll be showing you that brownstone on Garfield. You new around here?"

"We've been living over in Chelsea. But I've worked here in Brooklyn a couple of times." Seeing the question in Len's eyes, he added, "I'm an actor."

"That's interesting." Len struggled to mask his disappointment. An actor. His afternoon was as good as wasted.

Banks didn't give mortgages to actors, with their unpredictable temperaments and ninety-five-percent unemploy-
ment rate. There was little hope of a sale here. But you
never knew, some unlikely-looking people, even artists or
writers, sometimes had money. Optimism, Joyce always
said, a trick of the trade. So he asked cheerfully, "Stage?
TV?"

"Whatever they'll give me."

"What are you doing now?"

"Between jobs just now. I was in an off-Broadway thing
that folded last week."

"Oh. Tough luck."

"Not really," said Nick with a smile. "It was a turkey.
Glad to get out of it."

"Well, that's good. You'll like the Slope, it's got a real
pioneer enthusiasm. Do you have children?"

"Not yet."

"Me either." Len had a sudden warm vision of Nancy
laughing down at a little child. A little boy. His little boy.
Steady now.

The door opened and a woman entered. Tall, professional-
looking, a trench coat open over a gray wool suit, carefully
cut black curls, a red beret, a briefcase. The dignified
effect was marred by the overstuffed pastry she was chewing
enthusiastically. Len said, "Yes, ma'am, can we help you?"

"Mmph." She waved the pastry at him in apology.

Nick said, "Maggie, meet Len Trager. He'll be showing
us the house. This is Maggie Ryan," he explained to Len.

"Oh. You're together."

"Right," said the woman, having swallowed. "Is it okay if
I finish my Danish on the way over? I just have my lunch
hour."

"Sure," said Len. He was heartened by this indication of
a steady job, a job that required a suit. A bank wouldn't
give a mortgage to a young woman, of course, but an
owner like Abernethy might. He unlocked the box and
took out Abernethy's keys as well as the amber-tagged set
to Lund's building. "Car's around the corner," he said.

It was a short drive up to the park, a right turn to
Garfield, another right. "Transitional block," said Len.
"You can see the renovation going on."

Maggie nodded. The sense of change was almost tangi-
ble. Several of the brownstones had been cleaned and

repaired recently. Others were in varying states of disar-
ray, some with broken glass, graffiti, boarded windows.
The people were similarly various: a pair of stout Italian
matrons with shopping bags, a couple of black men with
exuberant Afros, an earnest young blond woman in flare-
bottomed jeans puttying a windowpane. A gray-haired
woman in a navy warm-up suit cycled past them. On some
blocks there were still elm trees, filmed now with the
flowery khaki-yellow that preceded leaves, but on Garfield
many trees had been lost, and the grandeur or decay of
each building stood exposed in the cool sunlight. Lund's
place looked okay on the outside, Len decided. But he
could already hear the booming syrupy tones of the Jesus
station. Damn. He parked and said brightly, "Here we
are."

The couple got out and stood on the sidewalk looking
up silently at the building. It was similar to the other
brownstones on the street—narrow, chocolate-colored, three
tall stories above a raised basement, a long flight of steps
up to a big double door. But its details were its own. Like
its Victorian builder, it was at once conforming and eccen-
tric, exuberantly individual within its rigid constraints.
Carved stone framed the window bay that ran from sidewalk to a florid cornice at the top. A third-story oriel
window and a band of vestigial crenellation under the
cornice completed the rugged trim. Nick said, "A forted
residence 'gainst the tooth of time."

An actor, Len remembered.

He said, "Well, shall we go in? Start at the bottom." If he
hit them with Mrs. Northrup first, they'd have time to see
the Abernethy place. He led the way to the two broad
steps that descended to the iron gate under the tall front
stoop, pulled out the keys with the amber tag, and unlocked
the door to a shabby hall that ran toward the rear of the
building. There were stairs against the left wall and a
closed door at the right that did little to block the rever-
berating voice of the radio preacher.

A sharp voice answered Len's knock. "Who's that?"

"Len Trager, ma'am. From Joyce Banks."

"Blast." The door opened a few inches to the length of a
stout chain and a pair of shrewd eyes glittered at them.
Then the door closed again and the chain rattled behind
it. Len wished that she would simply refuse to let them in.

That might give Lund grounds for eviction or something. But the door opened again and she snapped, "Well, come in!"

She was wiry, of medium height, with unkempt gray hair around a wrinkled face and neck, a smudged cheek. She smelled of alcohol. Her long cardigan was pilled and unraveling at the sleeves and neck. There were holes in it, a few of them carelessly darned with a darker yarn. Her feet scuffed along in pink terry-cloth slippers that were stained and burst at the seams.

She stood aside and they entered the dark and smelly apartment, which was ringing with the preacher's request for money. Len shouted, "Thank you! Mrs. Northrup, this is Nick O'Connor and Maggie Ryan."

Nick said, "Glad to meet you." He had no trouble being heard above the din. An actor.

Mrs. Northrup's voice was penetrating too. She gave Nick a sharp unfriendly look, icily inspected Maggie, and asked, "You together?"

"Yes."

"Living in sin, eh? One of those libbers. No bra, I bet. Well, it's your souls."

Len said hastily, "They're married. We'll just take a quick look, Mrs. Northrup, okay?"

"Have I ever stopped you?" she jeered. Maggie, rightly judging that a warmer invitation would not be forthcoming, moved on into the dim room with Nick. Len waited by the door. The smell wasn't just alcohol today, he decided. There was something rotting too.

Maggie asked, "Is it okay to open the drapes, Mrs. Northrup?"

"If it'll get you out any quicker."

"We'll be quick," Maggie promised, and pulled the draw cords.

Three big windows extended nearly to the ceiling in the street-side bay. A sofa, covered by a tattered quilt, held a jumble of newspapers, magazines, old clothes, and whiskey bottles. So did the bookcase, the rumpled bed, the desk, the television, the mantel, the floor, and every other surface of the room.

Len said cautiously, "You can see that it's spacious."

Mrs. Northrup snorted.

Nick had walked to the two doors at the back wall. "May I?"

"Go ahead, hurry up. Maybe Artie Lund will unload this place on you and I'll be left in peace. Artie thinks it's his, but it'll always be the Sweeney place in fact."

"Sweeney?" asked Len.

"Cornelius Sweeney. Invented a new furniture polish, made a little fortune, built this place. Artie Lund will never do as much."

"Few of us will," said Maggie. She picked up a couple of magazines from the heap on the desk, tossed them back, and studied the engraving of Lincoln hung above it. "You plan on staying here in the Sweeney place?"

"Sure. It's my legal right. My son is a lawyer."

"I see." Her face expressionless, Maggie joined Nick and they went through the butler's pantry to the kitchen. Len threaded his way among the bottles and dirty clothes after them.

Here, the noise was louder, the stench stronger, and the clutter, if anything, worse. Mrs. Northrup scooped up a whiskey bottle from the kitchen floor, inspected it, and apparently found something worth preserving. She scuffed her way over to the mantel and placed it there carefully.

Maggie crossed the kitchen to look in the bathroom, and Len stepped back to let her pass. His heel crunched on something. The bones of an old chicken leg, greasy and rotting on the floor. Damn.

Nick was at the sink, which was filled with dirty dishes. He tested the faucet, then looked out the window at a view of the underside of the back porch and a bare maple tree in the rubble-filled yard beyond. Someone on the radio began testifying raucously for Jesus. Maggie emerged from the bathroom, nodded at Nick, and they both looked amused. Maggie said, "Mrs. Northrup, Mr. Lund must be a terrific landlord."

"Lund is going to burn in Hades!"

Maggie frowned at her. Nick said, "But the plumbing and electricity are in pretty good shape."

"Yeah? Tell them how long it took him to get around to fixing that, Lennie."

Len cleared his throat, but the others were not waiting for a reply. Maggie was inspecting a cabinet door built into the wall at waist level. "Pass-through?" she asked doubtfully.

"Pantry," shouted Len. The radio was right next to the little door. "Converted from the old dumbwaiter car."

"I see." The door had a spring latch and a bolt that dropped down from the top of the frame. Maggie undid them and looked in. A little varnished chamber of sturdy Victorian craftsmanship was screwed into the walls. The pale ropes still hung on either side. A snarl of mops, buckets, dirty sponges, and rags had been crammed inside. Maggie closed and bolted the door, and turned back to the others.

Nick asked, "Do you like this neighborhood, Mrs. Northrup?"

The old woman looked surprised. She shrugged. "My friends are around here. And down here in the basement I don't have to worry about the leaky roof."

Nick smiled at her and said, "Well, thank you. I guess we're ready to go on, then."

Len was relieved. He said, "Fine. Thanks, Mrs. Northrup." The radio was now roaring out "Amazing Grace."

The old woman nodded silently and watched them make their way back to the door. Once outside, Len said, "There's no leak in the roof that I know of."

Maggie's grin was lively. "Hey, it's okay. She's got her reasons, poor thing. We'll believe our own eyes. Upstairs now?"

"There's a similar place I could show you, on St. John's," Len suggested. "At our nine-o'clock meeting yesterday morning, Joyce said the owner is now willing to finance. Plus, it's delivered vacant."

To his dismay, they shook their heads. "Mrs. Banks mentioned it, but it costs too much. Let's see the upstairs."

They walked up the stone steps to the double oak door with its frosted-glass design mostly intact. Len unlocked it and led them through a little tiled vestibule to a long, shabby stair hall. The walls were scuffed and smudged, the ceiling cracked, the varnish of floor and woodwork worn and dull. "Nice staircase," commented Nick, running a finger along the carving of the newel post.

"Yes, polish it up a little and it'll be beautiful," said Len, automatically professional. He unlocked the door into the peeling parlor. Inside, a recent closet built of two-by-fours and cheap paneling marred the proportions. But the room had high ceilings with elaborate moldings, and the mantel sported a bas-relief Victorian maiden of such delicacy that Len was always reminded of Nancy. "Amazing Grace," muffled but dominant, rumbled up through the floor.

They moved into the dining room, also finished with elaborate molding, and on into the soiled kitchen. "Hey, look, Nick, back stairs!" exclaimed Maggie.

Len felt a prickle of hope. He couldn't remember anyone else being this pleased by Lund's weary old brownstone, not after meeting the immovable Mrs. Northrup. Could there possibly be a sale here after all?

Not to an actor, he reminded himself.

They went upstairs. Loretta Lund's uncle, long ago, had divided the upper floors into separate apartments, with shoddily constructed kitchenettes backing onto the original plumbing wall. But the once-glorious Victorian bath still held a marble sink and a chipped clawfoot tub, and a small room at the front overlooked the street. Maggie smiled at Nick and said, "This could be a little study."

"One more floor," said Len. The steps to the top floor, the former servants' quarters, were narrower than the lower flights. Here the windows were smaller, and the ceilings lower. The front apartment on this floor had been most recently occupied—only Lund's disruption of the plumbing had finally forced the young couple on this floor to give up, accept his relocation money, and leave. For some reason a section of the hall had recently been repainted white, but in the main room the cheap paneling was blotched by the shadows of posters that had been Scotch-taped to the walls. The preacher's voice boomed incomprehensibly from below. Nick slapped his hand against a wall. "This isn't a supporting wall, is it?"

"No," said Len, giving the room a professional glance. "You may have a pillar or two in the stair wall, but not here. You're thinking of remodeling?" That was always a good sign.

"Maggie's a gymnast, and actors have to keep in shape. It would be great to have space to work out." Nick stepped to the doorway. "What do you think, Maggie?"

She was down the hall, looking into the little front room, the one that sported the oriel window over the main door. For a moment she remained there, still, not answering.

"Do you like the place?" Len prompted.

She turned back to them slowly, and Nick, suddenly concerned, took a step toward her. But it was Len she answered.

"Yes," she said, "it's a great place. There's only one problem. There's a corpse in it."

2

Julia Northrup sat alertly on the edge of her cluttered sofa, waiting, straining to hear their footsteps over that idiot preacher. They were audible only when old Reverend Goon paused for effect—first overhead, then on the stairs again, then, faint and far away, on the upper floors. It shouldn't be long now.

She had bagged the garbage and opened the kitchen window because the stench was so awful. Sometimes she was ashamed to think that she'd come to this. But she had learned long ago not to worry about what people thought of her. Except Vic. What would Vic think of this mess? He'd be horrified at first, curious, then amused. Furious at Artie Lund. But then he'd hug her, his hard arms gentle around her. Dear Vic. Would he be her lover still? Maybe. But face it, Julia, at sixty-eight you are supposed to be a neuter. Time kept gnawing away, working its evil transformations. Bright eyes into bleary. Cheeks into droopy jowls. Tits into dugs. Desire into—blast it, no, desire didn't change. It remained hot and rowdy inside the sagging skin, lingering on pointlessly after the mate was dead, after the breasts drooped and the uterus, she'd read, shrank to the size of a walnut. It remained long after one had become that most intensely nonsexual of objects, an old woman. And it made Julia Northrup, retired schoolmarm, sit here full of silly nostalgia for Vic, when she should be concentrating on her real problems.

Dorothy Parker's old lady said: *Contrition is hollow and wraithful, and regret is no part of my plan; and I think (if my memory's faithful) there was nothing more fun than a man!* True, Parker, true.

Sublimate, Freud said. Rechannel that id. But that too was easier before you retired. Then there was less money and more time, and all that sublimating had to be done on pennies a month. Artie Lund didn't help much with his stupid attempts to drive her out. At least it was a distraction, that could be said for him.

Actually she rather liked this afternoon's couple, though of course they wouldn't do. An interesting pair, the lanky energetic young woman with merriment in her eyes, and the pleasant balding man with his oddly familiar smile. Nick O'Connor, that was his name. A burly Irishman, as big as Vic had been and built even broader, all muscle. And gentle. He'd been concerned about her, not put off by her grumbling. And he was obviously in tune with young what's-her-name, his nice brown eyes constantly checking her reactions, talking without talk. A good man. Probably good in bed. She hoped young what's-her-name appreciated him while she could. But young women so seldom knew what they had. They looked in their mirrors and instead of smooth skin and thick hair and nice round lovable fannies, they saw fat legs and flat chests, and even the best of men had trouble convincing them of their own glory. It had certainly been that way with her. Too hippy, she had always thought, sliding quickly under the covers so Vic couldn't get a close look and be repulsed. Poor Vic loved a close look, she had learned at last. But they'd had some fine rollicking times despite her blushes.

Young what's-her-name, though, was tall and slim. Probably thought of herself as bony and thin. Scrawny. Bag of bones. Those were good words. Remember them. They would hurt.

Was that a step on the stairs? No. Julia pushed an annoying string of gray hair from her eyes, and waited.

On the phone Joyce Banks had said this couple was interested in moving into the place themselves. They'd want to glamorize it, no doubt, like that couple that had driven Pauline McGuire out of her Carroll Street apart-

ment into the dinky rear basement around the corner, or
the two men next door who'd brought in yards of lush velvet
and caused old Wilma Riggins to roll her eyes and warn her
grandsons to stay clear. The two men were polite enough,
always said good morning to Julia, but they'd paid too much
for the place and given Artie Lund big ideas. Now Artie, the
snake, figured he'd get rich quick. All he had to do was
throw out the poor folks and the rich would beat a path to
his door. Well, Artie, it hadn't been that easy, had it? Julia
smiled a tight-lipped smile. The funniest thing was how
frightened Artie was of Vic Jr. As if a lawyer would automatically do what his mother asked. Artie didn't know that Vic
Jr. too wanted her to move out. Vic Jr. had his eye on a
hopelessly dull apartment complex in Jersey for her. Ugh.

"O God our help in ages past," bellowed a young man
on the radio. Idiot station. *Toadying, in singsong, to a crabbed
god.* Parker must have known this station.

These blasted slippers were too tight, like cords around
her instep. Itchy, too, where the terry cloth was crusted.
Actually they were Pauline McGuire's old slippers, a size
too small to begin with. She wondered suddenly if Fred-
Law had had itchy feet. Sore feet. Feet were such an
important part of one's sense of well-being. What sort of
shoes had he worn? Wellingtons? And as a little boy in the
Hartford woods, probably those lace-up jobs. Bluchers.
His dad had been rich enough to afford shoes. But little
Fred-Law, out exploring, had probably been barefoot as
often as not. Julia wished she were barefoot, right now.

"Time like an ever-rolling stream bears all its sons away,"
sang the young man on the radio.

Listen! Here it came. She heard the steps, far away,
hurrying on the stairs. Unlocking the door to the basement stairs, clattering down just outside. Heels. It was
young what's-her-name, then. The knock was quick, urgent.

"Who's that?" snarled Julia.

"Maggie Ryan, Mrs. Northrup."

Maggie Ryan, right, that was the name. Irish to match
O'Connor. Julia shuffled toward the door. "I thought you
said you wouldn't bother me anymore," she said tartly.

"There's an emergency, Mrs. Northrup. A death. I have
to call the police."

Julia slowly undid the chain and bolts. "You'd better not
be kidding," she grumbled. But the young woman didn't

pause, just bounded across the room straight for the telephone. She must have noticed it before. Observant young creature. Julia hesitated, then went into the kitchen and switched off the radio.

When she returned, Maggie was saying, "Yes, a murder... In a vacant apartment, top floor, on Garfield Place, number..."

She raised her eyebrows at Julia, who said, "Two hundred sixty-eight."

"Number two-sixty-eight...that's right...No, I don't know who he is... Margaret Ryan... Yes, I'll wait here."

She hung up and dialed again without asking Julia's permission. "Merle? Is Dan back?...Hell. Okay, tell him I'm held up by the police, and if he'll cover for me at the Columbia meeting I'll fix him some crepes suzette...Merle, I don't know myself what it's all about. But a guy is dead and I'm a witness, sort of. I'll get back as soon as I can. Thanks!"

She hung up, raked her fingers back through her black curls, and turned back to Julia. They looked at each other warily. Then Julia said, "I want to see."

"It isn't pretty. He was strangled, Mrs. Northrup."

"This is where I *live*."

Maggie nodded and together they climbed the three long flights of stairs. The two men were standing in the hall, young Lennie looking a bit ashen as Maggie handed him the keys, Nick sad but composed. Julia asked, "Where is he?"

"This way," said Maggie. "Better not touch anything."

Julia shuffled to the door she indicated. Golden glass in the fancy little window warmed the thin sunlight, and she could see everything clearly. One year ago, Jack and Ann had painted the little room a warm buff and put in an old mattress with a dashiki print spread and pillows. Our African room, they'd told her. Come on up, Teach, and sit on the pillows and eat something Ethiopian. Heartburn afterwards, her old body grumbled at changes these days, but a nice evening. Soon afterwards, when the plumbing had gone, Jack and Ann had decided it wasn't worth it and moved out. But the old striped mattress, stained and missing its bright cover now, had been left behind.

Lying on it today was a man, young, with bright curly blond hair, his face and protruding tongue dark in bloated death.

"Do you recognize him?" asked Maggie, at her side, gently.

"That face?"

"I mean from the hair or clothes or anything."

Julia shook her head. "A million people dress like that." Jeans, a navy crew-neck sweater. She noted a bottle of Chianti lying in the corner, a dark red stain on the floor around it.

"The hair is distinctive."

"I don't know him." Of course he didn't really look like that. Maybe if they found a photo it might ring a bell. There would have to be some connection with this house or neighborhood, wouldn't there? She turned away from the little glowing ghastly room. Time like an ever-rolling stream bears all its sons away. "I want to go home."

"I'll go down with you."

Julia started to object but suddenly found that she wouldn't mind company. That ghastly dead young face tugged at her thoughts. Downstairs, she asked, "Coffee?" as she unlocked the door.

"Love some." Maggie didn't sound dubious at all. Frowning, Julia shuffled to the kitchen and found a couple of cracked cups. When she got back with the hot coffee the young woman had turned on the lights and was gliding around the jumbled room like a falcon after prey, as bold and as full of curiosity as she was herself. A tough adversary. Julia switched off the lights and pushed aside some newspapers to set Maggie's cup on the coffee table. Her own she took to the mantel. Beautiful carved wood, from the days when this was the Sweeney dining room.

"When Cornelius Sweeney's daughter Caroline was small," she said, eyeing the inquisitive Maggie, "she heard her dad bumping around in the kitchen one night. That very kitchen, right in there. She crept down to peek, but all she could see was that he was bent over doing something in the sink cabinet. He straightened up and she raced back up the back stairs to bed so he wouldn't catch her. But very early the next morning, before even the servants were awake, she stole down to look. And she opened the cabinet door and reached in and pow! Her fingers were caught in the mousetrap he'd been setting."

Maggie transferred a stack of debris from the sofa to the floor and sat down with a bland smile. "Cornelius

Sweeney's daughter would understand me very well. Tell me, Mrs. Northrup, can you think when that poor fellow might have died? Did you hear anything?"

"I wouldn't know. Artie Lund's noisy plumbers were here Monday and Tuesday, mostly down in the cellar whacking at the pipes. What's it to you anyway?"

"I don't think he's been dead that long."

"You some kind of expert?"

Maggie fished out the fragment of orange peel that Julia had dropped in her coffee and placed it carefully on an October issue of *U.S. News* nearby. Unperturbed, she took a sip before she said, "Didn't smell very bad, did he? I mean, Monday was four days ago."

Yes, a dangerous young woman. Julia snapped, "You've got a good nose for a slut."

"Why, thank you." The blue eyes met hers, amused. "Has anyone else been in? Besides those plumbers?"

"There are millions of people in this city. Some of them go past this door. Some make noise. Some come up the steps, even. Mostly Artie Lund and his noisy henchmen."

"Real-estate people too?"

"Not this week. Anyway, they count as his henchmen too. So do you, chippy."

Maggie grinned. "If we buy this house, he won't think so. We'll drive a hard bargain."

"You might buy it?" Julia found herself standing very stiffly, gripping the handle of her cup on the mantel, staring at this frightening young woman.

"It's possible."

"Even with that thing up there?"

"Are you moving out because of it?"

"Of course not!"

"Well, then, why should it discourage us?"

"What's here to attract you?"

Maggie stood and moved thoughtfully to the other end of the mantel. She stroked a finger along an ancient gash in the carved corner. "A good friend told me an Indian saying: You can't erase time. Seems true to me." She glanced around the wainscoted room. "I like the way this house sits here affirming the past and looking forward to the future. It's seen it all and it wants more. A hearty house."

Julia was silent, shaken to hear her own affinity for this

house of lusty age articulated. Maggie smiled at her tenta-
tively and added, "Mrs. Northrup, if we buy it we won't
need this floor. You'll stay on, I hope."

That's what they'd told Pauline too, and within months,
changed their minds. Julia shrugged skeptically and Maggie
went on, "Okay. Plumbers Monday and Tuesday. What
about yesterday?"

"I wasn't paying much attention. I didn't know anything
like this would happen."

"I know, Mrs. Northrup. Try."

She ought to throw her out. But Maggie was curious,
persistent, not easily deflected. Against her better judg-
ment, Julia was tempted to confide. But, Mrs. Northrup,
the interviewer would ask, why did you cooperate with
that brazen young woman? Well, Sonny, she'd reply from
her pallet in the shelter for the homeless, it seemed
important to clear up the murder too. She's brazen, yes,
but maybe bright enough to help with that. Aloud, Julia
said crisply, "Tuesday afternoon, Pauline McGuire came
over to celebrate the water being turned back on. The
plumbers were still here, carousing in the parlor-floor
kitchen upstairs, so we went up to tell them to hush. We
saw them out. Four-thirty or so. Then Wednesday morning a dark-haired fellow arrived, probably another plumber. I saw him walk right up the stoop and into the door. I
didn't know what he did because I had to go get groceries.
Can't make a full-time job of listening for murders to
happen."

Maggie went to the window, pulled back the drape to
check the view of the stoop, and nodded. "I see."

Julia said, "When Mary Sweeney was in college, a body
was found on campus once, under a hedge. The police
questioned all of the students. But it turned out that
the fellow had been in a drunken brawl in the
next town, and his friends had brought him all that way
before they noticed he had died. They panicked and
threw him out of the car under the hedge. Nothing to do
with Mary or her friends."

"You think this body was brought from somewhere else?
Up three flights of stairs?"

"Two people could have done it."

"You didn't see two. Well, the police will ask the neighbors. Two guys hauling a corpse around are conspicuous, even if the corpse is hidden in a box or something."

Julia shrugged and ran her finger around the chipped rim of her cup. In her mind the dead blond youngster stared at her. She shrugged and said, controlled, "Maybe. But he looked like a strapping young fellow. If someone started to choke him here, he would have made a ruckus. I'd have heard."

"Through the gospel music?"

Drat. Julia said, "I turn it off sometimes. I'd have heard."

Maggie nodded. "Unless it happened Wednesday morning while you were out. Or unless they cut off his breath before he realized it was an attack. Or bashed him on the head first with that Chianti bottle."

"Anything's possible," said Julia primly. Her coffee was unpotable.

"You don't like the idea of murder happening in this house. Neither do I. But we have to keep straight exactly what we know, and what we're guessing."

Julia said, "Let's let the police do the guessing. We're not overgrown Nancy Drews."

"We're not helpless damsels in distress either."

Okay, true enough. Julia repressed the stirring of comradely feeling for this brash, cool-headed young woman. She wondered if Nick could manage her, and decided he probably could hold his own. She gulped the last of her coffee and snapped, "Speak for yourself."

"Oh? Are you a damsel in distress, then?"

The probing annoyed Julia. She slapped her cup onto the mantel. "Look, who are you to come slamming in here, using my phone, pestering me with questions? Just who are you?"

"At last count, a slut, a chippy, and an overgrown Nancy Drew living in sin."

Julia snorted, pleased that her shots had registered after all. "You won't make a living for long that way. You're a bag of bones."

Maggie said, too evenly, "Right. Positively scrawny."

Bingo. Bag of bones was right on target. Julia asked, "So why the fancy gray suit? What kind of job do you have, Bonesy?"

"I'm with Goldman and Morrow. Statistical consultants."

"Sounds dull."

"Oh, feel free to embroider. Could be a front for a bordello, don't you think?"

Julia could smell victory now. She followed up. "And your bald friend? Your so-called husband with a different name? Surely he's not hoping for a family from a skinny tramp like you."

Maggie stood suddenly, stepped to the desk, and tipped her coffee cup over it, just short of spilling. Her eyes were opaque. "I'm sorry, Mrs. Northrup. What did you ask?"

Julia stared at the poised cup. Could she know? No, of course not. But it made her uneasy. She backed off, saying, "I was wondering about your husband. What does he do?"

The coffee cup straightened. "He's an actor."

"Unemployed, probably. Wait!" The connection suddenly surfaced in Julia's mind. She added eagerly, "Merchant's Bank?" That was where she'd seen Nick O'Connor's oddly familiar smile: on that fellow in the commercial, the one whose Aunt Mabel was supposed to have left him the shoebox of money.

Maggie took a sip of coffee. "Yes, that was one of his jobs. What do you do, Mrs. Northrup?"

"You mean what did I do."

"Is that what I mean?"

"I'm retired. I was a schoolteacher. Fifth grade. Little beasts."

"I bet you were good. Full of stories about the interesting Sweeneys. You taught history?"

Somehow Julia had lost the initiative. Voice gruff, she asked, "Who've you been talking to, Bonesy?"

"No one." Maggie stood again and pulled a thin square children's book from the bookcase. *Abe Grows Up,* by Julia S. Northrup.

"She's my aunt," said Julia stiffly.

"Mmm. A very interesting family."

This round was a draw. Better get back to business, Teach. Julia sat down on the sofa, folded her hands, and said, "I think Lund left the doors unlocked himself."

Maggie replaced the book and sat down again too. "Would he do that? He must be a terrible landlord."

No need to lie about this. Julia nodded. "He's done all the worst things he can think of. Bribed the other tenants to move. Made sure the furnace pilot light kept going out all winter, but I learned to fix that. The electricity was off for ten days. The water was out for three full weeks before he called the plumbers. I had to tell him my son would bring suit for punitive damages too before he fixed it."

"That's rotten."

"I got some obscene phone calls too. Finally I started calling his wife every time and quoting them to her. Poor old fluffy-top Loretta. But the calls stopped."

"All to get you to move out?"

"Yes. But he hasn't succeeded."

"No. I can see that you can't be forced. But I'm afraid I still don't understand."

"What is there to understand? Artie Lund's a rat."

"Right. So why are you trying so hard to keep him from selling this house?"

"I'm not!" said Julia indignantly. "I'd love to have a better landlord!"

"Look, Mrs. Northrup, I'm not blind. Number one, here on the coffee table is today's *Times*. Heaped on top of it are lots of older newspapers and magazines. Months older."

"So what?"

"Number two. This place was reeking of rotten garbage a few minutes ago. Now it's fine."

Drat. Julia said defiantly, "I just got tired of the smell."

"Good. So did I. Number three, there's no dust in your corners. No soap scum on your sink or tub."

"So who uses soap?"

Maggie smiled but continued inexorably. "Number four. In the kitchen, the sink and floor are clean under a layer of trash."

"What the devil are you getting at?"

"I'll leave aside the book you say your Aunt Julia wrote. I suppose those are her notes about Frederick Law Olmsted too, the ones called 'Fred-Law Grows Up'? The ones I almost spilled my coffee on? Anyway, we'll leave them aside too. We'll go straight to number five. A few minutes ago you were shambling around just this side of an alcoholic stupor. Then you whipped up and down three flights of stairs without a stumble, and held a long, coherent, cold-sober discussion with me about the poor fellow upstairs."

"So? I've always been able to hold it."

"Number six. Your clothes are neat and clean."

"You think so, Bonesy?"

"Yes. But you've roughed up your hair and smudged dirt on your cheek, and put on that hideous sweater. Then you came hobbling out to meet us. It's a costume, Mrs. Northrup, all the way down to the slippers."

Mouth tight, Julia tried for an instant to stare her down, but failed. Instead, she had to swallow a wild urge to giggle. Teach, old thing, you're losing your touch. You used to be able to stare down an entire fifth-grade class. And here you've been bested by this skinny statistician. She said snappishly, "They itch."

"The slippers?"

"Yes." Briskly, Julia got up and scurried into the bathroom to comb her hair and wash her smudged face. Blasted observant little chippy. Impudent. Julia found herself smiling at her reflection in the mirror. What the devil, the police were coming, and a little respectability wouldn't hurt. She stuffed the ratty sweater and slippers back into the box under the vanity cabinet and slipped her grateful feet into her loafers. Neat again, she emerged from the bathroom.

Maggie was inspecting the kitchen mantel, more workmanlike and simpler than the one in Julia's main room, but with graceful proportions. Servants had gathered in this room, not the elegant Sweeneys. She said, "Pleased to meet you, Mrs. Northrup."

Julia said severely, "Don't get ideas, Bonesy. I'm changing my attire for the police. You and I are still at war."

"Yes, ma'am. May I help?"

"Just stay out of my way." Julia grabbed the box from under the kitchen sink and pitched everything in. Bottles on the bottom, old cans and wrappers next, newspapers on top. Then she shoved the box back under to await its next use. When she straightened, she saw that Maggie was lounging in the kitchen doorway, eyes on her watch.

"Two minutes flat," she said in admiration.

"I can set up even faster." Julia scowled. "The dishes really do have to be washed, of course. And that"—she pointed an accusing finger at a smear on the otherwise shiny kitchen floor—"is where your oaf of a real-estate man stepped on a chicken leg."

"Clumsy of him."

"Out of my way, Bonesy." Julia shouldered her way past the younger woman to the living room, pulled another empty box from the closet, and whisked the room straight.

"One minute, forty-eight seconds, this time," announced Maggie. "But did you really want to stow away your brand-new *Times*?"

Julia dove back into the box, retrieved her newspaper, and tossed it on the coffee table. "Why don't you make yourself useful and open those stupid drapes?"

Maggie complied. "It was a good show."

"I know. It always fooled everyone. The real-estate people, the would-be buyers, even Artie Lund." Julia was flipping the bedclothes straight. "Everyone but you."

"I'm married to an actor," Maggie explained. "And I like to play games too. This was a good one."

"Humph."

"A very good one. But I'm still not clear about why you don't want a change of landlords. Lund sounds terrible."

Julia shrugged. "Artie's turned into a jerk, but he was okay at the beginning. Once he resigns himself to keeping the place he'll be all right again. I faced him down about the lights and the water. Why change now that he's broken in? It hasn't been that much trouble handling him, till now."

"What do you mean, till now?"

"Look," said Julia, ignoring the question, crossing to the big windows. "Here come the police."

3

The first uniformed officers were followed within minutes by the suited homicide detectives. Lieutenant Brugioni was short and swarthy, with a triangular face and flat intelligent eyes. He introduced Sergeant Cleary, a pink and smiling Irishman. Julia and Maggie followed them upstairs and hovered curiously as the detectives surveyed the scene.

"Any news?" Maggie murmured to Nick.

"Not much. You were right: no weapon in sight."

Brugioni turned to young Lennie. "Were all these doors locked when you arrived?" He had a deep rumbly voice.

"No," said young Lennie. He was upset, Julia could see, but was trying manfully to sound calm and businesslike. Brugioni sounded that way without trying; poor dear, this sort of thing *was* his business. Lennie explained, "We keep the parlor-floor apartment locked because there's woodwork worth saving, and the stairwell to the basement is locked because Mrs. Northrup is still living here. But the apartments on the two top floors aren't locked separately. They're empty, nothing worth stealing. Anyone who managed to break into the main hall could easily come on up."

"How easy is it to get in down there?"

"Not easy. Deadbolt locks on the front door and kitchen

29

door. The French door in the dining room has a full-length rod lock."

"Windows?"

"The usual latches, plus bolts and grilles on the ground floor and parlor floor. Someone might get in by climbing to the second floor and breaking a window, I guess, but I didn't notice any broken panes."

"We'll check for forced doors. Who has keys besides you?"

"The owner. Arthur Lund. And maybe some of the ex-tenants kept keys. They all turned their keys in, Lund said, but of course copies can be made. The workers Lund has hired recently might have been given keys. Plumbers, electricians. And Mrs. Northrup has keys."

Brugioni, noting it all down, raised his eyebrows at Julia. She said crisply, "I have a key to the basement street doors, and to my own apartment. That's all. The garden door in the laundry room is sealed shut. And I don't have keys to anything above my floor."

"So you're limited to the ground floor?"

"Ground floor and cellar. That's all."

"I see." Brugioni's flat dark eyes looked her over. "You're the only one living in the building now?"

"Yes."

"We'd like to talk to you in a few minutes. First let us give this area a once-over. Mr. Trager, can you come along with us to answer questions?"

They moved off. Sergeant Cleary went downstairs. Julia could hear young Lennie's earnest explanations about closets and flues and sealed dumbwaiter shafts and window locks. Maggie was down the hall peering curiously into the little room, while the young officer who had been first on the scene looked on nervously. Julia realized suddenly that Nick was watching her.

"You're looking very winsome, Mrs. Northrup," he said.

Winsome. Julia shrugged. "Impressing the police."

"Yes, I figured it was something like that." He smiled at her. He wasn't a handsome man, but his warmth was contagious. Ah, Maggie, you silly young thing, keep him happy, keep him charmed, because a warm man is hard to find and impossible to replace.

Winsome, he'd said.

Julia reminded herself that he was the enemy and scowled at him. "It's not to impress you!"

"I'll remember." He nodded solemnly.

Young Lennie and Brugioni came back into the hall as the medical examiner and the first of the police technicians arrived, led by Sergeant Cleary. Brugioni conferred with them briefly, then turned to his witnesses. "We're going to let these fellows take over. Why don't we move on downstairs? You can show us the other floors, Mr. Trager."

"May I wait in my apartment?" Julia asked.

"Okay. In fact, if you're willing, Mrs. Northrup, it would be best if everyone waited there. We'll talk to you one at a time. Mr. Trager first, since he'll be showing us the other floors anyway."

The technicians were taking photographs, measuring, drawing diagrams. Julia and Maggie and Nick went down to wait in Julia's ground-floor apartment. Soon young Lennie appeared, looking distracted, and informed Maggie that it was her turn. He phoned his office to tell Joyce Banks about the problem. It was clear from his reaction that the news upset his boss. When he finally hung up, he looked unhappily at the phone a moment. Only then did he glance around Julia's apartment with increasing surprise.

"Hey," he blurted, "the place looks good, Mrs. Northrup!"

Julia smiled at him, winsomely. But Nick, browsing in her Dorothy Parker books, didn't notice.

"What's going on?" cried a familiar husky voice outside, followed by a patrolman's polite murmur. Julia hurried outside and unlatched the wrought-iron gate under the stoop.

"Hi, Pauline. Can't talk now."

"What's going on, Teach?" Pauline McGuire leaned her bike against the steps. She was in her navy fleece cycling outfit, Nikes, short-clipped gray hair. Behind thick lenses, her dark eyes were bewildered.

"I'll tell you about it later. All right?"

Pauline glanced at the patrolman but refused to be intimidated. "Come on, Teach! You're as evasive as a teenager."

"Evasive as yours, maybe," snapped Julia. "In my opinion, your Audrey was better back then. She's turned glum since she got religion and moved away."

"I'll never complain about a rich and faithful son-in-law.

Now, tell me, did Artie—oh! You've got visitors?" She squinted into the darkness under the stoop behind Julia.

"I'm just here looking at the house." It was Maggie, blast her, still dogging Julia's footsteps somehow. "I'm Maggie Ryan."

Pauline took her extended hand. "Pauline McGuire. Friend of Julia's here. Well—sorry to bother you. Give me a ring when you can, Teach."

"Maybe, since you're here, you can tell us something," Maggie suggested. Julia noticed Brugioni peering out inquisitively from the door under the stoop. "You were here for dinner Tuesday night, right?"

"Um—yes." Pauline's glance at Julia was uneasy.

"The plumbers were making a lot of noise."

"Yes. We asked them to be quieter."

Brugioni joined them. "Lieutenant Brugioni, homicide," he said to Pauline, flashing his card. "Would you mind answering some questions about Tuesday?"

"Me?" squeaked Pauline. "Homicide?" She looked wildly at Julia.

"Yes, ma'am. Your name is McGuire?" rumbled Brugioni.

"Um—Pauline McGuire, yes."

"Since you're here, maybe you could give us some information."

"I just stopped to see if Julia was okay, because I saw the cop," explained Pauline.

"I'll see you in just a few minutes." Brugioni was firm. "Please wait with Mrs. Northrup while I finish with Mr. O'Connor."

"Um—yes, of course."

They followed him back into the building. When he and Nick had left, Julia waved a hand at her sofa. "Sit down, Pauline. I tried to warn you."

"What does he mean, Teach? Homicide?"

"They found a murder victim in the top-floor front," Julia explained wearily. "Young man. Blond, curly hair."

"Do you remember anything, Mrs. McGuire?" asked Maggie eagerly. "We were wondering if the plumbers were involved."

"The plumbers? A murder? Look, I'm all muddled!"

"We all are," said Julia. "Oh, I almost forgot. Pauline McGuire, this is young Lennie from the Joyce Banks agency. Trager, is that it, Lennie?"

"Yes. Glad to meet you." He was slumped morosely at the other end of the sofa, but smiled politely enough.

"Do you remember anything about the plumbers, Mrs. McGuire?" Maggie persevered.

"They were in the kitchen just upstairs, clowning around. But they were about ready to leave. We'd left the oven on so we came right back down when they left. Why are you so interested? Was he murdered with a pipe or something?"

"Nope. He was knocked out with a bottle, then strangled," said Julia.

Pauline's hand gave a sympathetic twitch toward her own throat. "God! Top floor, you said?"

"Yes. Front room. Remember where Jack and Ann served us that Ethiopian food?"

Pauline nodded, distressed.

"Hey, old thing, I know it's a shock!" Julia hugged her friend. "But be grateful you didn't have to see the body!"

"Did you see it?" whispered Pauline.

But Julia's attention had been caught by an angry voice outside. She hurried to the bay window, shielding herself behind the drapes. It was Artie Lund, arguing with the uniformed officer who was posted by the stoop.

"But it's my house!"

"Yes, sir, Mr. Lund. Just a moment, we're asking about it."

"But Mrs. Banks said I should come right over!"

Sergeant Cleary appeared at the top of the steps and identified himself. "I'd like to ask you a few questions, Mr. Lund."

"*You* want to ask *me*? Do you realize this thing could ruin me?"

"In what way, sir?"

"In what—my God! I'm trying to sell this place, you know!"

"Yes?"

"Well, my God, who's going to buy it with murders going on? Why can't you people protect us? Protect our property?" He was shouting and his face had grown crimson.

"Yes, sir," agreed Cleary politely. "Can you tell me who has access to this building?"

"Anybody can get in! No police around, any hippie or junkie in the borough could walk in!"

"You leave it unlocked?"

Artie sobered up a little. "No, of course not! Good locks on this building. Expensive. But junkies just break in."

"Yes, sir, but there are no signs of a break-in here."

"What? But then how—"

"It was probably done with a key, sir. Can you tell me who can get in? Who has keys?" Cleary was leaning against the main door, holding it open, while he took notes.

"Keys." Lund's face worked. "That old bag in the basement apartment!"

Julia's hand clenched on the heavy drapery fabric. You liar, Artie. You rat.

Cleary said, "Yes, sir, we're checking on that. Who else would have a key?"

Artie was too shrewd to push it. He mumbled irritably, "Quite a few, I guess. Realtors, meter readers. Plumbing foreman. Old tenants might have copies, I guess."

"You, too, of course?"

"Of course we've got keys! We *own* it, for God's sake! Wish we didn't."

"Yes, sir. When you say 'we,' you mean yourself and who else?"

"My wife."

"Name?"

"Loretta."

"Loretta Lund. And her occupation?"

"She's a beautician. Owns half of the Loretta Rose Salon down toward Midwood."

"Okay. And your occupation is landlord?"

"Hell, no! I'm an accountant. We inherited this thing from her uncle. He added those apartments upstairs, got it stuck under rent control. Thought he was doing us a favor, but my God! After a few years we could see we had to get our equity out. But in eight months we only got one offer, and that was contingent on delivering the damn thing vacant. The idiot must have thought we had rent control by choice. Look, officer, um, Sergeant, does this have to get out? It's so tough to sell the place already."

"Sorry, sir. This appears to be a homicide. Papers are usually interested."

"Hell."

"Maybe you'd come in with me, Mr. Lund, and see if you recognize the body."

Artie's eagerness to go in evaporated. "My God! Do I have to?"

"Well, sir, the sooner we get it cleared up, the sooner it'll blow over."

"Maybe so." Artie started reluctantly up the steps.

"Now, when was the last time you were here, sir?" Cleary was holding the door for him.

"Maybe three weeks ago. Top-floor tenants moved out, we came over to straighten up after them."

They disappeared inside. Julia turned from the window to find Maggie beside her. Nick had returned, but Pauline was gone. Probably talking to Brugioni.

"Well. What did the lieutenant want to know?" asked Julia.

"All the same stuff we talked about," said Maggie. "He's curious about the weapon, which seems to have disappeared."

"I wondered if that was what they were driving at," said Lennie.

"What kind of weapon?" asked Julia.

"Well, we're not really supposed to talk about what they asked," said Lennie uneasily.

Maggie nodded. "Except it's obvious that it has to be something to strangle with. They weren't asking about guns or blunt instruments even with that Chianti bottle right there."

"Why not bare hands?" asked Julia.

Maggie shrugged. "Why don't you ask them?"

"I will." She looked out the window again. "There he goes, poor thing." They were carrying him down the steps on a stretcher, a sheet over his still form. "So young."

"Young people die too," said Maggie, eyes dark with her own memories.

"Yes. Dorothy Parker thought she'd die young. 'You will be frail and musty, with peering, furtive head, whilst I am young and lusty among the roaring dead.'"

"Maybe so. I'd rather give frail and musty a chance, myself." Maggie's eyes were on the scene outside. Several pedestrians had spotted the police van from Eighth Avenue and had drifted closer to see what was happening. Four of Wilma Riggins's grandchildren were practically in the van themselves. The officer at the door moved to the curb to shoo them away in kindly fashion, then helped the others slide their burden inside. The van drove away. A moment later Artie came out the door, looking defeated, but before he crossed the street he glared balefully at Julia's window.

"Mr. Lund likes you as much as you like him," Maggie observed quietly.

Julia jerked around to face her. She said, "Cornelius Sweeney's son Mikey was a precocious child. He told the mayor his fly was unbuttoned, pointed out to the butcher that his thumb was on the scale, things like that. Everyone laughed and told him what a clever boy he was. One day a nice young couple came to town, and Mikey spoke up as usual. Mentioned that they seemed to be taking Mr. Jensen's money away from him. The nice young couple shot Mikey's leg off."

"Lucky for me that you and Mr. Lund aren't a nice young couple," said Maggie cheerfully. Young Lennie looked shocked at the exchange, though Nick's eyes were smiling.

There was a knock at the door and Brugioni entered, followed by a very solemn Pauline. "Oh, you're still here?" Brugioni said to Lennie. "I should have told you it's okay to go. Here are your keys." He dropped them on the bookcase next to the door. "Mr. Lund gave us his extra set. But we'll seal the upstairs for the time being, until the lab gives us the okay. So don't take any more customers through."

"Okay." Lennie began buttoning his trench coat as he started for the door.

"The rest of you can go too. Thank you all, you've been very helpful. Oh, Mr. Trager, you might tell Mrs. Banks that I'll stop by her office later today to get information on who's been through this building recently. Tell her about four o'clock, all right?"

"Yes, she was planning on being in the office later this afternoon." Young Lennie was dutifully noting the information in his little notebook.

"Thanks. Mrs. Northrup, may I speak to you now?"

"Yes, of course."

"Okay," he said to the others. "We'll be in touch if any more questions come up."

They left. Brugioni refused a cup of coffee but consented to sit next to her on the sofa. Julia studied him covertly as he arranged his notebook. A cop. A man's man, using that deep voice to good advantage, no nonsense. But he'd have a tough Italian grandmother somewhere urging him to be a good boy. And somewhere too he'd had a teacher like Julia; it showed in that touch of deference as he addressed her. He took her carefully over the same ground he had covered earlier with Maggie, making notes. Who had been around? When? What kind of noises had she heard? About halfway through the questions, there was another knock at the door. Cleary entered. "We've finished the rest of the house, Frank."

Brugioni cleared his throat. "Mrs. Northrup, the murder weapon is missing from the room upstairs. We're searching the premises. Would you mind if we looked around here?"

"Go right ahead, Lieutenant. But I think I would have noticed if someone left it here. What is it? What are you looking for?"

"We don't know, exactly. You saw the body."

"Looked strangled to me," said Julia bluntly.

"Yes, the medical examiner will probably agree with you, although of course we can't be sure until he's run his tests. The young man was knocked on the head first, I'd say, but basically we're looking for something thin and flexible."

"It wasn't done just with bare hands?"

"No."

"A garotte."

"Something along those lines."

"Well, I haven't noticed anything like that. But it could be a lot of things, couldn't it? Belts, neckties, necklaces, clotheslines? I own some of those things."

"Yes, we all do. We have to check, of course, Mrs. Northrup, but we have no reason to believe it was any of your things."

"Well, of course it wasn't. But look all you want. I want you to catch whoever it is. I don't like him getting into this house so easily." She tried a flutter of eyelashes: brave but fearful little woman. It worked. Brugioni became solicitous.

"We'll do our best, Mrs. Northrup," he rumbled kindly. "Don't worry. Of course I would advise you to keep all your doors and windows locked."

"Yes, indeed." She stood by in silence as Brugioni's men sifted through her things, looking behind her books, in her handbag, in her drawers, unmaking and remaking the bed, checking behind the pictures, in bottles and boxes, in canisters, in the garbage, in the stove and refrigerator, in the boxes of ratty clothes and old newspapers she had just packed away. Watching one detective politely inspect the baseboard, Julia said, "Lieutenant Brugioni, it looks as though you think I did it."

"No, no, this is just a routine check, Mrs. Northrup. We have to be sure the weapon wasn't left here."

"You mean the killer nipped in here, pried off the baseboard to hide the weapon, and then slipped away again without me noticing? Come, Lieutenant Brugioni, you can't believe that!"

A tiny smile tweaked his thin lips. "No, Mrs. Northrup. But you did explain that you'd been out of the house several times in the last couple of days. We can't overlook any possibilities."

"Oh, I understand. You're hunting for something, and if you find it, it either means that a murderer got into my apartment without my knowledge or else it means I'm the murderer."

Brugioni glanced away from her steady gaze and cleared his throat like a grotesquely deep-voiced fifth-grader. "Yes, ma'am. I'm sure we won't find it here. But we have to look."

In the end, the technicians solemnly signed out her toaster and iron with their scuffed cords, a dress with a fabric sash, a worn scarf, and three stockings, promising to return them all as soon as they could. The searchers had moved into the backyard and were checking the trash. She was impressed by their thoroughness. She would never have thought of some of the places they looked, and she had learned a lot from forty years of teaching fifth grade. She thought of fat little Bobby Cody, who had tried to hide his pocket money from the sixth-grade bullies by poking it up his own rear end. He'd been wriggly and miserable all morning, until Julia had pulled him aside privately and got the sordid little story from him. Well, so far the police had limited themselves to checking the premises, but she had no doubts that if the occasion arose they'd be equally ingenious at searching her person. After all, they dealt regularly with the full-grown Bobby Codys of the world, to say nothing of the full-grown bullies that the Bobby Codys feared.

She was glad now that Maggie had called her bluff and got her out of her wino costume. It was much better to meet the police as neat, grandmotherly Julia Northrup, one of the little old ladies who inspired every Boy Scout and rookie policeman to paroxysms of male protectiveness. Men were such romantics. The repulsive bag-lady Julia Northrup would not have fit those idealistic notions, would not have received such polite treatment.

But what she had won with the police, she had lost with Maggie, she reflected uneasily. Maggie had seemed amused, even delighted, with Julia's charade. Liked games herself, she'd said. There hadn't been any of the shock and revulsion that Julia usually inspired within seconds of meeting prospective buyers. Well, she'd just have to probe a little harder at the weak points. And there were weak points— the husband, the skinniness. Maybe others. But it would be tough.

Brugioni and Cleary left at last, urging her to call them if she thought of anything else, or if she heard any suspicious noises. She smiled and thanked them and said she would. Then she went to her kitchen, closed and bolted the window again, and got her handbag and coat and grocery list. In the mirror by the door, she looked herself over. Neat, frisky little old woman. Winsome, he had said. She smiled at her image. By golly, he was right. Humming, she locked the doors behind her and walked to Seventh Avenue. She needed bananas, orange juice, yogurt, bread. And one other thing.

"How're you doing, Mrs. Northrup?" Benny Bugliari, an ex-student, was now the proud owner of this shop, and of a few other enterprises that Julia preferred not to ask about.

"Fine, Benny. How's Carla?"

"Growing like a weed. A flower. A gorgeous kid."

"I meant, how's she doing in school," said Julia tartly.

"Okay. She's not much for math, though."

"Gets that from you. I thought you'd never figure out fractions. Look, Benny, send her over to me if she seems to be in trouble with it."

"Sure. Thanks, Mrs. Northrup. You're looking good today."

"It's the excitement, Benny."

"What excitement?"

"It'll be in the papers. They found a body in one of the empty rooms."

"In your house?" Benny's tone suggested that it had been found in Supreme Court chambers.

"Yes. In Mr. Arthur Lund's house."

"Really? A dead body? Who was it?"

"Nobody knows. A blond fellow. He might have died there, or he might have been brought in from outside. Benny, you tell me if you hear who it is."

"I don't want no trouble with the police."

"*Any* trouble. Don't bang those bananas down."

"Any trouble." Benny eased the fruit into the bag. "I really don't, Mrs. Northrup."

"There won't be any trouble for you, Benny. But listen to people. See if you can find anything out for me. Okay?"

"Okay. Can I come see?"

"They took him away already."

"I mean, can I see where it happened?"

"I don't have keys to that part of the house. Best I can do is show you the window of the room from the street, and give you a cup of coffee."

"Hey, maybe after work tonight."

"Bring Carla and I'll quiz her on math."

"Okay. Hey, take care of yourself, Mrs. Northrup!"

"See you, Benny."

Julia picked up her bag of groceries and the tape from the register and went back out into the cool sunny afternoon. She paused for a moment by the wire trash basket that Benny kept out front. It was nearly full; collection day was tomorrow. She dropped her register tape into the basket, spotted the wadded McDonald's bag two-thirds of the way down, and deftly pulled it out through the side of the basket. She dropped it into her grocery bag and went on down the street, skirting around a couple whose shoulder-length hair and neon headbands added brilliant color to the day. Vic Jr. claimed she'd end up a bag lady if she stayed in Brooklyn. Well, when the day came, she'd have the necessary skills. Mrs. Northrup, the interviewer would say, we are all impressed by your ability. Did you have to train long? Well, Sonny, she'd croak in reply, it helps to have a natural bent, but nothing beats long practice.

At home, she put away her groceries, then emptied the sugar canister into a bowl. Carefully, she placed the little

McDonald's bag in the bottom of the canister, then refilled it with sugar to its old level and threw the surplus away. Finally, she replaced the canister next to the others. She wasn't sure what to expect, but things here should be just as they were before. The police had been very competent and thorough, and they'd be back, to return her things if nothing else.

Probably not today, though. Julia took her screwdriver from her tool drawer and crossed the kitchen to the built-in cabinet. She unbolted and unlatched the door and took out the mops and buckets.

The idea had crystallized a couple of months ago. She'd been sitting with Jack and Ann and they'd told her they were thinking of leaving.

"Don't give in!" she'd urged them.

"Look, Teach," Jack had explained, his black face earnest. "Ann told you about our redecorated hall?"

Julia had nodded. That had been crude even for Artie: red spray paint forming a gigantic KKK outside their door. Jack had hit the ceiling—accosted Artie in his office, shouting threats that had been overheard by a lot of people. Artie, in fact, had appeared later that day and painted over the obscenity. But Ann feared that Jack's outburst had given their hated landlord additional weapons to use against them. Julia couldn't blame Jack—she remembered her own father's accounts of "No Irish need apply," the look of rage and impotence that tightened his kindly face when he spoke of it—and she knew that his emotional recollections of abuse were minor compared to what Jack and Ann's people had suffered, still suffered. "I can't tell you to turn the other cheek," she admitted.

"I know you don't want to give up," Jack said. "But med school takes all my time. And Ann is working two shifts to put me through. We can't take this hassle."

"Besides, the relocation money would pay the difference in rent for a year," Ann had added.

"And after that?" Julia had asked. But arguing was fruitless, she had known. They were young, with incomes going up rather than down. Why should they want to fight this particular battle? She'd stared at the wall and wondered if the thin panel was all that shielded the dumbwaiter shaft on this floor. She knew the other floors were sealed off with studs and wallboard. So when Jack came to the end of his earnest explanation, she said, "Oh, Jack, you're right. I just hate to give Artie the satisfaction. But let's change the subject. Have you people ever been up to the attic?"

"No, and I've always wanted to!" Ann enthused.

"You guys are crazy," announced Jack.

"Come on, Jack, where's our flashlight?" insisted Ann.

Julia and Ann had climbed up the ladder to the cramped little space under the eaves. The flashlight had gleamed on cobwebs, dirty insulation, and old machinery: the big wheel, the ancient frayed ropes. That week, without telling anyone, Julia had gone up again to oil the wheel, check the brake, replace the ropes and dust them with resin. The machinery was filthy, but still sturdy. Down in her own apartment, she had unscrewed the car from the walls and tested it. Piles of dust had come puffing down from the attic, making her sneeze, but the little car had creaked its way up and down once more. When Jack and Ann had left at last, she had adjusted both the counterweights, climbed into the car herself, pulled herself to the third floor, and tapped out the panel. It hadn't been hard for an ex-fifth-grade teacher to install hinges, a handle, and bolts on the inner side of the panel to hold it in place. Presto! A secret door. A priest-hole. A good toy for an old lady's second childhood. And most important, a way to keep an eye on Artie in case he decided to use those empty floors to plot against her.

Now she again removed the six sturdy screws that held the car in position in her kitchen, climbed into the compartment, tugged on the brake release, and began to haul herself up slowly with the hand rope.

The police were good and clever searchers, and with their photographs and fingerprints they might find something. But after seventeen years Julia knew this old house better than they did, and she wanted to make sure that they hadn't missed anything. Old eyes might not sparkle as much as young eyes, but they were a lot wiser.

She locked the brake, unbolted her secret door, and stepped out into Jack and Ann's low-ceilinged rooms to begin her search.

4

"My God, Len. You look ready to faint."

"I'm okay. But it was a shock."

Joyce didn't look exactly calm herself. No sign of her dimpled smile. She kept wiping nervously at a stray curl that had once been elegantly draped across her forehead. "The clients," she said. "Are they all right?"

"I think so. Acted very calm and sensible." Len didn't tell her that he'd thrown up, that Nick had gotten him into the bathroom just in time while Maggie took the keys to go down and call the police. Len added, "But we can't really expect them to come back after this."

"Oh, I suppose not. But I'm an optimist. I just hoped they weren't too horrified."

"Well, dammit, it was horrifying!"

"All right, all right. They reacted pretty well, all things considered?"

"Yes. If you want to worry about someone, worry about Lund. He was very upset."

"I know. After you called I decided we really should tell Arthur, so I called him. He rang back after he'd been there, and screamed a few minutes but ended up telling us to carry on. He accused us of being careless with the key. I said of course not."

"He's got no room to complain. He gives copies of those

43

keys to every cheap plumber and electrician and meter reader in the state."

"Yes, I pointed that out to him. And we've got no control over the previous tenants either. He refused to change the lock after they moved out, remember?"

"Yeah. You reminded him of that too?"

"Of course. He claimed he was waiting for Mrs. Northrup to leave too, but she doesn't have keys to the main floors anyway. Arthur quieted down eventually. But he doesn't seem to have any idea who the dead man is, so he's looking for someone to blame."

"No one has any idea. Not even the old lady."

"The old lady saw the body?"

"She came up to look, decided she didn't know him."

"Do you think she was telling the truth?"

"Oh, Joyce, I have no idea. I thought so. Maybe the shock sobered her up, I don't know. I couldn't think very coherently at the time. Still can't."

Joyce looked him over, poked feebly at the sagging curl on her forehead, and said, "You're right. Why don't you go on home early, Len? You're not going to sell anything until you sleep off that glazed look."

"It's early. And Lieutenant Brugioni said he'd be over later today."

"Not all that early. I'll cope with the police. Run along, now. Go home and have a stiff drink. You won't do us any good in that condition."

Early as he was, he found that Nancy was home even earlier. She had changed into jeans and a crinkly gauze shirt, and was calmly slicing vegetables at the counter. She did not look pregnant at all. He had thought he'd have a few minutes alone with a beer to collect himself, and her presence rattled him. When she looked up, she frowned at him in worry.

"Len, are you okay?"

"Oh, God, Nance!" He hugged her fiercely, kissed her hair and ears and eyebrows. She clung to him too. In a moment he sensed that she was sobbing. He said, "Oh, God, I don't want you to be upset!"

"You're upset too." She gave his chin a tearful kiss.

"Yes, but I saw the body. You didn't."

She became very still in his arms. "What body?"

He suddenly remembered that she didn't know. He said, "In the Lund place. There was a corpse."

"Len, you're kidding!"

"I'm not kidding. God, Nance, I can't think straight today. I don't want to upset you."

"Then tell me what the hell you're talking about! What corpse in the Lund place?" She swiped at her eyes with her gauzy sleeve, pulled away from him, picked up the knife again.

He said, "I need a drink. You want one too?"

"Yes. No. No, I'll skip it."

"Okay." He got a beer, swallowed some, and pulled his thoughts together. "A couple called about the Lund place, and Joyce asked me to take them over this afternoon. And after we'd seen the lower floors we went up to the top floor. And Maggie, that was the woman's name, she found it. Him. He was lying on an old mattress that the last tenants had left up there. He'd been strangled."

"God, Len!" The knife had stopped slicing again. "Who was it?"

"No one seems to know." He drank some more beer, then focused on the little pale face regarding him so anxiously. "Nance, you're back early too. Are you okay?"

"Yeah." She turned back to her carrots. "I just thought—"

He waited, but she was concentrating on the pile of orange disks and didn't continue. A vision of the hideous dead face floated into his consciousness again, and he gulped some more beer to try to banish it.

Nancy said, "It was awful, wasn't it?"

"His face. I mean, he'd been strangled, so it was— Nance, I don't want to upset you too!"

"But it is upsetting. Shocking."

"Yeah. Disturbing."

"Perturbing."

"Perplexing," Len continued automatically, then slammed the beer can down on the counter. "Nance, God, how can we play games? The man is dead!"

She reached over with a carrot-scented hand to rub him consolingly on the back. After a moment she said, "The game wasn't really about him. It was about John Leonard Trager, who is very upset."

"Yeah. Yeah, Joyce sent me home early. Probably afraid I'd get hysterical in front of her clients."

"Well, you should be disturbed! Perturbed. Whatever. Why don't you have another beer, and tell me about it?"

"Because I don't want you worrying about it too. Not now!"

She said defiantly, "And why not now?"

"Yeah. I know. You're right." He'd have to watch it. Nance's ethereal appearance was misleading. She would never allow herself to suffer from any condition that implied weakness or dependence. She guarded her freedom ferociously, determined to live life on her own terms. It was silly to suggest that anything, even pregnancy, would change that. Sometimes she even seemed to see her fondness for Len as a dangerous weakness, and even after three years of living together she insisted that they had no claims on each other. Hell, she could make any claims she wanted on him. But the one time he had mentioned marriage, long ago, she had disappeared for two weeks. He'd had to break the rules and hunt her down at the studio, interrupt her painting, and promise that there would never be any strings attached, before she would even admit that she'd missed him too. So now he said, "Let me do something useful too while I tell you."

"You can start the chicken. And tell me about his face. That bothered you."

He described the details to her. The shock of Maggie's announcement, the shock of what was in that little room: the bloating, the darkness of the puffed skin below the bright blond hair, the protruding tongue. His own nausea, he could confess that to her too. Every now and then he glanced at her warily. She was responding to his words almost viscerally, her vivid artist's imagination rebuilding the ghastly scene in her own mind. When he'd finished she embraced him, burrowing her face into his chest, and said, "Poor Len."

"Thanks for letting me talk. Maybe it'll help me get it under control."

"I hope so. God, Len!"

"Can I get you a beer or something?"

"Oh, dinner's almost ready now. I want you to tell me the rest, too. What the police said, and so forth."

She was right. It helped put it into perspective, put it into the context of a puzzle, of police work, of a system prepared to deal with violence. The image of the man still brought his mind to a shuddering halt whenever he thought of it, but he began to hope that someday, eventually, that would fade a little too.

After dinner she put away the leftovers while he scoured the pots. She said, "Len?"

"Yeah?"

"About me being pregnant."

He scrubbed at a frying pan. "Yeah?"

"Well, what do you think?"

Careful now. Len said, "I don't know what I think. Except I think you're the important one."

"Mm."

"And whatever you decide will be okay with me. You know that."

"But what would be best?"

He looked at her helplessly. "I can't tell you that, Nance." She seemed dissatisfied, and he added apologetically, "It's been a hell of a day."

She studied him a moment, then nodded, resigned. "A rotten day. A lousy day."

"A wretched day."

"A nefarious day."

He dried his hands and gently backed her against the refrigerator door so that he could look into her pained and loving eyes as he said solemnly, "A foul and scurrilous and most detestable day."

They both laughed. She linked her hands behind his neck and said, "Let's give up on it. Tomorrow will be better."

Lieutenant Brugioni said, "Mr. Trager, we've learned the identity of the murdered man."

"You have?"

The detective's dark face was smiling, crafty. "It turns out that he was a child. Your child. Do you know who would want to kill your child?"

"Len? Len, are you all right?" Nancy's soft hand was on his shoulder. He flinched away from her, rolled over, threw his forearm across his eyes to shut out the light. She sat up next to him and asked, "Bad dream?"

"Yeah."

"Yeah, I didn't sleep that well either."

The reality of the nightmare slipped away from him

slowly, thick and sluggish as candle wax. He moved his forearm a little and squinted at her, and for a moment hated her. No, not her. Her power. How could he have put his future in the hands of this unpredictable other person? He was trapped. A decision of enormous importance to him, and he was not allowed any say in it. No strings, she had said. But this was a hell of a string. A rope. A goddamn chain.

He swung grumpily out of bed and beat her to the bathroom. Shaving, a bit of sanity returned. She too was facing questions of time and money and emotion, of guilt, of potential, of relief. And she would suffer physically too, whichever way she decided. Her body, her career, her life.

But, dammit, his too! It was only a difference of degree.

He wondered who the dead man really was.

At the office, Joyce was already at work. She came in early a couple of times a week to catch up on the mail. She looked him over critically when he arrived and said, "You're better. Guess you had that drink last night."

"Yeah, I'm coping. What's up today?"

"Some people for you to call. The top two may be ready to list their buildings. Then we have the ad copy to call in. And this last fellow, Wilson, is never at home or at work either when Cronin calls. I'd like you to see if he's there when Trager calls."

"What's his problem?"

"Six weeks behind in the rent. You may mention legal steps, but with the usual great reluctance."

"Okay."

"And are you up to being a hero?"

"A hero?"

"The press started calling yesterday. I put them off, but you'll have to talk to them."

"Oh, God."

"So be prepared. Why don't you take a minute right now, and write out a statement of what you'll say. I'll look it over. We want to look like a dynamic business, in control, even in this sad situation. Okay? And stress that the owner was having work done on the building. Lots of people in and out."

"Right." Dynamic and in control. What a laugh, with the sterling representative of Joyce Banks Realty puking at his first glimpse of the corpse. Being rescued by the client. Still, he didn't think Nick would tattle on him, so he might as well try to do what Joyce wanted. The newspapers would make up their own version of the truth anyway. He wrote a brief, almost upbeat summary of the story, and Joyce skimmed it on her way out to a meeting on Wall Street.

"Fine. Remember, if they ask about details, don't give any more than this. Especially don't give out the clients' names or Arthur's name. They'll probably find Arthur anyway, but we shouldn't be the ones to point him out."

"What about Mrs. Northrup?"

"Leave her out of it. They'll track her down anyway, of course, and she'll bad-mouth everyone, including us, but let's not push them into her arms."

The door opened and a teenager with a crutch angled his way through it. He was handsome, dark-haired, with an ingratiating grin. "Hi, everyone!" he sang out, then hobbled to Renata to murmur, "Sis, can you loan me a hundred?"

"Are you kidding?" said Renata cheerfully, not looking up from her typewriter.

"Come on. It's important. I'll get it back to you soon."

"Tony, you owe me two hundred and twenty already." Renata, with a furtive, embarrassed glance at Joyce, lowered her voice. "Also, I'm not carrying that much. Now, get out of here!"

"Don't cop out, Sis! Once I can function I'll get the money quick."

"Yeah." Renata glared at him. "Very quick. Meanwhile, get out of here! I've got work to do even if you haven't."

"Hey, Sis, don't get uptight! I wouldn't hassle you, but something heavy came up. It's—well, it's not frivolous, I swear."

Renata stood up. Len could sense the terror bubbling under her cool surface. "Don't lay that on me! Look, Tony, I'll catch you tonight. But no more visits here. Ever! Now split!"

Tony shrugged, beamed a bright smile at the others in the office, and limped out. Renata said, "Sorry, folks," and returned to her typewriter, jaw clenched.

Joyce rested a manicured hand on her shoulder. "It's

tough when your brothers or sisters are in trouble," she
murmured.

"Yeah. And if you can't help. God, I'm sorry. I love that
kid, but he can't seem to get it together!" said Renata in a
tight little voice.

Joyce nodded, gave her shoulder a final pat, and swept
out to her meeting.

Two reporters phoned. Len read them his statement,
answered all their questions with paraphrases from it, and
felt a moment of satisfaction when they gave up.

There was no report of the Garfield Place murder in
the *Times*. Apollo 16, back from the moon, had splashed
down. Two factions of antiwar Columbia students were
taking over buildings from each other. North Vietnam was
battering Quangtri, and Nixon was pulling out American
troops. John Lennon and Yoko Ono were fighting depor-
tation. In the real-estate news, an unknown woman had
apparently been collecting fees from prospective low-income
tenants and guaranteeing them apartments in a new complex that were not hers to guarantee. Thirty-three cheated
families had taken over the Model Cities office. The woman had melted away. "How to make a killing in real estate,
low-income style," said Len to Joyce as she returned from
her meeting.

She glanced at the article. "She's got a lot to learn," she
informed Len as she took her coat to the closet in her own
office. "United is juggling low-income-area mortgages to
skim off federal money. Why fleece the poor of a few
dollars when you can fleece the feds of thousands?"

"Speaking of mortgages, how was your meeting?"

"I skewered them!" gloated Joyce. "This is one area
they'll never redline again! You should have seen that
bank president's face!" One of the secrets of Joyce's success was her inclination to treat business conferences as
Olympic contests.

The phone rang. Renata scooped it up. "Joyce Banks
Realty... Len, it's for you."

"Len Trager," he said into the receiver.

"Len, it's Maggie Ryan. We want to make an offer on the
Garfield Place building."

"You what?"

"Is there a problem?"

"Well, there's—no, I guess there's no problem."

"The police should be finished by the time we actually buy the place."

"Yes, of course. Um, you do realize that Mrs. Northrup will want to stay on in her apartment?"

"Oh, yes, she made that clear. It's not a problem. I like smart scrappy women."

Those were not the adjectives Len would have chosen to describe Mrs. Northrup, but he had long since learned to accept a client's word that a problem was not a problem. He said, "Well, that's great. Do you want to come by here to fill in the blanks, or shall I bring it to you?"

"I'll come by in a few minutes, on my lunch hour again, if that's okay."

"Sure. Will your husband be here too?"

"He has an audition uptown. But if you and I work out the details, we can show it to our lawyer today and return it signed. How late are you open tonight?"

"Someone should be here till five."

"We'll get it back by then or first thing tomorrow. See you soon!"

Len hung up. Hot dog! But he was stunned. A murder, added to Mrs. Northrup's filth and intractable malevolence, hadn't sent this couple elsewhere like all the others. Why not? Maybe they thought they could get it cheap. Certainly Lund was upset enough to be more reasonable than he'd been before. But there was still a long way to go. The offer, whatever it was, had to be acceptable to Lund, and a mortgage for an unemployed actor had to be found. Still, achieving even this first step was exciting. Len pulled out a purchase-offer blank and the information sheets on Lund's building, and began to fill in the legal description.

Maybe he'd make a little money this year after all.

Maybe, if Nancy decided to have the baby, he could add enough to his savings to buy a building too. Why should Fred's doctors be the only ones to make money? He was halfway to a down payment already. If he sold a few thousand dollars' worth more than last year, he could save nearly all the new money. He and Nancy could keep a roomy apartment for themselves, rent out the rest of the space to support the building, hire a top-notch sitter. A nanny.

Of course, if he didn't swing it, if they had to stay where they were, life would be a mess. A baby tucked into the corner of their bedroom. Soon a kid, needing clothes, doctors, a place for friends to visit, basketballs, ice skates. Schools. He always told clients the public school near their apartment was above average, but was that good enough? And there would be no nanny. A cheap sitter, maybe a recent immigrant with poor English. Would Nancy quit her job? She shouldn't, not now, not when her career was really beginning to move. It would be more reasonable for him to quit; he could pick up more easily later. But that was unthinkable too: with both of them working, they could pay for the two-room apartment, good food, necessary clothes, a little savings.

But he didn't want his kid to grow up on the streets of New York. A latchkey child.

Goddamn. It wasn't fair. Not to him, not to her, not to the kid. They just couldn't manage it now.

What would she decide?

"What are you mooning about, on company time?" teased Joyce. She had come out to fetch a cup of coffee from Renata's pot.

"Oh. Sorry." Len looked down at his half-finished form. "It's amazing. That couple yesterday, at Lund's? They want to make an offer."

"You're kidding!" Mug in hand, she stared at him.

"Nope. She's coming here in a few minutes to work out the terms."

Renata had looked up from her work too. "Hey, far out!"

"Fantastic!" Joyce crowed, dimpling. "I told you to be optimistic! You clever thing, Len, I'll have to put you on some of our other dog properties!" She sobered suddenly. "Do they understand about the Northrup woman? Not that you should belabor the point, but she'll be tough to remove. We did make it clear yesterday."

"So did Mrs. Northrup. No, they understood perfectly well. The wife thinks Mrs. Northrup is smart and scrappy. Even said she liked her."

"Really? No accounting for taste. The only sign of competence I've ever seen from that old lady is that rent check coming in like clockwork. Even when Arthur was trying to refuse it she registered the letters."

"Maybe she's okay when she's sober," said Len. "Joyce, I have another question."

"Mm-hmm?"

"I've been toying with the idea of investing in a building. Renovating it myself, and so forth, one of these days. Do you think that would be a problem with my work here?"

She regarded him thoughtfully. "Two reactions," she said. "First, you'd be better than ninety percent of the guys who try to do that. Second, when you're ready, I'll submit it to my investment team."

Len was elated. This was better than agreement. But before he could follow up, the street door opened and Brugioni and Cleary entered. "Good morning," said the lieutenant, nodding at them.

"Hello, Lieutenant Brugioni," said Joyce. "How can we help you?"

"A couple of things, thank you, Mrs. Banks. First, our people have come up with this sketch of the victim. They cleaned up the—face—and so forth, so it's closer to his appearance in life. We thought you people could give it a look, see if it reminds you of anyone."

"Sure," said Joyce. How sordid this whole affair must seem to her, Len thought. But if the house sold anyway, it would make anything all right in her eyes. Joyce added, "You'll probably want to show it to our office manager, too. Renata Giordano."

"Pleased to meet you," said Brugioni. His dark eyes crinkled a little at the blinding magenta of her miniskirt.

"And I don't think you've met Mr. Cronin, who handles our rentals."

Brugioni greeted Cronin, but handed the picture to Len. It wasn't as bad as he'd feared. A young man, wavy blond hair, blue eyes, square athletic good looks. Len shook his head. "No. No, I've never seen him."

"He was five-eleven, hundred and sixty-five, early twenties. He'd had wine for breakfast. No other detectable drugs, no medical problems."

"Sorry. That doesn't help. I just don't know who he is."

"Mrs. Banks?"

Joyce fingered the picture thoughtfully, then shook her head. "No. Never saw him before. You'll check with the plumbers and so forth?"

"Of course."

"God, he looks young."

"Early twenties," repeated Brugioni.

"What a shame." She turned away, clutching her mug with both hands.

"Yes, ma'am. Miss Giordano, would you look too?"

Renata inspected the picture, then shrugged. "Sorry. Doesn't ring a bell." Cronin, looking over her shoulder, shook his head too.

"Who else works here?" asked Brugioni.

"Karen Weld is showing a property now. And Fred Stein is checking something at the borough housing commission."

"I see. Have they had anything to do with Mr. Lund's building?"

"Not me," said Cronin. "It's a sale, not a rental."

"And not Karen," said Joyce. "She showed it once or twice when it was first listed, but that was months ago. She's been in Florida the last two weeks. Mr. Stein has shown it more recently. And of course Mr. Trager and I show it occasionally."

Brugioni was noting this information in his book when the door opened again. Maggie Ryan came in, tall, lively, and eating a rather sloppy hero sandwich.

"Well, hello!" she said, more pleased than not to see the police. "Is there news, Lieutenant?" A shred of lettuce was attempting to dribble from her sandwich, but she snagged it with a skillful tongue.

"Yes, we have a sketch of the victim that our labs put together. Why don't you take a look too, since you're here?"

"Glad to." She inspected the picture closely, munching on the sandwich. "No. Never saw him. Has anyone else recognized him?"

"Not yet," said Brugioni.

"And you must not have any I.D., or prints or a file on him, otherwise you'd know who he was. Interesting."

Joyce's blue eyes had been assessing the interloper. "Miss Ryan, I presume?"

"Oh, sorry," said Len. But Maggie was nodding at Joyce. "Right. Maggie Ryan. And you're Joyce Banks herself. I'd shake hands but I'm all over mayonnaise."

Joyce smiled, always gracious to clients, even those who brought messy heros to her office. "Len tells me you're interested in the Garfield building."

"Yes, we need more space than we can afford in Manhattan."

"You're a gymnast, Len tells me. You'll enjoy having your own space to work out. I always feel the edge is off when I miss my morning swim."

"Joyce and her sister were both Olympic-class swimmers once," said Len.

"Terrific!" Maggie's eyes flashed appreciation. "God, when I was about twelve I thought I'd get there too. But then I started growing. Got too tall for the tricky moves. Did you make the team?"

"Yes. I was off my form but I did manage a bronze," said Joyce evenly. "And I still hate to miss my morning swim."

A rumbling noise, Brugioni clearing his throat, brought their attention back to him. "Have you shown the sketch to Mrs. Northrup?" asked Maggie.

"No. We'll check her out when we finish here." He turned back to Joyce. "Mrs. Banks, I'd like to ask you who knows the house."

"Lund, of course. Ourselves. The various tenants. Is that what you mean?"

"Yes." Brugioni tapped his pencil against his front teeth. "What about the people who've looked at the house? As clients?"

"Well, I wouldn't say they know it, really. It's usually a quick tour."

"We'd know it enough to remember the layout," said Maggie. "A lot of row houses have similar plans. Stair hall on the left, two big rooms on the right and a third at the back on all the floors. Garden and parlor levels have entry halls, top two floors have little rooms at the front. That's where our blond friend was found. I might not get all the baths and closets exactly right, especially upstairs where it's cut into apartments. But I know it enough to remember that it's empty except for the basement level. If I needed a place to do something illegal, Mr. Lund's house would seem safe and private."

Joyce forced a little laugh. "Are you volunteering to be a suspect?"

"No, no. I'll be pretty low on the lieutenant's list of suspects. I don't have keys. I'd have to jimmy my way in."

"We didn't see any signs of recent forcing," said Brugioni. "So you see, Mrs. Banks, we're most interested in people who have access to keys. But just in case, we need a list of everyone who's seen the building."

"Surely you don't mean to bother all those people!"

"We may not have to. When we find out who the victim was, there may be an obvious answer. But right now all we have to work with is the house and the people who have had access to it."

"But these people are clients! We can't violate that relationship!"

Maggie, downing the last of her hero sandwich, said, "It won't be bad for business."

"Not everyone is as calm about murders as you are," said Joyce. Len could sense her struggle to keep her voice gentle—however annoying, Maggie was a client too, one who was about to sign.

"Most people will be fascinated," Maggie insisted. "And Lieutenant Brugioni is a gentleman. He won't go charging in, guns blazing, shouting that Joyce Banks put the finger on them."

Joyce's lips tightened. But Brugioni chuckled. "Miss Ryan is right," he told Joyce. "We'll be gentle. And we'll be sure to explain that you were cooperating with us when you gave out the information. And of course, it's possible that we won't have to contact them at all. But we do need the list."

His flat eyes met Joyce's. It was clear that further protests would only delay the inevitable. She decided on a tactical retreat.

"All right. Renata, pull it from the files. Names, addresses, phone numbers, date they saw the building, who showed it. But please, Lieutenant, there's a slump in real estate right now. Don't contact them unless it's absolutely necessary."

"We won't unless we have to. But you must understand, Mrs. Banks." The lieutenant was very serious again. "A murder investigation is not a pleasant thing."

5

Julia stared at the sketch. "No," she said at last. "I just can't place him."

"You think you might know him?"

"I definitely don't know him, Lieutenant. But there's something a little bit familiar about him. It's just that I don't know what."

"Do you think you might have seen him in the neighborhood?"

"I just can't remember. I should recognize that hair, but I don't. And there are just so many people on the street." She frowned at the picture again. "Maybe I saw his brother. Or maybe I taught him years ago and lost track of him, and this is his grown-up face. It's that kind of familiarity— not the familiarity of this particular person, but a closely related person."

Brugioni sighed and glanced at Cleary wearily. "I see."

"Maybe it's just that I saw him dead. Do you think that's all it is?"

"I don't know, Mrs. Northrup."

"I'm sorry, I'll keep thinking about it. 'Women and elephants never forget.'"

"What?"

"A poem."

"I see. Well, this picture should be in the papers today, so we may find out soon who it is."

"I hope so. I don't like dead bodies in my home."

"We don't either, Mrs. Northrup." The lieutenant slipped the picture back into a manila envelope. "Well, thanks for looking. And thanks again for letting us check your things." He and Cleary had returned Julia's toaster and iron and clothing, absolved of any involvement in the homicide. "Call us if you remember why he seems familiar."

"Of course."

Julia stood frowning for a moment after they'd left, but the tantalizing sense of familiarity did not crystallize into memory. Women and elephants my foot, Parker. Was it just her old brain? Dying, bit by bit, limping ahead of her body into death? Would a younger person remember? No, she told herself briskly. You're doing fine. You remembered Nick O'Connor being in that bank commercial, and he was wearing different clothes, and a whole different personality too. A good actor. A good actor, and you remembered him.

But where could she have seen this dead young man?

Give it up for now. Let the subconscious work on it. Freud would say there was a reason she had forgotten, some worry or buried fear from her childhood. Dear old Freud, with his fertile imagination, would have invented a splendid and plausible link between her childhood and her present failure to remember. And who knows? Maybe he'd have been right.

Brugioni had said there would be a story in the papers today. Julia decided to go see Benny. It was warming up, and she went a block out of her way so she could walk along the edge of Prospect Park. Fred-Law had been proud of this park. He'd be horrified by the graffiti-sprayed walls urging peace and drugs and by the vandalized lampposts. But the underlying frame of meadow and woods, berm and valley, remained sound and lovely. There was talk of restoring it. That would be good. But the biggest problem just now was that spring was so late. She hoped it would be warm Sunday for his big birthday celebration in Central Park.

"Heard anything, Benny?" she asked as she handed him fifteen cents for the *Times*.

"Not yet, Mrs. Northrup. But I saw the story and the pictures." He tapped a forefinger on the little inner-page item that she had already opened to. "I'll keep my ears open, but I sure never saw him before."

"Well, I hope he's nothing to do with any of us." If Benny hadn't seen him, the dead man had not been a neighborhood regular. But then why did she feel that nagging familiarity?

Vic Jr. called later in the afternoon.

"Mother! What the hell is going on there?"

"You suburbanites wouldn't understand."

"It's in the paper, Mother, don't try to brush it off! A man strangled, it says. At your address!"

"Hasn't anybody ever been murdered in Jersey?"

"Not on this block. Mother, for heaven's sake! Loyalty to your old friends is fine, but I told you years ago that the Slope was on its way down!"

"And you were wrong. It's getting better."

"Better!" squawked her son. "Mother, you're out of your mind! Absolutely!"

"Calm down, Vic. Nothing's going to happen to me. On the other hand, you should watch out for your blood pressure."

"Oh, quit telling me what to do! I'm forty years old, Mother!"

"And I'm sixty-eight," snapped Julia. "And which of us is telling the other what to do?" Though he was right too; she shouldn't needle him on such a sensitive topic. His father had died of a stroke.

"Oh, hell. Listen, I'm coming over."

"No need." But he'd hung up. Julia sighed as she put the receiver in its cradle. It was all very well to encourage your children to be individuals, to live their own lives, to become responsible adults. But it was a shame when their individuality led to stuffiness. To bossiness.

On impulse, she dialed Seattle.

"Hello, Jean?"

"Yes. Mother? Is anything wrong?"

"I'm fine. But I thought I'd better call you before Vic Jr. did. He's overdramatizing again."

"Vic is? Old Sobersides?"

"Well," admitted Julia, "he might have cause this time, I guess. They found a dead body in the empty apartment upstairs."

"Oh, my God! A renter?"

"No, no. Even Artie Lund isn't crude enough to strangle a tenant. It's a mysterious stranger, and the police are still trying to figure out who it is."

"Mother, are you scared?"

"A little. But I don't think anyone's out to kill me. Not even Artie, drat him."

"You seem to think it's exciting!" Jean accused.

Julia laughed. "Beats those dreary sitcoms."

"True."

"What are you up to, honey?"

"I just accepted a part in a film."

"A film?"

"Isn't that a hoot? The university is making a publicity film, and they asked three of us from this office to take screen tests. The guy in charge of casting needed a middle-aged, motherly-looking administrator. He also said I had good bones. So I guess I beat out Joe and Wayne for good bones and for motherliness."

"You introduced me to Wayne, right? Desk next to yours? He's a lot more motherly than you are," said Julia. "You're a tough cookie."

"Sure. That's in the genes. But we don't look it, do we? Anyway, I won't argue with their sexist attitudes if it gets me onto the silver screen."

Julia laughed. "Fame and riches and Hollywood next, huh?"

"Natch. But listen, Mother, you're not in trouble, are you? Do they suspect you? Didn't you say you were the only one still standing up to Lund?"

"Yes, but that's all they could possibly have against me. I don't even have keys to the upstairs."

"Mother, Mother! If they knew you as well as I do!"

"Shhh. No need to defame my character. But there's a nice sober young Italian lieutenant in charge, and he'll do a good job. My biggest problem is that Vic Jr. has decided to worry about me."

"Poor Mother. Well, if he complains to me, I'll try to straighten him out. I wish we lived closer."

"I'd like that too. But anyway, don't let his sermons

worry you. The investigation is in good hands, and the whole thing is entertaining."

"God, Mother, I think you would have got first-row seats at an auto-da-fé."

"Right next to you."

"Of course! It's good to hear from you."

Julia hung up, smiling. Too bad Vic Jr. wasn't more like his sister. But there probably had to be a few sober folks to keep the world rolling along.

The Hunger Committee was meeting at the church at four o'clock. She had closed her history of Hartford and was gathering her material on third-world agriculture when the bell sounded. From the window she could see Ann, seething with anticipation, standing at the door under the stoop. Julia hurried out to open the door.

"Ann! How wonderful! It's been so long!"

"Oh, Teach, you know what a bitch moving is. You're still here, huh?"

"I'm not leaving."

"Boy, you've got more grit than I have. Listen, is that article true?"

Julia waved a hand at her sofa as she closed the apartment door behind them. "Yes. You missed all the excitement."

"Not all of it, honey." Ann lowered her elegant form onto the sofa. She was wearing big feather earrings, a slim cream-colored mini-dress. "Artie Lund kept things hopping for a while."

"He sure did. After you left, it was obscene phone calls."

"Ain't that a bitch. I'm just as glad we missed that. When Jack found that KKK in our hall he was ready to throw Artie down the stairs. But tell me about this murder! The paper didn't give many details."

"Details. Well, the body was found in your African room."

Ann squealed. "Really? God! Jack will freak!"

"On your old mattress."

"Oh, my Lord!"

"You want some coffee?"

"Oh, Julia, I have to run. I'd better not. But I wanted to ask about it. Jack will absolutely freak!"

"Even I was surprised. I mean, some landlords try arson, or let the top-floor pipes break and ruin everything. But Artie has hopes of getting his money out of the building now that the young folks are buying these places. So I thought we'd already run through all the bad things that could happen in this house."

"Well, even freaking Artie wouldn't do that! Would he? It's terrible advertising. God! Our African room! Aren't you glad you're way down here?"

"I sure am. And glad the locks are there."

"Could Artie have left things unlocked on purpose?"

"Maybe. But I'm not dumb, Ann. I've checked. And it's generally locked."

"Julia! Remember that dumbwaiter we found? Could someone come down that, if they got into the attic?"

Ann didn't know Julia had made herself a private elevator. Julia shook her head. "No, it's too tight a squeeze with all that machinery in the attic. Besides, the car is very sturdy, and it's screwed in place down here. It would be easier to saw through the floor than that hardwood cabinet."

"True. But doesn't it give you bad vibes? A dead body!"

Julia shrugged and said sanctimoniously, "Time, like an ever-rolling stream, bears all its sons away."

Ann laughed. "Well, I'd rather be borne away in my sleep than strangled. But speaking of time, I've got to split."

"I'll walk you to the corner. I'm off to church."

They strolled together through the warmth that had finally, grudgingly, arrived. Julia asked, "Ann, did the sketch in the paper look familiar to you?"

"No. Not at all. Why? Did you recognize him?"

"No. But there's something—Did you two keep keys?"

"Jack did. He had some idea of going back to get even with Lund but I told him he'd be crazy if he did."

"Good. The police will be around to talk to you, you know."

"They will? Oh, God, of course they will! What should we say?"

"Just answer their questions. Tell the truth. Who knows, you may have the missing clue. But you might want to throw away those keys. And I wouldn't bring up the KKK episode. Though it wouldn't be natural to say he was anything but a rat if it does come up."

"Yeah. Well, we'll tell the truth—we're glad he's out of our life and hope he stays out. But God, Julia, how can you be so calm?"

"I never noticed that shrieking and jumping about was very good for solving problems."

Ann laughed warmly. "Always the schoolteacher! Hey, it's good to see you, Teach. Take care of yourself, hear?"

"Same to you, Ann." They parted at the corner.

The World Hunger meeting got off to a slow start because everyone wanted to discuss the murder and Julia's exciting predicament. "The neighborhood just isn't safe anymore," declared Pauline McGuire, adjusting her glasses.

"Nobody's ever totally safe," said Ellie Voorhees. "I think there was more trouble around here four or five years ago than now. But we'll never get rid of all the crazies in the world."

"True." Pauline nodded energetically. "But I wish we could keep them out of our homes! Any idea how they got in, Teach?"

"No one's found any signs of forcing," said Julia. "So the crazy who did this had to have a key. Or a friend with a key."

Ellie Voorhees puckered her forehead and said, "All those real-estate people and plumbers. Could be anyone. And they haven't found the weapon?"

"No, though I could—well, you don't tell police what to do."

Pauline frowned at her, alarm in her dark eyes. "Maybe the plumbers have an organized-crime connection!"

"Or maybe Artie does," said Julia. "Yes, I've thought of that. It's a convenient empty house. Warmer than the docks."

"Okay," said Ellie Voorhees, who was chairing the meeting. "But now we ought to get to work. One out of maybe five thousand of us gets murdered every year, and he was the one. But in India one out of eight babies dies. We'll save a lot more lives if we talk about our mission there."

"I'm not a baby," grumbled Pauline, but they got to work.

After the meeting, Pauline cornered Julia by the exit. "Hey, Teach, I'm going to Utah, so we can't have dinner Tuesday. But I bought some nice fresh scrod today. Want to help me eat it?"

"Utah!" exclaimed Julia. "You're off to see Audrey?"

"The kids sent me airfare." Pauline was beaming.

"Lucky you!"

They walked down the avenue toward Pauline's building. One of the new young people on the block was painting her iron gate and gave them a smile. Julia smiled back, but with mixed feelings about this wave of too-industrious youth rolling into her neighborhood. Pauline said, "Yes. But they didn't give me much notice for a two-week trip. That makes a hole in your life."

"I know what you mean. It's great when your children want to be nice to you. Except they also want to run your life."

"Especially those two! They give me pamphlets all the time. Trying to save me before I ship out among the unchosen." A feeble, uncharacteristically vulnerable smile flitted across her face. "Maybe they're right. Maybe I'm a goner."

"Oh, shut up, Pauline," said Julia forcefully. "We're all sinners. Don't let those green kids shake you up. You know a lot more about life than they do."

"Yes. But I still have to read their pamphlets. To be polite."

Julia thought of the Reverend Goon's program, always a surefire way to turn away Artie's buyers. Until the unruffled Ms. Ryan appeared. She said, "I sympathize."

Pauline's apartment was pleasant, thought not as spacious as her Carroll Street floor-through had been. Her furniture and plants looked a bit cramped here. Well, Julia had felt a bit cramped too after Vic had his stroke and she'd had to move him and his wheelchair to a ground-floor apartment. A cheap ground-floor apartment, since his so-called benefits had been eaten up by the medical expenses. But she'd come to love her place, where a touch of the glamour of its days as the Sweeney dining room still hung in the air. Pauline, too, was grateful for her son-in-law's subsidy that enabled her to stay in a safe, familiar area. Without rent control, she needed that subsidy.

Pauline was still glum as she hung their coats in the closet. "But don't you think sometimes we're just in the way? I've got bad teeth and varicose veins. Even the mighty Teach is visited by arthritis in the knees. In the old days we would have died years ago."

"What do you mean, in the way?" objected Julia stoutly. "It's other people who are in *our* way. We've got a few thousand babies in India to save, and a few thousand

American kids to tell about Fred-Law Olmsted's vision, and so forth."

"Maybe. But I still don't know how you can stay in that apartment. Even here around the corner, I get the shakes about it."

"That place is already full of ghosts for me," explained Julia. "Benevolent ghosts. They won't let this upstart bother me." Though, in fact, that bloated young face kept seeping into her dreams. She changed the subject, picking up a snapshot from Pauline's coffee table. "Hey, look how those grandchildren of yours are growing! You're right to keep in touch. They'll grow up fast. Time like an ever-rolling stream."

"I know." Pauline, taking the wrapped fish from her refrigerator, smiled at the photo. "I dote on those kids. I'd do anything for them."

"Grandchildren are one of the great inventions, all right," Julia agreed. "And look at your begonias! They've grown about two feet!"

Pauline joined her at the window. "Yes," she admitted with pride, "they're going to be great this summer."

Julia touched a graceful young leaf. "Aren't you worried about leaving them for two weeks? Even a plastic bag is not enough when they're growing so fast. Want me to take care of them?"

"They do need watering every day," Pauline admitted. "But I don't want to bother you—"

"Don't be silly. I'll make you return the favor when I visit Jean."

After they had eaten the scrod and cleaned up the tiny kitchen, Julia shouldered her bag and picked up the two pots of begonias to walk the half-block home. As she approached the door, a man emerged from a Buick parked across the street and hurried across. Julia sighed, exasperated.

"Mother! We were so worried!" Vic Jr. was tall, with his father's strong nose and gentle eyes. Behind him, a miniskirted blond woman and a teenage boy were getting out of the Buick.

"For heaven's sake, Vic. What are you doing here?"

"I told you I was coming." He took the plants from her.

"You didn't tell me when. Have you been sitting in that Buick an hour and a half?"

"No." The boy approached them, yawning and stretching his arms coltishly. "We grabbed a hamburger. Hey, did it happen in your pad, Grandma?"

"No. All the way up on the top floor. See the oriel window?"

"What's oriel?"

"That little window that sticks out. You probably don't have them in the suburbs."

"Oh, yeah. I thought that was a bay." A very cool, sophisticated thirteen.

"It is. If it has its own bracket you can call it an oriel too."

"Did you see the stiff?" The boy reverted to the real topic of interest.

"Greg, hush!" Diane, scandalized, joined them.

Julia ignored her and answered Greg. "Of course I saw him. You couldn't keep me away from something like that."

"What did he look like? Yucky?"

"Greg, that's enough!" said Diane.

"He looked pretty awful, Greg. He'd been strangled, so his face was puffy and sort of dark."

"Yuck!" Greg was delighted, forgetting to be cool. "Was there a lot of gore?"

"Vic, make him stop!" pleaded Diane.

"It's no use. Mother's egging him on," said Vic tiredly.

Julia put her arm around Greg's shoulder. "No. Not much gore. But his tongue stuck out a little from being strangled."

"Yuck!"

"I was scared."

"You were?" Greg's quick glance held a furtive question. She'd been right, then. What really preyed on a thirteen-year-old mind was not so much that evil things happened; that fact was boringly obvious. The worry was how people should react to the evil things.

Julia said, "Every one of us was scared. There were four of us who saw him before the police came. And we all felt pretty sick. I think one of the men really was sick when he saw it. I heard the toilet flushing as I was going up to look."

"Did you want to run away, Grandma?"

"Sure. We all wanted to. But there were things to be done, so of course we stayed."

"Yeah."

"I'm not ashamed. People should feel awful about someone dying. It's a very serious thing. But it would be shameful to run off and not report it, or not help the police as much as you can."

"Yeah."

"It's brave to feel sick about it and still do what has to be done."

"Yeah. I'd do that," Greg decided, full of resolve. "I'd get it together. Call the police and stuff. Even if I felt sick."

"Yes. I know you would, Greg." Julia turned to Vic and Diane with a twinkle. "Well, if I've answered everybody's questions, let's go in and have some coffee."

Diane didn't smile, but Vic grinned sheepishly and followed her in. Julia fixed the coffee and sat in the chair near the sofa. "Greg, there's a new Central Park book on the fourth shelf," she said.

"It's okay. *Beat the Clock* is on," he said, switching on the television set and folding himself into a gangly heap two feet away from it. Julia, with an uneasy thought about the future of books in Greg's TV generation, turned her attention back to Vic and Diane.

"Vic, I'm not going to move, so let's talk about something else," she said. "Did you recognize the picture in the paper?"

"God, of course not! Or—was it someone we know?"

"No, I just thought he might be someone from Jersey."

"Mother, I just don't understand. Your friends are moving away."

"Not many of them. And not of their own free will."

"Lund has made you a very generous cash offer to move."

"Pah! How much cash would it take to get you to move from that place in Jersey you're so proud of?"

"That's different, Mother. We own that place."

Julia sighed. Even at forty, Vic had not learned that places could own people, could wrap them in intangible, unbreakable filaments of friendship and familiarity, of memory and expectation. He would have to learn it for himself; explaining would be futile. She said wearily, "I'm not moving."

"But, Mother, it was murder!"

"If anyone wanted to murder me they could have done so long since. Just don't worry about it."

Diane said, "It's just that we care about you."

"Yes. It's hard on us too," agreed Vic. "Don't you understand? Won't you do it for us?"

Julia's voice softened. "Vic, I know you care about me. But at this time of my life I can't do things for you anymore, I have to do them for me. I don't really need anyone to take care of me. And I want to stay here. This was your father's and my home."

"Damn."

"It'll be all right."

"Please think about it, Mother."

"I've thought, Vic. I'll be careful, of course. But the murder has nothing to do with me, and I like this place. I'm not moving."

There was an awkward silence, punctuated by excited squeals from the *Beat the Clock* contestants. Then Vic swallowed the last of his coffee and looked at Diane.

"Well, honey, our trip was in vain."

Diane sighed and stood up, tugging down her miniskirt. Silly style, Julia thought. In the twenties when they'd gone in for short skirts they'd kept the waists loose too, so dresses slid right back into place when you stood up. None of this twitching your skirt down whenever you moved. But Diane was in her mid-thirties, a fragile time for a woman. And she did have nice legs. Let her pretend to be young for a while. The ever-rolling stream would catch her soon enough. Diane said, "Let us know when you do want to move."

"You'll be the first to know," Julia assured her. "But don't expect it soon."

"We won't," her son said grimly. "Hey, Greg, c'mon."

"Aw." Greg made the expected complaining noises but stood up and moved slowly to the door, his eyes still fastened to the TV screen.

"I'll see you all Sunday in Central Park," said Julia.

"We'll pick you up," said Diane.

Julia started to protest but decided to let them win this one. She nodded.

"Will there really be a birthday cake?" asked Greg.

"An enormous cake."

"Hope it doesn't rain again," said Vic Jr.

"It won't. Not on Fred-Law's day," promised Julia.

She watched them from her window as they crossed the street. Greg turned to look back with frank fascination at the oriel window, and Julia smiled as each parent, separately and furtively, glanced up at it too before settling into the car.

Beat the Clock was over. She switched off the television and went to her desk to write about Fred-Law and the poison sumac.

"So there's nothing fishy about it?" Nick asked the lawyer.

"Not from the legal standpoint. Standard contract, reasonably fair to both parties, unless there's some hidden problem with the house. You're sure there's only one tenant left?"

"Yes." Maggie, in blue jeans, had been doing stretches, but now had lighted fleetingly on the lawyer's brown carpet and was sprawling back against Nick's shins. He sat quietly, feasting on the warm touch of her back against his legs, on the shine of her black curls. An astounding woman. After his first wife had died, he'd resigned himself to a solitary struggle in his brutally unpredictable profession. Nick the Lone Ranger. But this mischievous statistician had somehow entangled herself in his soul, luring him into more unlikely roles than his job did: Marriage. Spy games in Central Park. Even buying a house where a murder had occurred. Not what he would have predicted for himself at all. He hoped he would be ready for what she'd thrust upon him next.

Maggie was saying, "All the furniture was gone, except for the one mattress with poor dead Blondy."

"I can't say I understand your taste in brownstones. I'd think you could have found one without a corpse." The lawyer, a pleasant hazel-eyed young woman named Ellen Winfield-Greer, was wearing jeans too, because the play they were going to attend that night was a long way off Broadway. "Do you think this Mister Whosis—Lund—will really take back the mortgage for you? Of course you can get out of the contract if he doesn't."

Maggie, grounded too long, rolled away from Nick into a handstand and walked a few steps on her hands as she answered. "We don't know for sure if he'll loan it to us. But Len thought he'd agree because Nick's giving him such a big down payment."

"True. It's a big percentage. You two aren't as penniless as I thought."

Nick said, "I saved it all up from my dishwashing jobs. That's the secret to financial success for an actor, Ellen. Don't act."

"I'll tell Jim." Ellen too was married to a frequently unemployed actor. "It's true, I've never heard of an actor getting a mortgage from a bank."

"No. Not till he was worth more than the bank."

"Exactly. And our upside-down friend here may have letters after her name and fat paychecks, but she's a woman of childbearing age and therefore, say the banks, liable to quit her posh job at any moment."

Maggie eased into a split on the carpet. "Well, I am liable to quit."

"What? Are you kidding?"

"Not for a couple of months. But Dan and I are thinking about starting our own statistical consulting firm."

"Well, for God's sake, don't tell Mister Whosis!"

"That's not the only thing we won't tell him."

"Why are you quitting? I thought you liked this job!"

"I do. But I'd like more control over my own hours."

"Too many years on campus, I'd say," sniffed Ellen. "You're spoiled."

"Never claimed I wasn't. But listen, Ellen, one thing still bothers me about this deal."

"What's that?"

"Mrs. Northrup. Why doesn't she want us?"

"That's easy. She's afraid of you."

"But why? I like her, and though she won't admit it, I really thinks she likes us."

"She probably does."

"And she's furious at Lund and his dirty tricks."

"Of course. But he has one great virtue that you and Nick don't have."

"What's that?"

"He doesn't plan to live in the house himself. You see, one of the very, very few ways to evict a rent-controlled tenant is for the owners to need the space for their own personal use."

"So Lund can't dislodge her. And even though we won't, she's afraid because we have the power." Maggie was on her feet now, bending to touch her toes.

"That's right. They're talking about tightening the law, making you prove need before eviction, but they haven't done it yet. Even then, you could withdraw it from the rental market and bounce her."

"I told her we wouldn't need the space. But I guess she can't quite trust the promises of a stranger."

Nick said, "That one wouldn't trust the promises of George Washington himself."

"A woman after my own heart," declared Ellen. "And I especially wouldn't trust Maggie." She ducked the good-natured roundhouse swing that Maggie aimed at her.

"Well, if we have any money left over when Lund gets finished with us, we'll have you draw up a lease or something that'll set her mind at ease," said Maggie.

"Okay. And if you don't have any money left over?"

"You'll just have to give us credit for a while."

"You're crazy." Ellen stood up haughtily and turned to the window. "I'd never extend credit to an actor and a woman of childbearing age."

"You lawyers are all heart." Maggie joined Ellen at the window. "Look, O woman of childbearing age, isn't that your actor coming now? Let's drop this purchase offer in Len's box and then go see *Alice in Wonderland*. After we eat."

"You statisticians are all stomach," observed Nick, and this time it was his turn to duck.

6

"Dennis Burns." Joyce shook her head. "I never heard the name. But Renata is checking the files for you."

"Anyone else?" asked Lieutenant Brugioni, glancing around the office. Len and Cronin shook their heads, and so did Renata. Fred Stein was off this Saturday, Karen taking a listing.

"He was a waiter at the Henry Hotel for a couple of weeks. Have any of you been there?"

Again the heads shook. Joyce said, "I never even heard of it."

Renata said, "A client we had maybe five years ago was staying there while he looked for a place. I remember the envelopes. But that's the only time I heard of it."

"Well, it's strange," said Brugioni. "No one reported him missing, so he must have irregular hours, or maybe he's living alone. The headwaiter said he was at work Monday, and when he didn't show the next few days he was annoyed but not surprised. He tried the number Burns left but the guy who answered said he'd never heard of him, so he threw it away. Waiters aren't all that dependable, he says. He saw the picture in the paper yesterday afternoon and identified him."

"What was he doing in Lund's building?" asked Len.

Brugioni shrugged. "We've still got a lot of questions. Let us know if you think of any connections."

Sunday was a glorious warm day, as though April was trying to atone on its last afternoon for all the cold and gloom that had gone before. Standing in the Bankses' penthouse garden, Len felt he could almost see the leaves opening, ready to leap from bud to summer. Below them, Manhattan glistened, the winter's grime suddenly irrelevant next to the sparkle of sun on glass and water. Closer at hand, crystal stemware twinkled, in honor of the unannounced anniversary that everyone knew about. Around Len and in the dining room behind him, men in dark suits and women in bright miniskirts or flaring party pajamas chattered in the soft air. Len too was wearing his best suit and holding a glass of twelve-year-old Scotch as he discussed Vietnam strategy with Fred Stein and a man from the mayor's office. On a wrought-iron bench near him, Nancy, in a dress of tender blue, was smiling politely at Gordon Banks.

Len was almost fond of Banks, certainly grateful. After college in the late sixties, lucky to have drawn a high number in the draft lottery, Len had hit the streets with his highly unmarketable degree in art history. He'd finally found a job as assistant to an assistant in the tiny New York office of one of Banks's resort projects. For a year he had run errands and answered phones, and even sold a few package weekends to groups. One day, writing up a sale, he had noticed some discrepancies in the books. After a bit of soul-searching and a deep discussion with Nancy, he had reported it to the division head. The next week came the news: the resort was sold, the office was permanently closed, they had all been fired, and Len was summoned to Banks's Wall Street office.

"Thinking of shedding that one anyway," Banks had said. "Don't want you feeling guilty about those fellows. Not your fault. Though you helped explain the lousy bottom line. Not worth prosecuting him, though, you see. Evidence pretty slippery unless we subpoena customers, and we don't want to do that."

"Yes, I see, sir."

"Don't 'sir' me. This isn't the army. Where'd you grow up?"

"Brooklyn. Near Ebbets Field."

"So did my wife. Do you like selling, Trager?"

"I didn't do much selling. I guess I'm not really a salesman. I don't like pushing people. But when they came to me I liked it. I was good at finding them the package that suited them. I liked helping them."

"Perfect," Banks decided abruptly, scribbling on a card. "You're a Stewart."

"What?"

"Jimmy Stewart. You look sincere."

"Oh."

"Joyce needs someone sincere in Brooklyn. Park Slope." Banks handed Len the card. "She'll give you something to live on while you're training and a percentage of commissions, and your buyers and sellers will generally come to you."

Joyce had directed him to the cheap, desirable apartment he and Nancy shared now. A nice fringe benefit. But not big enough for a baby.

The man from the mayor's office moved back to the bar for a refill. Fred bobbed his gray head to sip his drink and left the topic of Quangtri abruptly. "Len, have you had a chance to think about my development plan?"

"Fred, I'm flattered you asked. But at the moment I don't want to start anything without Joyce's approval. I'd better say no."

"But this would raise your income in the long run, Len! You know Joyce is never going to entrust the big dollars to anyone else but herself. We'll be limping along with these little fifty-thousand properties forever. Dr. Carr's group is solid. And asking for you."

"Just because of that sketch?"

"Exactly! The problem with developers, they say, is that they have no vision. And God, I agree, but I know I can't do it either. But you just sketched it out and half the stuff was there already when they pulled down the paneling."

There was more here than met the eye, Len felt. Reluctant to hurt the other man, he said, "Fred, it's an appealing idea. But why don't they get an architect? What's so urgent about getting me? I can't afford to antagonize Joyce. I owe her and Gordon. And anyway, if I say no, it's not the end for you, is it?"

An uncomfortable smile twitched at Fred's mouth. "Well, it would take a while to find another partner."

"Is Carr in a rush?"

"Well, you know, strike while the iron is hot."

"The doctors don't need it instantly, but you do. Right?"

"Well—I'll manage, really. Loan coming due. Balloon."

"Boy, I can sympathize with that! Bankers don't take any excuses. But there must be someone else who can help, Fred. I'm in Joyce's good books now. I can't sacrifice that."

"Don't count on that lasting forever," said Fred darkly.

"I know, but now isn't the time for me to move. Maybe you should put out a few feelers to other guys you know."

"Well, the truth is, Len, I know I can work with you. So think it over, okay?" He bobbed off toward the bar.

Len drifted toward Banks and Nancy. She had not been enthusiastic about this party. For four days, she had been subdued and pensive, and he knew that the decision she faced filled her with pain. When they were together he avoided the subject, tried to keep things pleasant, to smooth her life as much as he could. He wondered how much longer she could delay before she had to decide, but he didn't dare ask. Time rolled on; after a while, no decision was a decision. He ached for the choice to be made, so that he could do something, take action, come to grips with whatever she decided. But he mustn't pressure her. He had to wait helplessly on the sidelines.

"Well, hello, Trager!" said Banks, with tipsy enthusiasm. He had been leaning very close to Nancy, but now sat up straighter. He held a drink in one hand, a cane in the other. Beneath the flawlessly tailored trousers his legs were in steel braces, but his forceful enthusiasm could still dominate any conversation. "Your fiancée here has been explaining advertising layouts to me."

Damn. Len tried to look an apology to Nancy, but she was inspecting her drink, tight-lipped. To Banks he said, "Yes, she's doing very well now."

"She is indeed. I'm looking forward to seeing the MacIntyre catalog. In fact, our Grosvenor division may want to try your firm, Nancy."

"You wouldn't regret it," said Len. "It's a talented outfit."

"Now, Nan, tell us your complaint about the Pine Island campaign."

"The campaign's fine," Nancy said. "It's the logo. The

campaign is stressing elite, solid, upper-class values. Golf, luxury hotels, yachts. But the logo is still in those thin light-blue letters with little seagulls dotting the I's. Very insubstantial."

"That's true." Banks's shrewd eyes fastened on her. Perhaps he wasn't as tipsy as he'd seemed. "You think the symbol should be more upper-class?"

"Not only more upper-class, but more solid, dependable. Seagulls are fine if you just want to say freedom. They don't say wealth or status."

"You're right. Holcomb!" A thin gray man detached himself from a nearby group and joined them.

"Yes?"

"Tell Wayne Marks we're getting a new logo for Pine Island. I've decided I don't like that Jonathan Livingston Seagull look. They're to commission Glow Graphics to design it. I want to hear from them tomorrow."

"Right." Holcomb had noted it in his little book.

"That's all," said Banks, and Holcomb moved obediently away.

"Wow!" Nancy's face crinkled into her heartwarming smile. Len relaxed. "You move fast, Mr. Banks!"

"When something needs doing, don't hesitate," he said, beaming back at her. "That's the secret of success. Well, one of the secrets."

"We won't let you down."

"I know you won't. Trager," said Banks, "Joyce tells me you were asking about apartment development. That's not a bad idea here. Good way to support a family."

"Excuse me," said Nancy, standing up abruptly. "It's time for the powder room. See you in a few minutes."

"Yes indeed." Banks smiled after her as she retreated toward the French doors. "Splendid young woman, Trager. Splendid."

"I think so too." Len took her place next to him on the bench.

"Splendid fiancée."

"Um, yes." Len couldn't tell him that "fiancée" was one of the words that spooked Nancy. So was "family." Don't even mention marriage. But to someone like Gordon Banks, who celebrated anniversaries, her views would be anathema. Len felt a sudden pang of anxiety. If she had the baby, what would Banks think? And Joyce?

"You know," Banks was saying, "she reminds me of Joyce."

Len was startled. Delicate Nancy didn't seem at all like the statuesque Joyce to him. "Blond?" he hazarded.

Banks laughed. Yes, he was definitely a little soused. "Well, that too," he said confidentially. "I've always liked a handsome blond. My first wife was blond too. But I was thinking of the ambition, the drive. I like that in a woman. Makes them interesting. No dull moments."

"That's certainly true."

"You have to give them their heads a little," Banks went on in boozy good fellowship. "It can be very hard for a woman sometimes. Very difficult. You should help them along, help them find goals, help them toward those goals."

"Yes. I try to." Nancy, of course, found her own goals. But Len saw that it was paternal-advice time. He tried to look filial. Through the branches of the potted trees, the sun sparkled cheerfully. Nancy had disappeared indoors.

"You're still young. You don't have any big problems yet," Banks informed him. He had finished his drink. "But when the problems come, you have to help them along." He looked hard at Len. "You don't follow."

"Well, I'll certainly try to help her," said Len lamely. "But sometimes she's pretty independent."

Banks clapped Len on the shoulder, adjusting his braced feet and bending closer. "No, you don't quite follow. It's my Nixon, Joyce calls it." He was nodding, a bit embarrassed, a bit amused. "My Nixon."

"I'm—I'm sorry, I still don't follow."

Banks frowned, concentrated on communicating. "The diabetes," he said. "You knew I had diabetes?"

"Joyce mentioned it once."

"Yes. Does a lot of strange things to a fellow. Joints give out. Numbness, flat feet, now braces." He nodded down at his gleaming shoes. "Get along pretty well, actually. But it's important to a woman, you know. My Nixon."

"Your Nixon," repeated Len, uncomprehending.

"Tricky Dick, you know." Banks laughed. "Joyce is a good sport. Calls it Nixon. But a woman like that, full of energy, she needs something to do. Fulfillment. She was an Olympic-class swimmer, you know, she and her sister." He looked out over the great city. "It's ironic, in a way.

First wife had Lou Gehrig's, you know. Died young. I
didn't plan to marry again. But I wanted a family, and
Joyce came along. I was still in fine fettle then. We both
wanted kids." He blinked at the view. "No one to leave this
to, you know. A nephew who lives on a commune upstate."

Len felt that the older man was slicing at his heart. He
didn't want to hear this. Not now. But he could only stare
at his drink as Banks continued. "Joyce feels twice as bad,
of course. I remember the day old Doc Gable told us. Not
his real name. Real name was Clark, so he joked that I
ought to call him Gable. He'd tested us both. Everything
they knew how to do in those days. Nothing wrong with
either of us, he said, keep trying. Joyce cried. We've been
trying for four years, she said, and after all those tests all
you can say is keep trying? Well, I wanted to shoot the doc
too. But that's the way it is sometimes."

"Yeah," said Len. And sometimes it was not that way at
all, but heartbreaking too.

"And of course I knew that with old Nixon we couldn't
keep trying forever," Banks continued. "So I encouraged
her to go into business. Didn't tell her why, of course. She
doesn't complain. But I can be useful to her there. And it
gives her an outlet. Very important for a woman."

"Yes. And she's very talented. Wonderful businesswoman." Len was uneasy. Why had he been entrusted with
Banks's unhappy little secret? Nancy, he decided. Probably
a sort of apology for the keen attention Banks had been
lavishing on Nancy. Don't worry, young man, no danger
that I'll lay your fiancée, I'm a diabetic eunuch. There was
a sour taste in his mouth.

Banks was nodding in agreement. "Yes, Joyce is good. A
good sport. A fine mind. You ought to follow up that
apartment-house idea, you know."

"What do you mean?"

"You know she has an investment corporation. She
thinks with you in charge, an apartment project would be
a sound investment. Bit of a slump now, but it'll right
itself. She's done it before, for other good managers who
are short of capital."

"Well, that would be wonderful! If I could just get a
start—"

"I know. Pump-priming. I always tell Joyce, the best
place to put our money is in bright young people."

"Well, I appreciate that."

"But of course, she won't come to you. Pick a property, work up the statistics. Sell her." Banks shifted on the seat, found his cane, and shoved himself erect. He looked down at Len with dignity. "When something needs doing, don't hesitate. Be prepared for opportunity."

Len stood up too. "Yes. Thank you."

"And make sure that splendid young woman stays busy and happy."

"I'll do my best."

"You need a drink too. Let's go fill 'em up."

Joyce caught them near the bar. "Len, there's someone to see you in the foyer. O'Connor."

"That was fast." Joyce had told him to have them drop by if they wanted, but he had just left Lund's counteroffer with them only at noon.

Joyce dimpled, glamorous in designer chiffon and pearls. Mrs. Gordon Banks this anniversary afternoon, not tailored Joyce Banks, realtor. She said, "It's all right. Sanchez almost didn't let them in, but luckily I was powdering my nose and overheard. I told him it was all right. They said they couldn't stay, so I told them I'd send you out." She shook her head. "I still can't imagine how you talked them into it. A murder, and that horrible old woman."

"They talked themselves into it. And Northrup changed her clothes, you know. Even cleaned up the apartment. She just wasn't the old slob she usually is."

"Really?" Joyce seemed startled. "I wouldn't have predicted that."

"I know. But she was sharp that day. Maggie seemed to think she knew something about the murder. They were comparing notes about the weapon and everything. Listen, you said they're in the foyer?"

Joyce nodded absently. "Yes. Hope it's good news."

Len went through the glass garden doors, across an elegant dining room that glittered with gifts of crystal, and through a hall to the marble-floored foyer. Nick and Maggie, both in blue jeans and holding gym bags, were sitting on a gilded bench. From the vestibule, Sanchez squinted at them disapprovingly.

"Hi, Len." Maggie bounced up.

"So you found us," said Len. "No small feat."

"Yes, we got past the gatekeepers." Nick waggled his

fingers at Sanchez, who smiled sheepishly. "Here's the counteroffer. Lund accepted our basic offer but he wanted a thousand more in cash. So we said, hell, we'll hock the guitar, and signed it. Is that all you need?"

Len took the papers, trying to contain the elation spreading through him. He said, "Everything looks okay. He's agreed to hold the mortgage."

"Right."

"Great. I'll keep after the two lawyers and we'll set up the closing as soon as we can. Oh, Nancy!"

She had come out of the bathroom off the foyer and joined them with a brave smile. "Hello."

"Maggie Ryan and Nick O'Connor, this is Nancy Selden. They're buying Lund's place on Garfield, Nance." He tapped the papers.

"Great!" She shook hands. "Len told me about it. Some excitement there."

"Quite a bit. Are you a realtor too?" asked Maggie.

"No, I'm in graphics." With a touch of bitterness she added, "And in this house my official title seems to be Len's fiancée. Though it's nothing that formal, really."

"Oh, I know. We had that problem too. No good words. I could never bring myself to say that old bald Nick here was my boyfriend."

"Right." Nancy smiled a fleeting smile.

Len said, "You must be on the way to the gym."

"Yes."

"Well, thanks for coming by. You're getting an excellent value here."

"Yes, with free bonuses," said Nick, twinkling. "A rent-controlled tenant and a corpse."

"Three for the price of one," agreed Len, and Nancy giggled.

"Well, at least they've got his name now," Len said. "Dennis Burns. Brugioni dropped by the office to ask if any of us recognized it."

"And did anyone?" asked Maggie.

"No. Only one person had even heard of the hotel where he worked."

"It's a strange case."

"I hope they find out something soon. I was frankly a little surprised when you decided to go ahead. I mean, it's a good value, but a lot of people might just want to forget the experience."

"We decided to ignore popular prejudice," explained Maggie.

"That doesn't surprise me. I can tell by your party clothes," said Nancy. "I wish I had the guts to come here in Levi's."

"We're buyers. We can do no wrong in Mrs. Banks's eyes," said Nick cheerfully. "Just ask Sanchez over there."

"Well, you're right, you are wearing haloes just now," Nancy admitted, smiling. "But generally, Levi's won't do. When I went into the restroom just now, Joyce was in the lounge section adjusting that thousand-dollar dress she's wearing. And you know what? Even her pantyhose are Givenchy."

Len grinned. "I'm not surprised."

"Suddenly my own best dress felt like a Salvation Army reject."

"You impressed Banks even so," said Len fondly. "He admires your ambition."

"Also my fair hair," Nancy pointed out. "Oh, he's a sweet old moralistic lech. And who knows? Maybe when I'm stinking rich I'll spend some of it on designer undies too."

Nick asked, "You said you were in graphics?"

"Yes, layout and so forth. And I paint a little on the side."

"She's marvelous," said Len warmly. "Oils especially."

"Abstract?"

"The label I'm most comfortable with is 'gestural,'" said Nancy. "But unfortunately, painting is no way to become rich. Not that graphics is either, but it's a little more dependable. And I enjoy the work."

"Same here," said Nick. "I'm an actor. But this side of superstardom, there's not much money around. Except in television. Commercials, sometimes soaps."

"Do you like TV?"

"Sure. I'm good at it. It's not exactly soul-satisfying, but it's a lot better than the alternatives."

"Yes, exactly." Nancy had clearly found a kindred spirit. "And it keeps you sharp, in practice, right? I think actually my painting has improved with the discipline I've learned in graphics."

"Do you have shows?"

"About once a year, at Bianchi's. Next one will be in July."

"Send us an announcement, okay?" said Nick. "But right now we ought to let you get back to impressing these people. We'll hear from you soon, right, Len?"

"Yes. I'll keep you posted. If nothing unusual turns up, we should be able to schedule the closing within a few weeks."

"Fine. We want to start fixing it up as soon as we can. We have to do most of it ourselves in our spare time, so it'll take a while."

"Yes. Three floors is a good-sized place to renovate by yourself. A lot of space for two people."

Maggie smiled. "Don't tell Mr. Lund, because it might worry him needlessly, and we'll keep up his payments. But we'll be more than two. The baby is due in October."

Len said woodenly, "Congratulations," and then, not woodenly at all, "Goddamn!" Nancy had bolted past Sanchez and out the front door. Len started to follow, then stopped helplessly.

"What's wrong?" Maggie touched his sleeve, puzzled.

"It's okay. Not your fault. Goddammit!"

"Oh hell," she said quietly. "A miscarriage? No. An abortion?"

"I don't know. She hasn't decided, dammit. Hey, what are you doing?"

Maggie was disappearing through the door too. Len ran a step after her, only to be stopped by Nick's firm hand. "Better wait," said Nick. "It'll be okay."

"But why—"

"She didn't mean to upset her."

"I know. Nancy knows too. She doesn't have to apologize."

"It's as much for Maggie's sake as Nancy's. Here, sit down a moment." Nick led him to the little gilded hall bench and Len realized his own legs were trembling. Nick asked, "Do you want to talk about it?"

"We'll be okay," said Len without conviction.

"Sure, but it's still tough at a time like this." Nick sat comfortably next to him. Len wondered if he should have run after her. Dammit, he was so useless! He couldn't think how to help her. He noticed he was kneading his hands together, rubbing his knuckles.

"Listen, I'm sorry about this. But we're both half crazy with this thing. It's worse than that dead man."

"You don't have responsibility for the dead man."

"Yes." Len pressed his knuckles into his palm. "Um, Nick, was your wife sort of depressed and distant when she got pregnant?"

"Not this time. Not at all. Elated."

"Oh, hell." Len looked at the door.

Nick said gently, "Maggie is very happy about this baby. But a few years back she had a very bad experience. She coped somehow, of course. But she grieved too. She'll understand what Nancy's going through."

"God, I wish I could!" said Len violently. "A guy is helpless, you know? I mean, dammit, it's my kid too!"

"I know what you mean. We're responsible and helpless, all at once."

"Yeah. God, it's ironic. Gordon Banks was just saying how hard he and Joyce tried to have kids, to no avail. And Nancy and I try to avoid it, and here we are. I mean, she's just getting launched at her firm, and I'm just beginning to build a career with Joyce. But right now we're basically scraping by. A kid now is out of the question. I guess."

"But it's still not an easy choice."

"How should I know? I'm not allowed to choose!" He punched his open hand with his fist and shook his head. "Oh, I'm not being fair. It's her decision. I know that."

"Have you talked with her about it?"

"Not really. It's painful for her. And I don't want to pressure her in any way. We sort of avoid the subject."

"I see."

"Well, you saw her just now."

Nick nodded. He was bulky and out of place in his jeans on the antique golden bench, but he had a sympathetic strength that was somehow comforting. Len felt that the man beside him had made difficult choices too. Nick said, "It's a hell of a decision for anyone to have to make. God-playing, no matter which way you choose. I hate God-playing."

"Yeah. I want to help Nancy, though. I don't know how."

"Hold her."

"What?"

"Hell, sometimes all answers are wrong. All we can do is

hold each other. Pray, and sing, and tell old tales, and laugh at gilded butterflies."

"Yeah. Dammit all."

After a while Maggie reappeared. Len jumped up. "Is she all right?"

The fury in her voice was barely under control. She said, "I'm authorized to tell you that she took your car, and that she won't be back till late."

"Oh, hell. Why?"

Arms crossed, lips tight, she said, "She's trying to think things through."

"But—oh, hell." Len sat back down and bowed his head, fingers splayed across his eyes. But he was still dimly aware of Maggie's accusatory stance before him, and of Nick's comforting presence next to him.

Nick was speaking to Maggie. "Is thinking things through alone a good idea for her?"

"I think so."

"Len?"

"Yeah. If she thinks it's best."

Nick glanced at Maggie, puzzled, then back. "Len? Does Nancy know you want to help?"

"I keep telling her."

"Telling her!" flared Maggie. "Jesus! You worm! You keep—"

"Maggie!" Nick's sharp tone checked her. More gently, he said, "Just explain what the problem is."

"The problem is—" She broke off again as a group of women, eyeing the blue jeans with the same enthusiasm Sanchez had, crossed the dining-room hall. When they had disappeared, she said in a lower, scornful voice, "The problem is that Nancy is facing one of the ugliest dilemmas anyone ever has to face. And she's all alone. Because the guy who should care, who should be helping her, is wrapped up in his own problems and ignoring her."

"That isn't true!" Len exploded. "What can I do? The only way I know to help her is to stay out of her way! Dammit, I can't do anything! That's the goddamn problem! You think if I could do something, I wouldn't?"

Nick said, "Maggie, it's not like—"

But she was hurling her response at Len. "You could talk to her!"

"I try, for God's sake! But it's hard to distract her."

"Distract?"

"What do you expect? Hell, it's the same with me! I think about it all the time. I dream about it, for God's sake! I try to cheer her up, but she's obsessed with it as much as I am. So what can I do?"

Maggie looked at Nick and said, "Whoops."

Nick said, "Yeah. We've got a misunderstanding here. Maggie isn't talking about distracting her."

"She isn't—" Len too had to wait while a pair of women returned to the dining room. "You think Nancy wants to talk about it?"

"Wouldn't you?"

"But it's her decision! I can't think of anything to say that doesn't seem like pressuring her. Like a condemnation of one choice or the other. And she's so jumpy. I mean, that's natural, but it makes it tough."

Maggie's rage and scorn had evaporated. She stepped closer, put a hand on his shoulder. "Len," she said, "it's just the same for her. Wildly conflicting emotions. It's a decision that's going to hurt someone, no matter what she decides. There's no painless choice. But you could help her think things through. And for God's sake, tell her that this is what you're upset about! She thinks you're wrapped up in some other problem. The murder, or your job."

"I thought—God, yes, I see why she'd think that it was the murder. Both things hit me the same day." A bad day, a nefarious day. He looked at the two of them and tried to smile. "Okay, I'll try. But God, it seems I'm dumping all my problems on you. The dead man, and now this. Not a very professional way to treat clients."

"We don't mind being friends too."

"Okay. Thanks." Maybe what they said was right, but he'd have to go slow. "You don't really have to nursemaid me. You want to get to the gym."

"No rush."

"We'll be okay. And I'll get busy on your house tomorrow. Special attention."

"Thanks. You're sure we can't help?"

"We'll be okay."

He watched as Sanchez held the doors for them, first the glass ones and then the big steel one. Nick's arm was across Maggie's shoulders. She seemed to need comforting too. Len turned back to the party to say good-by.

There weren't many trains on Sunday, and the subway ride home was slow. Even so, he had a long restless wait in the apartment before she appeared. He occupied himself with going over apartment properties, as Gordon Banks had advised. He finally settled on a decontrolled eight-unit building that was shabbily kept by its elderly owner, but was in a block that should benefit from the historic zoning. The owner's asking price was a little high, but none of the offers so far had even come close. Len decided to take a look at it again tomorrow.

Nancy finally arrived near midnight.

"Nance, are you okay?"

She shrugged.

"Where were you?"

"Painting."

"Yeah. Nance, look, I know it hurts like hell. It's bothering me too."

"Yeah?" she said, skeptical.

"Yeah. Would it help you to talk about it?"

She looked haggard, rubbing absently at a spot of white paint on the back of her hand. "Right now we're both exhausted," she said at last.

"Yeah. But tell me when."

"We're both tired now," she repeated.

But she did let him hold her.

7

Julia poured everyone a last cup of after-dinner coffee. Well, no, not coffee exactly; it was decaffeinated to avoid irritating sixty-year-old nerves at night. But it was hot and strong, a good finish for the three-hour fest of cooking and eating that she and Ellie and Ruth had just completed.

"So no one knows this Dennis Burns." Ellie leaned back in the sofa and reverted to an earlier topic.

"If so, the police aren't telling me," Julia said. "Brugioni was back twice, hoping I'd remembered something." She shrugged. "But I've never even heard of that hotel where he worked."

"The detectives are working very hard," said Ruth. "They even came by to talk to me, because I live on the block. Nice young officer. Irish."

"I just wish I could remember," said Julia. "There's something so familiar about that unfamiliar face. The lieutenant has decided it's just that I saw him after he was dead."

"Well, that sounds reasonable," said Ellie.

"Oh, yes, he's probably right. But if he isn't—"

Ruth said, "He was a handsome young fellow, judging from his picture. If you saw him and forgot him, Julia, you're slipping."

"Nah, he was too young for my taste," said Julia tartly.

"I'm willing to ogle kids my son's age, but not kids my grandson's age."

Ellie giggled in scandalized delight. "What would Reverend Peters think of you two?"

"Reverend Peters claims to be thirty, but he's already older than I'll ever be," retorted Julia. "Anyway, Ellie, you're one of us. A healthy red-blooded American geriatric case. You can't deny that an occasional salacious thought does cross one's mind."

"But I don't brag about it!"

Ruth, amused, called a halt. "Julia, tell me about the birthday party."

"Oh, that's right! It was great. Wonderful weather yesterday, of course. Fred-Law must have ordered it himself."

"Straight from heaven. Were there a lot of hippies?"

"Sure. Happy Birthday, Happy Earthday. There were hippies, kids, dogs, Frisbees, retired schoolteachers, even Vic Jr. He held down the dignified end of the spectrum."

"And food?"

"A giant green birthday cake. Huge. It wouldn't fit in this room. It looked like Central Park and was made of green cheese."

"Ugh," Ruth laughed. "Wish I could have seen it."

"Yes. And there was an actor playing Fred-Law. And there was dancing. Scott Joplin on the greensward. Too bad Pauline is in Utah. She loves Joplin."

"I bet Vic Jr. didn't dance."

"On the greensward? Don't be silly! But Greg and I sure did. He's going to be as good as his grandfather."

"Must have been fun." Ellie put down her mug. "But Ruth and I should be moving along before it gets dark."

Ruth glanced out the window at the lengthening shadows. "Yes, we'd better," she agreed. "Say, are those Pauline's begonias? They look great! Well, I'll see you Thursday at the library meeting, Teach."

"And be sure to show up Friday at the mission meeting, because Pauline won't be there and you're the only other person who understands those missionary budgets," ordered Ellie.

Julia assured them both that she would be there, refused their offers to help with the remaining dishes, and walked them out to the sidewalk. She watched the departing pair and wondered how the world would get along without widows. They taught school, ran companies, counseled teenagers, raised funds for hunger missions, for libraries, for hospitals, for historic and literary and civic organizations. Her friends were bright, dedicated, compassionate, efficient, hardworking people. All sublimating like hell, Freud might think. Maybe. But when you thought about the babies dying of preventable diseases in India, or the twelve-year-old prostitutes stumbling into Father Ritter's underfunded haven in the West Forties, or the old people right here in Brooklyn slowly dying of malnutrition because they couldn't buy decent food, the motive made no difference. The work had to be done. And along with the heartbreaks and frustrations came the warmth of being needed and the joy of being with friends.

Right at the moment, though, the work that had to be done was cleaning up.

She had just put the pots in to soak when the bell rang. Drying her hands, she went to the front bay to look out the window. It was Maggie Ryan, lanky and vivid in a bright blue blouse under a tweed jacket, inspecting the underside of the brownstone stoop. With a pang of premonition, Julia went to let her in.

"Well, if it isn't Bonesy!"

"Hello, Mrs. Northrup."

"I suppose I should ask you in." Julia retreated along the hall to the apartment door and motioned Maggie to the sofa. "There's still some coffee," she added grudgingly.

Maggie said, "Thanks, but I don't think this will take very long." She sat down with the grace that was always surprising in such a tall angular person. "Nice new plants."

Julia sat erect in the chair. "Pauline McGuire's. She's visiting her son-in-law who pays her rent. Now, what is it?"

"Three things. First, we're going to buy the house."

"So you think." Damn. Damn and hell.

"Second, we know that we can claim that we need this space for our own use, and try to get you evicted."

Julia bowed her head. Silly of her to think that bright young people wouldn't know that. Yet, foolishly, she had clung to the wan hope that they would be ignorant of their rights. She said in a low voice, "I'll fight it, you know. I went through every step when Pauline was evicted, and I know the ropes. And my son is a lawyer."

"No need to bother him, Mrs. Northrup. We admit we
don't need it and we're not going to try to evict you. Please
try to believe me. Once we own the property we're willing
to sign a lease or whatever you want that will guarantee
your right to stay here."

"Once you own the property. It's a long way from here
to there. And anyway, I don't know many leases that are
better than rent control."

"We could model it on rent-control regulations. Make it
good for, say, thirty years."

Julia could not afford to believe her. She said sourly,
"The papers will crucify you, you know."

"Oh?"

"For throwing out a ninety-eight-year-old widow."

Maggie laughed. "Fifty years, then!"

"You think it's funny."

"Mrs. Northrup, I'm dead serious. Look, I know it's
hard to get used to the idea when you've fought against it
for so long. But we signed papers yesterday, and so did
Lund. It's as close to inevitable now as these things ever
are."

"You can still get out of it, somehow. You won't like it
here. I'll play the radio loud and throw garbage in your
windows."

"Do anything you want that's allowed in the rent-control
regulations."

"And before you move in I'll pour cement into all the
upstairs drains. You won't want it then."

The deep blue eyes darkened. "You said you didn't have
a key to the upstairs. How will you get in?"

Drat her. Julia mustn't forget that this young woman
was bright as well as audacious. Talking to her was more
dangerous than talking to Brugioni. "I'll get in through
the broken windows, of course. Did you think I'd leave any
glass in the place?"

"Oh, of course. Silly of me." But she was still regarding
Julia a little too thoughtfully.

Julia said, "Well, then, Bonesy, I think we understand
each other. Any more good news?"

"No. The rest is bad."

"Oh?"

"I thought I'd give you some time to prepare. We have a
piano, and a dog."

"St. Bernard?"

"A little black cocker named Zelle. Nick also has a guitar, and I have a flute."

"And your best friends are probably the Rolling Stones."

"How did you guess? Also, one of these days we'll have children. It won't be a quiet household."

Julia was silent. Despite herself, she was attracted. She told herself sternly that it was impossible. They'd change their minds, just like the people who had promised Pauline she could stay and then promptly evicted her. With children, especially, they would decide they needed more room, and bounce her out. The disposable woman. Parker said, *three be the things I shall have till I die: laughter and hope and a sock in the eye.* Well, laughter and hope were fading fast.

And yet the impossible picture appealed to her. Tall good-natured Maggie, a baby, a little dog. Nick up there playing Irish songs on his guitar, a strong and reassuring presence when there were noises in the night. And Julia was in the picture too, winsome, tweaking the baby's cheek or patting the dog while Nick's warm eyes smiled at her. Silliness. This was a worn-out brownstone in Brooklyn, not a rose-covered cottage in Pleasantville USA.

She stood up and walked to the window. Across the street, a red-haired girl, teenaged, was staring at the house. Half the neighborhood had walked by this week-end, tourists gawking at the scene of the crime. Madame Tussaud's chamber of horrors, starring Julia Northrup. Because the ugly facts remained: she was a widow, living alone, soon to be evicted. And, Brugioni's sweetness not-withstanding, a prime suspect in an unsolved murder that stuck in the craw of the NYPD. Those were the facts. Babies and guitar music and a warm Irish landlord were foolish dreams.

Maggie said, "I'll go now. I just wanted to give you a chance to get used to the idea before we move in."

"Thanks," snapped Julia. "I'll buy the cement tomorrow."

Maggie grinned, and was gone.

Julia moved automatically to the door and, unseeing, fastened the bolts and chain. Not Jersey, anyway, she decided fiercely. There had to be someplace around here. She'd ask Benny to keep his ears open. They might be able to throw her out of her home, but never out of her neighborhood. She'd sleep in Fred-Law's park first. A snug little bench on Prospect Park West. A fashionable Gold Coast address.

She went back to the kitchen to finish scrubbing her pots. And for the second time was interrupted by the bell.

It was Maggie again. But this time her arm was around the red-haired teenager that Julia had seen across the street. The girl was sobbing. Julia hurried to open the door.

"What we need," said Maggie, "is some Kleenex and some coffee." Without taking her eyes from the girl, she guided her to Julia's sofa.

Julia produced the requisitioned coffee while Maggie fetched tissues from the bathroom. "Here, dear, blow your nose," the older woman coaxed. The young redhead obeyed meekly. She was a pretty creature, long luxurious hair, freckles, not much over a hundred pounds.

"Now drink your coffee," Julia instructed her.

She took a deep breath and swallowed a little, the big sad eyes glistening above the rim of the cup. "Thank you," she snuffled. She was clutching the cup in both hands. Julia noticed that she was wearing a wedding band and an engagement ring with a huge fake stone. She sat almost primly in her flared jeans and hiking shoes and L. L. Bean windbreaker jacket that clashed with the gaudy ring.

"Better?" asked Maggie.

The girl nodded. "I'm like really down. Sorry."

"Everything will be okay. I'm Maggie Ryan. And this is my friend Mrs. Northrup."

"Pleased to meet you."

Julia said, "What's your name, honey?"

"Oh, I'm sorry. Amy Burns."

"Have you had any dinner, Amy?" Maggie asked smoothly, not even a flicker to show that she recognized the significance of the name.

"No, I'm not hungry," said Amy, and snuffled again.

"Sure. You've had a terrible shock," said Maggie, taking some coffee too.

"I never wanted him to leave. He had to, I guess, but I didn't like it."

"He probably didn't like it either."

"No, he didn't. But he said he had to. It was the only

way to like get ahead, in his business." She pushed back a long strand of hair.

"He was a waiter, wasn't he?"

"A waiter? No! He was an actor!" Amy stared accusingly at Maggie. "You mean you didn't know him? Then how come you said you did? You won't go to the police, will you? Curt said not to go to the police! If you're a friend—"

"We won't go to the police, Amy," said Julia. "Not unless you want us to, or Curt wants us to."

Amy's big eyes shifted from one of them to the other, back and forth. Finally she said, "Curt won't want you to."

"Well, don't you think he wants them to catch the murderer?"

Amy repeated obstinately, "Curt won't want you to."

Maggie looked straight at Julia and said viciously, "Curt's a numbskull."

"He's not!" said Amy hotly.

"Of course he's not," said Julia soothingly, darting a glance at Maggie to confirm that this was the right response. "He's a good friend, right?"

"Yes!" Amy turned to her gratefully. "And he's like really smart."

"I don't see anything smart about him," snorted Maggie.

Julia turned on her in indignation. "He knows a lot more about it than you do!"

"Yes!" Amy agreed. "He knows what's going on around here! He thinks someone was jealous of Denny because he just got this terrific part everyone wanted. You know how it is in show business!"

"That makes sense," murmured Julia sympathetically.

"Denny was doing so well."

"Not in show business!" exclaimed Maggie. "Nobody makes money in show business! Not for years!"

"Well, Denny did," said Julia.

Amy nodded vigorously. "Yes! He sent me hundreds of dollars a week ago! It wasn't easy. And he had to be away a lot, that was bad. But he said last time that it wouldn't be long. He did Curly in *Oklahoma!* at our school, he was really good. And he was onto something big, he said. He meant this part he just got, I guess."

"Probably," said Julia.

"And then this happened." She dabbed at her nose, then

glanced fearfully around Julia's comfortable room. "Was it in here?"

"No, honey. It was on the top floor, in an empty room. No one was living up there."

"They just like lured him up there?"

"Maybe. The police are trying to find out, but of course they don't have much to go on. They think he was a waiter."

"That was only part-time."

"I know, honey. But I wondered if they should know he was an actor, so they'd understand the motive."

Amy turned to Julia earnestly. "But Curt thinks he can find out more by himself, because the guy who did it will feel like safer if the police aren't asking around. He might tell Curt something, you see. Then later Curt can tell the police a lot more."

"I see," said Julia.

Maggie sneered. "That's really not very bright of you, Amy. How do you know Curt is telling the truth? You don't, do you?"

"Of course he is!" Amy looked a little frightened of Maggie.

"It's stupid!"

"No, it's not," said Julia. "Curt's a friend. But he knows if the police are investigating, everyone will clam up."

Amy responded eagerly to Julia's TV jargon. "That's exactly right! So you see, you mustn't tell them."

"We won't," Julia promised. "Not until you or Curt says it's okay. We want the guy caught too."

"Yes." Amy took another Kleenex. "We were only married six months, you know. Dr. Burns died—his dad—and we had to postpone the wedding, of course. And my parents—well, we had to keep it a secret."

"Oh, that's a shame," said Julia. "And you had to live apart a lot."

"Yes, we were only together for like a couple of months. And my dad was so—Anyway, Denny decided to join Curt in New York. But he was so good. He came to see me, and brought money. Especially at the end."

"Was Curt making money too?"

"Well, I don't know," she said, hesitating. Julia's charms were wearing thin. Maggie attacked again.

"Of course Curt was making money! He's probably a

rich banker with loads of expensive things. Probably has an apartment on the Upper East Side!"

"He does not! He plays drums and he lives—" Amy stopped suddenly, seeing the trap.

Vitriol dripped from Julia's voice. "Bonesy, get out of here. You're upsetting her."

"Upsetting her? I'm trying to help her!"

"Well, you're not helping! Get out!" She turned to Amy solicitously. "Here, honey, have some more coffee." Maggie glared at them, banged her coffee mug down on the bookcase next to the door, and slammed out.

Amy accepted the coffee distractedly. "Curt's nice, really," she reassured Julia.

"Of course he is. She doesn't know him, and you do."

"Yes. And Denny liked him a lot. They were best friends in high school back in Winston. Denny'd trust Curt with anything." She snuffled. "Oh, God, I can't believe he's dead! He was just getting started and already had this big job. He'd had to put it off, you know, when his dad died. Had to help his mother like close the office and everything. Heavy stuff. And now—I just can't believe it!"

Julia put her arm around Amy's shoulder. "It takes a while, honey. Took me a couple of years, and even now I miss him. Don't be afraid to cry."

Amy began to bawl. Julia held her tenderly and felt fury at the murderer who had killed this sweet youngster's husband.

A husband who had been onto something big. What? And what did it have to do with Artie Lund's place?

But before she could figure out a way to work the conversation around, Amy jumped up. "Oh, God! I'm supposed to be at Curt's in twenty minutes! I've got to hurry!"

"Do you want me to call a cab? Where are you going?"

But it didn't work. Amy said, "No, no, it's all right. The subway stops near there." She gave her reddened nose a final swipe before opening the door.

"Sure, honey. Come back anytime." Julia locked the door behind her, frustrated that the much-praised Curt's last name or address had not surfaced. She went to the window and watched Amy run toward Seventh Avenue. And, as she suspected, a rangy woman in tweeds, dark glasses, and a scarf emerged from beside a stoop and followed.

She finished scrubbing her long-neglected pots, but hadn't started on the mugs when the phone rang. "It's Bonesy the Bad Policeman reporting to headquarters," said Maggie breezily. "Did Amy tell you Curt's last name?"

"No. She just cried."

"Yeah, poor kid. But you're such a wonderful good-policeman, I'd hoped that she might let something slip."

"Denny and Curt went to high school up in Winston. And Denny helped his mother after his dad died. But we don't need character references. We need clues."

"We sure do. I tracked her to what's probably his building, but only last names were posted. No Burns, but then Denny was visiting Curt, right? So I've got him narrowed down to one of about fifty possible names."

"Drat. Still, knowing the building is a start." Julia knew without asking that Maggie was as excited as she was about this new knowledge. "I take it he doesn't live on the Upper East Side."

"No, it's a medium-sleaze block not too far from Union Square. Could be worse."

"We know he's a drummer, probably from Winston."

"Right. And he hung around with an actor. Or a would-be actor. Wish we could tell the cops."

"You mean you won't?"

"Hey, we promised her! But Nick knows a few things about actors. I'll ask him to nose around a little."

"You think Denny really got a big part?"

"No. Anything's possible, but my feeling is that Denny or Curt invented the part to account for money that was earned some other way."

"Maybe so. Do you think Curt killed him?"

"A lot of people might have killed him. Including Amy."

"I know, I know."

"Including you," observed Maggie.

"Of course. Or you. We'll all have to be careful."

"Right. I'll see you soon. Keep your doors locked."

"Caroline Sweeney's Great-Aunt Lizzie kept her doors locked. When the burglar came, he slid down the chimney."

"Must have been a right jolly old elf."

"He was a skinny twelve-year-old. She boxed his ears, scrubbed him down, and sent him on his way."

"Admirable Aunt Lizzie. I'll let you know if Nick discovers anything."

"Tell him to be careful."

"Okay. And think about what we talked about."

Julia drew a long breath. "I won't grovel," she said bleakly.

"Jesus Christ, woman!" flared Maggie. "The day you start groveling, we *will* evict you!" And the receiver crashed in Julia's ear.

8

Julia hung up, mind and heart at war. *I am old, and good and bad are woven in a crazy plaid,* said Parker. How could she decide what to think about this brash young woman who suddenly loomed so important in her life? Was she good luck or bad? Well, if bad, hoping and trusting too much would make it worse.

There was still some daylight left. Julia decided to go hunting again. She knew there was probably nothing left to find after the police search. But there was always the chance. She changed to her old skirt.

She had already searched the whole third floor, inch by inch, shortly after the police had left. There had been nothing at all. But she had only given the lower floors a glance. She was locked out of the parlor-floor apartment, of course, but the front stairs and the halls were accessible. She was sure that the murderer had used the stairs, to lure or drag the victim up, and to escape. So she opened the dumbwaiter, dropped the top bolt down to keep the door into her kitchen from closing behind her, undid the screws and dropped them into a corner, and pulled herself up to Ann and Jack's old room. She left the panel slightly ajar so she could get it open again without breaking a fingernail, and then went all the way downstairs to the first-floor hall to begin her search.

First, the little vestibule. Light still entered the frosted
windows from outside, and she didn't have to use her
flashlight at all. The house itself was quiet, but she could
hear sounds of harsh music, a children's ball game down
the street, cars, and dogs. She looked carefully into the
crevices of panels, into tiled corners, into the hinges and
latches of the outer and inner doors. Nothing. The police
had been thorough too, and anything obvious would have
been found already. But there was still a faint chance that
something less obvious might still be here.

She moved on into the hallway. It was wide at the
entrance, then the long elegant flight of stairs ran up the
side wall. In the 1890's Caroline Sweeney had come sweetly
down those steps to meet, and later marry, Tim O'Rourke.
Always thought I'd fall on my face, she'd told Julia. The
hall itself continued back beside the stairs to the door of
the kitchen and back stairs. That door was locked because
it was part of the first-floor apartment now. Without hope
she tried the door and the parlor door, but the police, or
Artie Lund, or young Lennie, had remembered to lock
them.

But the door under the stairs was unlocked. She went
in. It was a small square area, really the top landing of the
stairs to her basement rather than a true closet, though
the seldom-used door to the steps was locked and the
brooms Artie had left here made it seem like a closet. It
was clear that there were no garottes here. No purloined
letters either. A purloined broom, perhaps? Well, if there
were any purloining going on these days, Artie would be
just the one to do it.

The downstairs side of the closet was another door that
led to the basement steps and the hall outside her own
apartment. This, too, was firmly locked, with a sturdy
deadbolt that dated from the early days when she was still
on good terms with Artie. None of the tenants had keys to
that lock. But the police had been through the door
during their search, of course, and Maggie had come
through it using Lennie's keys when she'd run down to call
the police from Julia's.

There was a scrap of paper by the baseboard next to the
door. Julia scrutinized it in the beam of the flashlight.
Shucks. Overgrown Nancy Drew foiled again. It was not a
scrap from an incriminating diary. Not even a laundry

ticket with which she could trace the murderer's shirts. Just a small square sticky Woolworth's tag that said "89¢." No wonder the police had left it behind.

On to the hall, then. She was thorough, as befitted little Bobby Cody's former teacher—checking the baseboards, the carving in the newel post, the corners, the door hardware. Nothing. Much cleaner than it had been when it was still a busy dwelling-place. The police were better housewives than Artie and fluffy-topped Loretta; they'd swept up every bit of dust. Caroline Sweeney O'Rourke would be proud of them. Probably they'd taken it to their lab. She started up the stairs, checking every corner, every scuff mark, every banister. Nothing.

Halfway up, she stood and stretched. Working on all fours in the dim light was not the easiest task for sixty-eight-year-old bones and eyes. Or knees. Especially knees. As she approached the top of this flight, it was even darker. Not only was the daylight almost gone, but even the streetlight that glowed through the frosted panes of the main door did not reach this high. Well, the flashlight would have to be enough. She bent again to her task.

Below her, the back-porch door closed quietly.

Julia froze. Had she heard right?

Could it have been next door?

Outside, the children called to each other still. A car passed.

And then, closer, another doorknob turned. The locked door to the first-floor kitchen.

And the damn flashlight was still on! Julia switched it off hurriedly, and in doing so bumped it against the step.

Silence.

With damped breath, Julia strained to listen. Cars passed. The children shouted. A bicycle bell. A dog. Far away, a siren.

The back-porch door closed again, quietly.

Gone? Had the noise frightened him away?

Faint music from next door. A man passing on the street, reminiscing with someone about the Dodgers. From the street too, metallic clanks. A garbage can?

Was that creak from inside?

Julia's grip tightened on the flashlight, ready to use it as a club.

The dog, far away, barked shrilly. Another car passed. Willa's voice, faint, calling her grandchildren.

Another car.

No noise from this house. No motion. Nothing.

Whoever it was had left. She'd scared him away. Well, she'd scared herself away too. Time to go home.

Quietly, she climbed the stairs. Solid stairs, nearly silent as she ascended the two flights. At each creak, however, she stopped in terror, but then forced herself to go on. Don't be silly, Julia. Even if he's still down there, you'll be safe in your dumbwaiter, the panel latched and invisible on the third floor, the walls solid on the first and second.

She hurried across the landing to Jack and Ann's room.

The fabric that fell around her was dense, soft against her skin. No light came through. She stumbled, fell painfully to her knees, and the cloth tightened around her arms. She tried screaming, but the pressure on her mouth increased, the thick material was crammed between her teeth. Weight on her stomach. Her ankles bound. Then steps hurried away, down the stairs.

She could still breathe. A little.

She spat out the cloth and tried screaming again, but knew that the fabric muffled her voice into incoherence. Her heart pounded. Even if a neighbor somewhere were listening, he wouldn't know there was a problem. Some kid playing, he'd think.

Could she move? Escape into the dumbwaiter after all?

She couldn't walk with her feet tied. But maybe she could roll. A new kind of potato-sack race. Field Day on Garfield Place. Which way? What direction was she facing? Well, she had a chance of hitting it if she moved, none if she stayed still. She rolled vigorously in the direction she thought most likely.

Thump. What was it? A wall, of course. Through the binding material, her fingers explored the wall. Smooth, but of course with the intervening fabric she couldn't tell if it was plaster or wood paneling. She could feel a little baseboard. Aha! The plaster walls up here had six-inch heavy baseboards. This little flat one must be the paneled wall. Okay, she had her bearings now. She could heave herself along, a giant inchworm, feeling with her feet for the hinged panel.

Those steps again, hurrying back upstairs. Rubber soles,

but the steps were audible now that there was no attempt at stealth. Julia hunched her way along frantically, determined not to panic. There! The open panel, against her loafers, still ajar. She pushed her foot into the gap eagerly, widened it, started to wriggle her way in.

Hands hauled her upright again. Loosened the ankle ties. She kicked out wildly and her attacker grunted but did not let go. Julia braced herself, hooked a foot behind the upright of the dumbwaiter frame so she couldn't be dragged away, and thrashed wildly. The thick fabric slid up a little along her back. Was she winning? She freed an arm, grabbed wildly, blindly, at her opponent, but her hand closed only on hair. Then there was a sickening blow to her side. She fell back into the dumbwaiter, aware only dimly of the cloth sliding off, the panel closing as the heavy material was withdrawn, still shielding the assailant from Julia's teary eyes. The black wave of nausea crested, and waned.

Footsteps hurried away.

Trembling, Julia fumbled at the bolts, locked the panel closed.

Footsteps on the stairs.

She took a deep breath. Time to go home.

The flashlight had disappeared, but even in the dark she knew the dumbwaiter. Groping, she found the brake rope and released it. Her other hand, she noticed, still clutched those strands of hair. Carefully, she tucked them into her blouse pocket and began to ease herself down with the handrope. Was her enemy going down too? To meet her in her own apartment, perhaps? But she hadn't been killed when she was tied and helpless. Why not?

Maybe it wasn't supposed to look like a murder. Maybe an accident would be staged.

Be careful. More careful than before. Somehow, he'd gotten upstairs past her, to Ann's room. How?

Oh, blast.

Senility, Teach, that's your only excuse. Stupid! While she'd been crouching there cautiously on the stairs after the back-porch door had closed for the second time, waiting to be sure he had gone away, he'd run up the back stairs in those rubber-soled shoes. He'd run up, noticed the panel that she'd left ajar, and found the dumbwaiter. Then he'd just waited calmly for her to come blundering up the stairs at last. Ah, Teach, you're failing. You would never have overlooked that if you'd been dealing with fifth-graders.

But he hadn't killed her. Did he think he was safe because she couldn't identify him? Or was he planning a different death for her, something that looked accidental?

And why had he come? She hadn't expected him to come. What had she missed? And why had he risked climbing to the third floor to ambush her? Was he afraid she'd actually find something? Did he suspect Amy had told her something? Why this sudden attack?

And why had he tied her and run down before coming back and pushing her into the dumbwaiter? That's where she wanted to go anyway. He'd tied her, then freed her completely at the end. Not even a scrap of that fabric left. No record of the encounter at all, except for some very sore ribs.

The hair. She had some of his hair. That would do it, wouldn't it? Brugioni would be proud of her. Julia Northrup, the winsome sleuth.

She hoped he didn't know she had his hair.

The dumbwaiter car inched down toward the door into Julia's kitchen. She saw the crack of light at the top of the frame, and slowed. No sense dropping feetfirst into another ambush. Weapons? She had her loafers and the six big screws that fastened the car into place for its function as a closet. Not much of an arsenal. She picked up two screws and adjusted her position so that she could kick out viciously at anyone who opened the door. Then, gripping a screw in each hand, she cautiously pulled on the handrope, letting herself down gently into position.

The door was still closed. Was he outside, waiting?

Well, she could wait too. But it would help if she didn't have to keep holding on to the handrope. She adjusted the brake, then, cautiously, screwed in one of the big screws as tightly as she could get it with her fingers. Not snug, she needed the screwdriver in her kitchen for that, but it would help hold if she had to struggle.

Near at hand, there was an enormous crash. The little car shivered. For an instant Julia thought he was trying to destroy the car. Then she realized what the crash had meant. Frantic, she groped to find the next hole, shoved another screw into place, and then a third, twisting them furiously into the frame, ignoring the sharp metal ripping the skin of her fingertips. As she jammed in the fourth, the second crash came. Again, the car shuddered—but it held.

Julia closed her eyes in relief. She'd won that round, just barely. Her enemy had cut through the ropes that held the counterweights and sent them hurtling to the cellar. But by pushing in the screws, Julia had not hurtled after them. She was still here, on her own floor. Not lying wounded in a smashed car down in the closed cellar shaft.

Shakily, she started to put in a fifth screw, then stopped. What are you doing, Teach, you idiot? To cut the counterweight ropes he had to be up on the third floor in Ann's room, or even in the attic. He couldn't reach the ropes anywhere else. So he's not in the kitchen! Get out, old dummy! Run! Run to the hall, into the street! Call Brugioni! You've won, you've got his hair!

Was he rushing downstairs even now, ready to assault her again? He had staged his accident. What would he do when he realized she hadn't crashed?

Ambush her in the kitchen, perhaps. But he'd have to get there first. It was a race. So get a move on, Teach.

Julia contemplated the cabinet door into her kitchen. She'd burst out, she decided, feetfirst, screws in hand, to surprise him if he was there. Continue at the same pace out to the street, to Willa next door, to a telephone. Hope he wasn't between her and the door. Sprint like you've never sprinted, Julia. She drew a deep breath and launched herself at the door.

Smashed against it.

It did not move.

But it had to move! She remembered dropping the upper bolt into place with the door open, so it couldn't close and latch by itself. There was no way it could be locked now!

Unless—

Oh, damn.

She shoved again, but the immobility of the door no longer surprised her. Julia leaned back into the corner of the little car, dazed. So that was why he had kept her tied for a few minutes before pushing her into the dumbwaiter. He had run down to bolt her kitchen cabinet exit closed, while Julia, in pathetic eagerness to escape, had struggled and strained to reach this little car. This little car, disabled with its counterweights destroyed, and its exits blocked.

The accident had been staged, and this was it.

She was trapped.

9

"Hey, man, you gone musical on me, or link up with the mob?"

Nick set the guitar case carefully on the bar stool next to him. "Nah. You and me, Franklin, we're the wrong nationality."

The bartender's shrewd black face creased in laughter. "Right about that, man. Want a drink?"

"Maybe a strawberry daiquiri."

"Shit, for that I gotta send away to my fag uncle in Miami." Franklin picked up the two bills on the bar. "So, you donating this to the Orphan Bartender Fund?"

"I'm looking for a guy who plays drums."

"Music after all. Black drummer?"

"White, I think. Named Curt."

"Where's he hang out?"

"If I knew that, I wouldn't be here. Don't know what he looks like either. He's supposed to live on the nice side of Union Square."

"Ain't no nice side." Franklin waggled the bills thoughtfully. "Try Palomino," he said at last. "He know that scene, got musicians on the premises. Eighteenth, near the Square."

"Thanks."

"Your new woman keeping you happy?" Franklin had been a dealer for Nick's first wife, whose drug habit had

106

contributed to her death five years before. He still considered Maggie new.

"She's fine," Nick replied. "Going to have a baby."

"No shit!" Franklin beamed. "Knew you wasn't shooting blanks, man!"

"Happened after I switched to strawberry daiquiris."

Franklin guffawed and tucked the bills back into Nick's shirt pocket. "You go buy your woman a present from old Franklin, hear? And if she bring in the baby, they both get a free hit."

"Aw, Franklin, you orphan bartenders are so sentimental."

Palomino's, halfway down the island, had a crowd as mixed as Franklin's. On a tiny stage tucked in the corner, a black jazz trio sweated. Amateur night. Except for the pianist, Nick decided. He wasn't bad. Through the smoky haze he saw a space at the bar and made his way to it.

The bartender, black but with a startling pale Afro and an astonishing amount of jewelry, was cautious at first, eyeing Nick's brawny build and his guitar case with uneasiness. But the mention of Franklin's name, and a little cash, brought acceptance.

"Yeah, maybe I hear about someone like that."

"Had a friend named Denny. From Winston."

Palomino looked at him sharply. "No trouble here, man."

"No. No trouble. Is Curt here now?"

"Here? Old Curt? Old Mr. Clean Jeans? Shit, man, Shirley Temple come around first." Delicately, he ran a finger along the heavy gold chain around his neck. "But somebody here know him, maybe."

Nick dropped another bill on the bar. "Okay. I'm going to the coffeehouse on the corner there. I'll wait for him."

"Yeah." Palomino seemed relieved to be rid of white affairs. "He be along."

It was already eleven when Nick entered the coffeehouse. He ordered a cup from the tired waiter and went into the phone booth to call Maggie.

"Progress?" she asked.

"I think I'm on the scent." He told her what Palomino had said.

"He was afraid of trouble?"

"I'm a big guy, Maggie. Doing my tough act, complete with guitar case. Dropping Franklin's name. Asking about a murder."

"Yeah, wow, I'd be scared too."

"How easy is a bush supposed a bear."

"Well, bush, watch your back. You're waiting for Curt now?"

"Yeah, I'll have some supper and see what turns up."

"Oh, God, it was my turn to cook, wasn't it?" They hadn't seen each other since the morning. She'd called home excitedly after tracking Amy and sent him out on this chase. "I'm afraid I'm not a very reliable roommate."

"I know," said Nick. "It wasn't your well-ordered domestic life that attracted me."

"Likewise." He could hear the smile in her voice. "God, Nick, I hope our kid doesn't turn out stuffy. Poor thing'll be miserable with the two of us."

"We've got an old Irish saying: Stuffy to stuffy in three generations."

"Well, it won't come from my side of the family," she said confidently. "See you later, love."

He bought a burger and a Greek salad and ate slowly, the guitar case propped next to him in the booth. Would their child be stuffy? Poor little thing. Wrong family for that. Of course, babies were all stuffy in their way, insisting on frequent meals and dry diapers. But they liked surprises too. Peekaboo games. Being swung in the air by proud fathers. And he knew that even the stuffiest, most unpleasant baby would receive lavish and sensible love from Maggie, who had craved a child for years. She remained childlike herself in her vast enthusiasms, in her relish for games and new challenges. This baby, sweet or stuffy, was lucky in its mother.

And father? Maybe. He still couldn't imagine himself a father. He supposed he would love the baby, whatever it turned out to be. Even stuffy. But it didn't seem at all real to him yet. His childless first marriage and his beloved but unsettled profession had killed any illusions he may once have had of becoming the all-American family man. Now, suddenly, in his late thirties, balding rapidly, he had been informed that he would soon be a father. And couldn't quite believe it.

Did Maggie believe it? She was still slim, lively and lusty as ever, not the bloated broody hen that she cheerfully promised to become. There were baby books now on her desk among the computer manuals, and there was her sudden ravenous desire for a bigger apartment. Maybe she believed in the baby. But to Nick, the child was still mythical, like Peter Pan, someone he could talk about but couldn't imagine meeting in the flesh. 'Tis a wise father that knows his child. Men were so distant from their offspring. A spasm of pleasure and then, long months after, a strange little being that, people said, was yours. How could he believe such a story?

Maggie, of course, could get him to believe almost anything. Even that the corpse on Garfield Place had had a red-haired wife, and a friend named Curt, who would come meet him here in this coffeehouse.

Not that Nick's own curiosity wasn't strong too. Maggie had said that Dennis Burns had been an aspiring actor too. Young, Nick knew, even younger than Nick had been when he'd started. What kind of preparation had Dennis had? Those first months were always a devastating shock as you found that your highly praised school successes counted for nothing in New York. Nick and his first wife had struggled together, working as waiters, janitors, temporary clerks. It had not been healthy for her; alcohol and drugs could be very alluring when the alternative was facing crumbling dreams.

Had alcohol and drugs attracted Dennis Burns? Wine for breakfast the day he died, the lieutenant had said. And drugs could get you into deep trouble. Could get you killed. Even if you were very young.

He opened the guitar case, which held nothing more lethal than a script, and made himself concentrate on it. He had an appointment in the morning at the CBS casting office at Black Rock, a callback for a police drama shooting in the city. He wanted to have a clearer sense of who the principal characters were. The part he wanted was juicy—the bad guy who died horribly in a flaming car at the show's climactic moment—but to play the scenes intelligently, he had to know who he was playing *against*. There was much more work in this business called playing than most people realized.

He was munching one of the last olives, wondering if he should rouse the sleepy waiter to order something else, when the street door opened and a young man entered. Mr. Clean Jeans, Palomino had said. His dark eyes skimmed the coffeehouse, snapped to a stop on the guitar case in

Nick's booth, then moved on to Nick. Nick beckoned him over.

"Curt?"

"Yeah."

"I'm Nick. Glad to meet you. Have a seat."

Curt was tall, broad-shouldered, with neatly trimmed brown hair. Jeans, desert boots, corduroy shirt. Maggie had mentioned L. L. Bean. He slid into the booth, tense, looking furtively at the guitar case, at Nick, back behind him at the door.

"Coffee for my friend," said Nick to the waiter, and watched him bring it and depart before he added, "I hear you've been asking about Denny."

"Yeah. You knew him?"

"I'm an actor too. Met him in line at a cattle call. A while ago now."

"You know something about him?"

"I might. I don't know if I know."

Curt nodded, as though Nick's hedging made sense, but remained cautious. "Were you like a friend of Denny's?"

"Not a friend, exactly. Acquaintance. But I don't like to see acquaintances get killed."

"And you know who did it?"

"Hey, not too fast! I've just got little bits and pieces. Enough to make me wonder. I thought maybe you and I could compare notes." He saw the doubt in Curt's face and added, "Maybe it's worth something to you."

"I see." Curt was no friendlier, but the doubt was gone. He could believe a hustle. "I don't have money to throw around."

"We've not talking big money. We're talking fair. Your bits and pieces for my bits and pieces, and maybe a few bucks if I tell you something really useful."

"And if I already know?"

Nick shrugged. "That's the breaks. No charge. Like I say, I don't like to see acquaintances get killed."

"So what do you know?"

He'd been afraid it would come to this. But Nick was an actor, deep in the role of a small-time hustler, and there was complete conviction as he leaned forward and said, "First, I know his dad left him money or something."

Curt snorted. "Money? You're crazy! His old man like

drank it up those last years. Not even enough left for Denny's mom."

Nick backtracked. "Okay, maybe not money. He said something valuable." That should cover it, he thought. Sage advice, even.

But Curt was nodding. "Sure. The stuff for his big job. But that's what we're talking about, right?"

"Right." Better leave that topic until he had another clue. What else did he know about Denny? He said, "And there's a woman."

"You know her name?" asked Curt eagerly.

Not Amy, then. Nick said, "I might know her, yes."

Curt squinted at him thoughtfully, stroking his jaw. "Well, he said she was like older, and you're going bald."

"And what's wrong with that?" Unsure of his next move, Nick stalled. "Yul Brynner's bald."

"Nothing's wrong, man. So tell me about this woman."

"Telly Savalas. Ed Asner."

"Yeah, yeah, screw all that. What's her name?"

"No, your turn first."

"My turn?"

"Sure. I gave you this woman. Before I say more, you give me what was going on in Denny's head. I'm not asking about the stuff his dad left, just what he was thinking."

"I don't know, man. He got this call Tuesday. He said she was uptight so he was supposed to get a disguise. Like goddamn Halloween, you know? He thought it was funny." Curt swallowed. "Next morning he split early, eight-thirty. Took a bottle of wine to celebrate. He was a little high, man. Not spaced out. Said he was going to win another one for Amy, and to take good care of the stuff. God, he was happy!" Curt's young face gave an unmanly twitch before he mastered it.

"Yeah. He had a sense of humor," said Nick gently. "Where'd you meet Denny? Here, or back in Winston?"

"Winston. We were going to come into the city together. He's an actor. Starred in *Oklahoma!* his senior year."

"In high school."

"Yeah."

A lot of us have done that, thought Nick. He'd played Curly once himself, back when he had hair. This fact had not overwhelmed New York casting directors. "So what happened?"

"His dad got sick. Denny told me to go ahead and split, get started here, and he'd show later. But when his dad died—Christ, it was a real bitch, the way the old man had piled up the debts. Denny had to help his mom sell the house and everything. It was six months before he could come."

"Did he have any luck with auditions?"

Curt's face sagged, suddenly old. "Hey, it's not real easy to get a start."

Nick felt a surge of sympathy for the well-groomed, blustery young drummer. "Not easy at all," he agreed. "But listen, you said the woman who called was uptight. How come?"

Wrong move. Curt's eyes narrowed. "Hey, look, you being straight with me? You really know her?"

"Sure. But we aren't bosom buddies," said Nick smoothly. "More a friend of a friend. We do each other favors sometimes."

"And are you doing her a favor right now, maybe?" Curt glanced at the guitar case.

"No. She doesn't know I'm here," said Nick. Shocking to find himself telling the truth about something. "But listen, you still haven't told me what Denny was going to do. His big job."

"He never told me about it."

"Not her name, I know. But you had a pretty good idea what he was planning. You know what his dad left him."

"Screw that, man! We have a deal! You tell me the woman's name, and I'll show you the stuff. I've got it at home."

"You're trying to trade promises for facts. How do I know you've really got it?"

Curt was firm. "You go first or we can the deal. I was his friend, dammit!"

Nick only had one card left to play. He said, "Maybe I ought to ask Amy."

Shielded from the somnolent waiter by Curt's casually outflung arm, the little revolver glinted suddenly against the Formica tabletop. "You say one word to Amy, and it's all over!"

"Hey, all right, take it easy!" said Nick. "We'll leave her out of it if you want."

"So are we going to do business, or not?"

Curt was too young and too nervous. Unpredictable and unreasonable. Nick found himself wishing he had rein-forcements. But the restaurant was empty, except for the waiter. He said soothingly, "Look, this is bigger than I thought. We don't want to make a fuss here. But I'm going to have to think about it."

"Screw that! Come on, let's hear the freaking name!" Curt waggled the little barrel.

The man coming in the door was about six-six, lavishly tattooed, with a wrestler's thick neck and a submachine gun. He started slowly toward their booth. Nick said as calmly as he could, "I can't tell you anything if I'm dead, Curt. Look, I promise to leave Amy out of it. Now, I've got the name, you've got the evidence. We need each other, right?"

"Maybe." Curt's attempt to be tough was grotesque against his nervous downiness. "But tell me the name first."

The tattooed man was drawing nearer. Nick the hustler was trying not to look at him, trying to concentrate on the little blue-black gun. But somehow, subtly, he must have given it away. Edgily, Curt glanced back over his shoulder. Back at where the tattooed man would have been if he hadn't been just a vivid figment of an actor's practiced imagination. Curt's distraction lasted only an instant, but that was long enough for Nick to shove the barrel of the revolver aside with one big hand as he chopped down hard with the other on Curt's gun hand. Triumphantly, he scooped the weapon into his own lap.

"Yeah? Want something?" called the waiter, awakened by the thumps.

"Another coffee for my friend. And the check," Nick said. "You see," he explained to Curt while he removed the ammunition, "I need a little time. There's threats all over, and I'm thinking I should cover my tracks better."

"The mob, huh? Heavy scene." Watching his own gun uneasily, Curt bowed to the inevitable. "Well, okay, let me know when you're ready."

Nick pocketed the bullets. "I need a phone number."

Curt gave it, and added, "When'll you know?"

"Couple of days. And you might think about getting a couple hundred together. Just in case you like what I say."

The coffee and check arrived. Curt gulped thirstily. He said, "Can't get that much. But what I said about Amy still goes." This time, though, his words were more wistful than threatening.

"Understood. I'm not trying to mess you up. Or her."

"Okay."

Nick slipped the empty revolver across the table. "Here. Take better care of it. I'm not the mob. But they wouldn't have been very impressed either."

"Yeah. Well." Curt stood up, shrugged, tried for nonchalance. "See you, then."

Nick watched him leave, a neatly dressed handsome kid from Westchester County, trying to swagger his way into fame and fortune. But he'd never make it if he kept looking over his shoulder at imaginary men. Nick paid the waiter and went home.

Maggie, wearing a big striped barbecue apron and nothing else, greeted him at the door. A curly black spaniel was bouncing at her feet, and she held a plate of fresh madeleines. *"Avec les compliments du chef,"* she said.

"Mmm." He ate one while he patted the dog. "Do I get a bonus if he pulled a gun on me?" He handed Maggie the bullets.

"Merde!" She stared at them. "God, Nick, I wish we hadn't had to promise her not to call the police."

"I'm not sure the police would have helped. He's very young."

"What on earth did you say to get him that excited?"

"Suggested that I might tell Amy about a mysterious woman with gangland connections."

"About who?"

"Hell, I don't know who! I came on very confidential and suggested there was a woman involved, thinking of Amy. But he instantly asked if I knew her name."

She was pouring coffee to go with the madeleines. The barbecue apron didn't quite meet in the back, which Nick found highly entertaining. She deftly removed his exploring hand and pressed a mug of coffee into it. "And then?" she prompted, sitting on the sofa.

"Um. Yes. Then we talked about Dennis a little. Poor kid. His dad was alcoholic, apparently. Here he is, eighteen, ready to embrace the future. And his father dies. Leaves him a load of debts and responsibilities."

"You survived that." Her blue eyes looked intently into his.

He nodded slowly. "Dad didn't leave any debts to speak of. But I still felt—well, sad, of course. He was fun, a worthwhile guy. But I also felt angry that he'd abandoned me, left all those responsibilities. My mother, my sister. I know now it helped me through the grief. But I was mad that I couldn't just chuck it all. Leave high school, become instantly rich and famous."

"That was your original plan?"

He smiled and grabbed another madeleine. "Actors are insane. Diseased. You know that. But when Dad died it did force me to take responsibilities seriously. The whole man-of-the-house bit. I finished high school, even did what Mom wanted and went to college. Got married. Got the Army out of the way. And then, having proved how stable and reliable I was, I chucked it all."

"I'm glad," said Maggie firmly. "Insanity suits you. Reliability too."

"I'm glad, too, now," mumbled Nick through a mouthful of crumbs. "But at Denny Burns's age, I was mad and resentful. He stuck it out six months, Curt said, then came to New York in February. New York did not roll out red carpets. I don't understand quite what happened next, but the mysterious gangland woman is involved. I couldn't find out much because Curt wanted to trade."

"Trade?"

"He'd show me something or other that Denny's father left him if I'd tell him the woman's name. I said fine, it's a deal. But then we got into kind of a stalemate about who should go first."

She chuckled. "I can imagine." As she leaned forward to put her mug on the coffee table, Nick sneaked a very appealing glimpse down the bib of her apron. He took another madeleine to distract himself.

"Mm-hmm. We went back and forth awhile. Then I tried to break out of it by mentioning Amy, and he whipped out his piece."

She frowned. "Knight-in-shining-armor stuff? Do not sully her fair name?"

"Exactly." The madeleine hadn't worked as a distraction. Nick began undoing the barbecue-apron ties.

"That's odd. He was a punk, right? A would-be hood?"

"Not at all. More a knight-in-shining-armor type."

"Really?" She was unbuttoning his shirt now.

"This kid was all-American clean. Hair trimmed. He could do Ivory Soap commercials. I can't think of a single band that would want him for a drummer, except maybe Lawrence Welk." Nick tossed the apron aside.

"Strange. But I'm glad to think he may not really be a hood. For Amy's sake."

"I'm glad to think that too," he murmured to her left breast. "But right now I seem to be thinking of something else."

Later, resting, he laid his hand gently on her smooth belly. Was it a little firmer, a little denser than before? He asked, "Maggie, does this baby seem real to you?"

"It seems familiar, somehow. Not exactly real. But soon, I think."

"I believe in it, but only with my head."

"I know, love. Soon," she promised.

Len was still awake, working up the figures on the apartment building. He'd stopped by it again that afternoon, looked hard at the mechanical systems, checked the roof. It was run-down, yes, but not gone. And with Nancy's touch in a demonstration apartment, her gift for bringing light and excitement into all those gloomy corners, they'd rent fast, for lots of money. But he was sobered by the amount he'd need to start. It was clear why the offers that had come in so far had been lukewarm—the investment necessary for success was large. Did he dare ask Joyce for such a loan? The office market was down, would residential slide next?

But, hell, where else could Joyce get such a return on her money? Not at first, of course. Things looked bleak for the first two years, but she could probably use a tax write-off. People like Joyce always needed tax write-offs. And by the third year there should be profits. So, what the hell, he might as well ask.

He had almost finished copying the figures onto a clean sheet of paper when Nancy came in.

"Hi, Nance." He kissed her unresponsive face. "How are you doing?"

"Oh, Len." She lifted her hands and let them drop again in an abbreviated gesture of despair.

"Dammit, Nance, I wish I could help!"

"But you've got other things on your mind."

"Sure I do. But I don't think about them, much. I think about this."

"Really?" She folded herself slowly into a chair, exhausted eyes on him. "I'm sorry, Len. I shouldn't—well, I'm sorry."

"It's not your fault, for God's sake! It's nobody's fault." He knelt before her, pulled off her shoes. "Can I get you some coffee?"

"No. Maybe something cold. A Coke."

He found one in the refrigerator and brought it to her. "Here. Relax a little."

"I'll try. God, Len. There's no answer, you know? No right answer! Anything I do will hurt someone!"

"Nance, Nance..."

"I'm not a person who hurts people."

"I know."

"I never thought this would happen! And if it did, it seemed it would be easy to be rational about it. But it's all mixed up—I mean, it's you and me. Maybe that shouldn't make any difference, but—And there's the potential. It's not actual yet, I know that, but it could be—" She twisted her hands around the aluminum can. "I mean, I always thought someday there might be children. When there was time to be a good mother, and money. What about those children? What about their potential? And yours? And mine?"

"I know, Nance."

"For years, I've been trying to be independent. Lead my own life. Not harm anyone. And now, suddenly—" She shook the cloud of blond hair.

He squeezed her shoulder. "Look, let me say something. This isn't the answer, but it might help a little. Maybe not."

"What?"

"I've been turning it over in my mind for a while. I thought we could buy a building. Fix up the apartments together. I could be a contractor and manager, I know the ropes, and we could make quite a bit on it after the first couple of years."

He could see her pulling her thoughts to this new topic, struggling to see its relevance. "Buy a building?" she said. "But we don't have that kind of money! You said so before!"

"Joyce has an investment corporation. She'll back me if I find the right property."

Nancy was puzzled. "Len, I don't understand. You'd have to go into debt to her, right?"

"Sort of. Our corporation in debt to her corporation."

"But your money would be on the line? Ours?"

"Sure. We'd get a lot back on it. So would Joyce, after a couple of years."

"Okay." She gestured at his notes. "You've worked it all out."

"Yes."

"Okay, then. But is that what you've been brooding about these last few days?"

"One of the things. There's been a hell of a lot."

"Why, Len? I don't understand. Why are you doing this now?" She put the Coke can down on the end table. Her face was white.

"Because—" Careful, Len Trager. Don't make it sound as though you're looking for a place with a nursery. He kissed her forehead. "I've been thinking about this for a while. It would be work, but in the end we'd be more comfortable. And I thought if I could get it settled now, you'd know there would be money, and space. You wouldn't have to worry about those things."

"Money and space. Do you mean you want me to have it?"

Damn. "Nance, I don't mean anything, one way or the other. But I thought if I did this you'd have that much less to worry about. You'd be free to decide."

"Free?" She laughed suddenly, close to hysteria, leaning forward in the chair and hiding her face in both hands. "God, Len, I can't believe it!"

"What?"

"Free, you say! Free to decide! Weren't you listening? You want me to be free to decide to ruin everything we've worked for? Or free to decide to destroy this new life?"

"Nance, please don't! All I'm saying is, whatever you decide, it'll be okay with me. We'll be okay. Either way."

She shoved her feet back into her shoes. "Okay. I hear what you're saying. You don't care."

"Goddamn, Nance! I care so much it hurts! I just don't want to tell you what to do!"

"I know. You want me to be free to decide." She was at the door again. "Okay. Okay, dammit, I'll be free!" She ran out.

Len stood at the window, cursing, and watched her get into the car. What could he do? What the hell could he do? Why didn't she just have the goddamn abortion, put them all out of their misery?

Free to decide to destroy this new life.

Jesus. How could she stand it? How would she live with her choice, either way?

He poured himself a Scotch and sat down on the sofa. After a while he brought over the bottle and poured himself a second, and a third. Nancy's paintings glowed on the walls. The big luminous twist of warm pastels over the mantel. Or, if he leaned forward a little, he could see the one in the bedroom. *Spring Storm*. That had been the first. God, things had always been a bit prickly with Nancy, hadn't they? As a couple they were rough and soft, tense and yet harmonious in some deep way. Till now.

He poured another Scotch. He'd still been working for Gordon Banks's resort office back then. He'd been sent downtown to pick up a stack of forms from a lawyer, and the lawyer hadn't had them ready yet. Stupid lawyer. Messing up people's lives. Dunce.

Len took the Scotch into the bedroom, stripped, flopped back against the pillows, and stared at the painting.

The lawyer's receptionist had been pleasant, he remembered. "Sorry, Mr. Trager, really sorry. We'll have them ready in thirty minutes. Unless you'd rather wait till after lunch?"

He'd told her he'd be back in thirty minutes, and he'd gone out to look around. With his eyes closed he could see the block even now. A narrow storefront. A lingerie shop, actually, but propped against its window was a cheerful hand-lettered sign: "Bianchi Studio—Show and Sale" and a big arrow urging him into a narrow door that opened on a dingy staircase. On impulse he climbed it, was directed by another sign to the extreme rear of the building, and eventually found himself in a long room hung with a variety of modern paintings. A few people at the far end of the room were laughing and sipping coffee. He picked up a badly Xeroxed program, was informed that the paintings were by students of L. Bianchi, and that the program numbered them counterclockwise. Len started around the room, not exactly with interest, but with a sense that this would be the best way to kill time until the lawyer had the documents ready.

One of the paintings, a tense curl of pale green and aqua and violet on a white ground, attracted him. *Spring Storm.* He paused in front of it, enjoying its complexity, the interplay of filmy color with the rough muscular design.

"What's the verdict?" She was small, wearing white bib overalls and a hand-woven headband to hold back a cloud of pale blond hair.

Len said cautiously, "It's interesting."

"Interesting. Mm, yes."

Was she mocking him? He explained, "It's very lively and active for such delicate colors."

"Active?"

"It sort of swirls." He felt foolish; but he didn't want her to go away.

She was frowning at the painting thoughtfully. "No, it sort of jerks."

Yes, she was mocking him. He said enthusiastically, "Exactly! It jerks! You might even say it flounces!"

"Flounces?"

"It lurches! It staggers! It wheezes with effort!"

Astonishment, followed by a rueful grin that illuminated the whole room. "God. I asked for that, didn't I?"

"Well, yes."

"You looked like a businessman. Slumming."

"Therefore, I don't know art, but—"

"I know what I like." She finished in chorus with him, and they smiled shyly at each other. Then she asked, "Are you some sort of artist in disguise? Or a critic?"

"Neither. I'm a vacation-resort agent in my natural garb. I can't paint, but I like to look."

"How do you know you can't?"

"I've tried. Did okay in high school, but in college I grew up enough to realize what the competition could do." He gestured at *Spring Storm.* "So I became a fan rather than a player."

"I see."

"Are you a player?"

"Sort of. I'm looking for a job in graphics, actually. I keep sane here in Bianchi's classes."

"Are you by any chance N. Selden?" He read the name from the corner of the painting.

"Nancy, yeah."

"I'm Len Trager. It doesn't really wheeze with effort. Will you have lunch with me?"

"Lunch?" She glanced at the group of coffee drinkers at the end of the room.

"I'm sorry. Do your friends have a claim on you?"

There was an endearing flash of truculence in her blue eyes. "Nobody has a claim on me."

"Good. Tell you what, I'll even take off my jacket and tie so I won't embarrass you in front of the counterculture."

She laughed, a heartfelt silvery laugh that reminded him of children playing, and said, "Okay, Len. Why not?"

Why not, indeed? Maybe now they were learning why not.

He opened his eyes again and gave the painting on the bedroom wall a bleary look. He waved his Scotch at it companionably. "To Art," he said. "Why not?" and fell asleep.

The alarm clamored at his aching head the next morning. Tuesday. He lurched awake, stumbled to the bathroom, dunked his head in cold water.

She wasn't home.

He dressed, fixed himself strong coffee, and only then noticed the note on the refrigerator. So she'd come again, and gone, and him stewed as a wino. The note said, "Len, I'm moving out for a while. Maybe it'll help."

Her clothes were gone.

But she'd left the paintings.

He took his aches and worries and his neat columns of figures to the office.

10

Julia was thirsty.

There were lots of other problems, but thirst had gradually worked its way to the top of her list of complaints. She took off her watch carefully and held it to the gray light that seeped through the narrow crack between door and frame. Quarter to three. Still Tuesday afternoon. Her last drink had been last night, that cup of coffee with Amy, about eight o'clock or so. Eighteen, nearly nineteen hours ago. And what she wouldn't give right now for another cup! Or tea. A tall glass of iced tea. Clear russet liquid, dewy glass, cubes of ice, maybe a slice of lemon. Or a sprig of mint. Mint, she decided. She'd order one with mint.

She was sawing at the lower hinge with one of the six big screws. Her fingertips were bloody, first from jamming the screws into the wall of the car to keep from crashing into the cellar, and now from the hours of work chipping away at the wood around the bottom hinge. Drat those Sweeneys, they built for the ages. Old Cornelius could have used cheaper wood for the blasted dumbwaiter, you'd think. Or Caroline, who had redone the plumbing— why hadn't she installed a faucet in here? Or a Coke machine. Julia smiled; but the problem was real. A modern pine door would have given away long since. Oak just wouldn't. Of course, a screw was not a saw or a crowbar. It

122

was, unfortunately, merely a very small bit of metal with a sharp spiral around it and a bit of a point. She could use it to dig and rasp at the area of the lower hinge, but it was hardly efficient, and it managed to dig and rasp at her fingers too.

Her first thought the previous night had been to kick the door out somehow. She had braced herself firmly, put her feet against the door, and shoved. But when, in response to her straining, a little movement had finally occurred, it had not been in the door. It had been the car that shifted a tiny bit, its loosely driven screws inadequate to hold it. Julia stopped shoving. Maybe later she'd be ready to risk plummeting to the cellar, to see if the sealed shaft down there was any easier to escape than this bolted door. But not just now. Now digging out the hinges made more sense.

If only she weren't so thirsty.

She had thought carefully about who might come looking for her, and the results were not encouraging. Pauline McGuire generally called Tuesday and they planned a meal together. Pauline, unfortunately, was in Utah kowtowing to her prissy son-in-law. And Julia was supposed to be watering her beloved begonias. Sorry, Pauline, but something came up.

Then there was Vic Jr. He phoned frequently, but in her eagerness to stay independent, Julia seldom informed him of her exact plans, even when she had them. Anyway, she'd seen Vic Jr. and his family on Sunday at Fred-Law's birthday party. No, he wouldn't call until tomorrow or Thursday; and if no one answered, he wouldn't be surprised. His willful mother was always going out unexpectedly. He'd start checking, maybe, this weekend, after a number of calls had gone unanswered.

The phone had rung this morning, once, and again at noon. Probably an offer for cut-rate photographs, or a free introductory dance lesson. Just what she needed now.

Jean was even less likely to be calling than her brother. She checked in once or twice a month, and they'd just had that little talk last week. If she phoned and no one answered, Jean would not be worried either. Probably just go back to studying her film script. Jean in a movie, what an idea. And even if Jean did worry, what could she do from Seattle? She'd call Vic Jr., and he'd complain about how unpredictable Julia was and how she ought to move to Jersey. No, her children were of little use to her now.

Well, then Benny! Benny would notice her absence sooner. She saw him most days, picking up groceries or at least the newspaper. But she'd missed days before for various reasons, and he'd have no reason to worry for a while. He probably wouldn't begin to ask around until next week.

There was a chance, she supposed, that Lieutenant Brugioni would uncover something he wanted to ask her about. She was certain that it was the murderer who had locked her in here, and now just as sure that it wasn't because of Amy's visit; it was because there was something here that he didn't want found. Well, she'd looked hard, and hadn't found it; trapped in the dumbwaiter, she'd heard her assailant hunting around the stair hall and in her apartment for close to an hour before he left via the kitchen porch again. Maybe he'd found it, maybe not. Julia hadn't seen anything to find. Maybe, whatever it was, the police had found it in their thorough search, but hadn't yet realized its significance.

If someone in their lab figured it out, maybe Brugioni would come back to check with Julia, and maybe he'd stick around banging on the door, and maybe he'd hear her if she shouted. But more likely he'd give up when she didn't open the door, and decide to come back again later. Or he'd call to see when she could see him. Maybe by next week he'd be worried enough to check. She didn't think she could wait that long.

The real-estate people, and Artie Lund's plumbers and electricians, had come popping in at irregular and inconvenient intervals for months. But now, thanks to that meddling Maggie Ryan, the building was sold. There was no reason for any of them to come back for weeks. If Artie came he'd just leave her in here. And if Maggie decided to keep on meddling, it probably still wouldn't help. She was always careful not to violate Julia's territory. If no one answered when she knocked, even she would go away. Meddling when she wasn't wanted, nowhere to be seen when she was. Julia felt rather cross with Maggie, as well as with Vic Jr. Where were these inconvenient bossy people when she needed them?

And how about her friends? She had nothing scheduled

with them today or tomorrow. Thursday noon, there was the library meeting. Ruth would wonder where she was, because Julia had promised just last night to be there. Ruth might even call. But people did miss meetings, and usually no one panicked, and usually it turned out to be something benign: a visiting niece, maybe, or at worst, a flare-up of arthritis. Everyone knew about Julia's knees.

Friday, the World Hunger Committee was meeting again at the church, but not till four o'clock. Ellie would worry. After all, Julia had promised faithfully to explain the mission budget. Ellie would call about ten after, and when no one answered, she'd decide Julia was on her way over. She would call again after the meeting. She would call again in the evening. Then she would phone Ruth. If it were still early enough, they might come over to check. Then, when there was no answer, they'd go home. Maybe to bed. Maybe to call Vic Jr. He'd come. He had a key, he had insisted on that, bless his stuffy little heart. So—if Ellie began to worry, and if she thought to call Vic Jr., and if he were home when she called, they would come. Late Friday night. Or Saturday, if Ellie wasn't worried enough, or if Vic Jr. wasn't home when she called. But be optimistic; say, Friday night. Three nights from tonight. Four from last night. Four times twenty-four hours. Ninety-six hours, plus the four that took her back to the cup of coffee with Amy. One hundred hours without liquids.

Too long, Julia knew, to wait for her mint tea.

So it was up to her. Alone. She had three unpleasant alternatives: Give up. Kick at the door and probably crash into the cellar, still trapped. Or weaken the door somehow. She'd chosen the third.

She'd worked blindly in the dark for hours last night, digging at the solid hardwood with a screw, dropping it sometimes when her hand cramped or the blood from her torn fingertips made it slip from her grasp, then groping, in mounting desperation, for the little piece of metal on the floor. Once when Jean was little she'd gotten her hand stuck in the iron filigree work of a fireplace screen. Vic had set her on his knee and begun to work with a file, gently, trying not to hurt the tender little wrist, telling her stories and singing her songs. It had taken hours, but his patience never waned. Even when the metal was finally severed and he had carefully pulled it away, shielding the

little girl from the cut edges with his own fingers, he had
not moved, but sat there long enough to finish the song.
Julia, who had busied herself taking care of Vic Jr. and
trying not to dither, couldn't hold back tears of relief.
Little Jean, puzzled, had piped, "It's not a sad song,
Mother."

Julia had snuffled a little last night too. Sing me a song,
Vic, sad or not. I need a song now. About a hundred
hours long. Time like an ever-rolling stream.

She'd scratched away at the hinge until, exhausted, she
fell asleep.

This morning, she had awakened stiff and creaky and
sore. A little gray light was coming through the crack. She
wound her watch, causing her fingers to bleed again, and
held it to the light until she managed to figure out that it
was six-thirty. The sun is amazing, she used to tell her
fifth-graders. Source of life and energy. Powerful beams
starting so far away, pushing through clouds, bouncing off
buildings, bouncing under the high back porch and through
her thin curtains, bouncing around her kitchen and through
the crack, so that even Julia, incarcerated in the middle of
a solid old house, received a little light. Maybe she'd join
the sun-worshipers if she got out. Maybe she'd write a
book. *Old Sol Grows Up.* She smiled as she replaced her
watch.

Even with Old Sol's help, though, she couldn't see much
of what she'd done last night. There was a faint, lighter
shade where she'd scraped off all the old varnish, but
she'd still have to work by feel today. Not that there was a
lot of feeling left in her scarred fingertips, cut by the
sharp edges of the screw head. The screw! Where was it?
Had she lost it? Frantically, she felt around the little
cabinet. There it was, back in the corner. Thank God.
She'd have to be more careful tonight, put it in her pocket,
along with the hair.

She was so stiff. The little cabinet was thirty inches
square, maybe three and a half feet tall. Lucky she didn't
suffer from claustrophobia. She'd slept all night slumped
in a stiff curl, and this morning her shoulders and neck
and back and arthritic knees were all raucously unhappy.
No way to stretch out, of course. But maybe she could
change positions. Laboriously she pulled her feet under
her, straightened her legs carefully while bending over at

the hips. When she was younger she could touch her toes. Maybe she'd learn again now. She swung her arms around to loosen up. It helped a little. She checked her pocket: the precious tuft of hair was still there.

Okay. Back to work. The old salt mines, the teachers had called their classrooms. The old rat race. The daily grind. And here she was, hard at work again at sixty-eight. Mrs. Northrup, the interviewer would say, it's so exciting! Whatever made you decide to embark on a new career at the age of sixty-eight? Well, Sonny, it's just my philosophy. Live life to the fullest. You can't imagine the sense of purpose and direction that a career in hinge removal can give to those of us with limited mobility. Ah, Mrs. Northrup, Sonny would reply, you are an inspiration and a role model to us all.

Gradually a new problem presented itself. Besides being hungry and thirsty and cramped and aching, Julia realized that she needed the bathroom. Phooey. What could she do? The hinge was still a long way from removable—waiting until she got out was not an option. She'd be here for hours yet. But thirty inches square was not your usual luxury apartment with Jacuzzi and bidet. Last night she had solved the pee problem, after a fashion, by remembering that one of the forward corners by the handrope was lower than the others. She'd once spilled a bottle of window cleaner on the floor of the cabinet and it had flowed quickly to that corner and out. So by arranging herself as close to the corner as she could, she minimized the problem. But this was not so easily minimized.

Julia considered and decided to sacrifice her skirt. It was old anyway. The blouse would be softer but she needed the blouse pocket to keep the hair safe. She took off the skirt, squirming and wriggling in the little space, and ripped it into several pieces. Most she folded carefully into the back corner. Then she spread one square in the low corner and squatted over it. Poopy-pants, chanted the first-graders who didn't yet understand the more adult obscenities, pointing fingers at some unpopular classmate. God, though, they were right, those little first-graders. This was a lot less attractive than sex. Ugh. She wrapped her mess in the piece of skirt and pushed it gingerly to the corner as far as it would go, trying not to breathe much. Too bad she hadn't thought of this when she was trying to

discourage buyers. Even the meddling Miss Ryan might
have thought twice about buying a place that smelled this
revolting.

But the torn pieces of skirt had given her an idea. She
took another small piece and wrapped her sore fingers.
They slipped a little more on the screw head, but it was
slightly more comfortable. She settled to her task. *Work is
the province of cattle*, said Parker. How true.

She chipped away at the hinge all morning. Uncovered
one screw. Started on the next.

And grew thirstier.

Come on, Teach, Beat the Clock.

In the afternoon, the ringing phone broke the silence.
Who was it this time? Someone new? Or the same person
who had tried before? Probably just the free introductory
dance lesson again. Congratulations, Mrs. Northrup, you
have won our grand prize. Well, maybe she'd accept this
time. She needed to get out of the house more, right?

In the twenties she'd been a good dancer. So had Vic.
He was bashful and in those early days at the college
socials Julia had ignored him. Sort of nice-looking, she
and her girlfriends had decided, but hard to talk to. Julia,
not a flapper, really, but just a touch flirtatious, had
preferred John Randall or the handsome Bennett brothers, all of them pleasant and ready with compliments for
her. "You look good as ice cream, Julia!" John Randall
would say. "Your eyes sparkle like champagne!" Tom Bennett
would whisper wickedly. Vic managed to say, "You look
real pretty tonight, Julia," but after that it was up to her to
think of conversation. She would chatter about the people
around them or the decorations or the food, and Vic, back
then, would smile and answer in friendly, boring monosyl-
lables. But when he danced with her there was no need
for words. They were the best pair there. Waltzes, fox-
trots, Charlestons, the whole range. Their bodies instinctively
understood each other. One night, desperate to break the
silence that descended on them between numbers, Julia
had babbled something silly about the American Revolution.

"No, Julia," he'd answered seriously, "it had less world-
wide effect than the French Revolution, but then, the
French Revolution was partly inspired by ours." Startled,
she'd rallied a few thoughts from her world history classes
in response, and discovered that he could talk perfectly

well about ideas even though he was a bit short on silly compliments. Ideas and dancing. Were those such bad reasons to marry him? Bad or good, it had worked for thirty years. Most of the time, anyway.

The phone was still ringing. Nine rings. Ten. Eleven. "Sorry, dear," she said to it, "but I don't have a partner anymore. And anyway, I'm too busy to go dancing today. I have to work late." God, her mouth was dry. She could hardly get the words out. Her voice sounded so rough. Would she be able to scream if someone came? She tried. Okay, she could do it, but it was getting raspy. Her throat was drying out too.

Maybe she'd die.

Stop it, Teach. Don't think thoughts like that. Work on the hinge, get out of here, have a drink, take the hair to Brugioni. Beat the Clock.

But if she did die, she didn't want the murderer to get away. There was still some light coming through the crack, filtering dimly against the back wall of the dumbwaiter. She turned her back to the cruel oak door for a moment, and scratched big letters into the varnish of the back wall: HAIR IN POCKET.

Then she turned back to the hinge, and kept on sawing.

The phone rang twice more before the light disappeared, but Julia ignored it. She just went on scratching.

And grew thirstier.

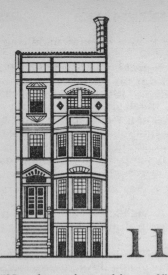

11

"Hey, how about this one?" said George, his gnomelike face leering. "Belinda Belden. Specialties: German dialects."

Nick inspected the bikini-clad woman in the photo and shook his head solemnly. "I don't think it's him."

They had skimmed through Equity directories and cast lists from non-Equity productions. No Dennis Burns. Now they were sifting through George's files. As an actors' agent, he received a deluge of photographs with résumés from would-be actors, in addition to letters, cards, balloons, flowers, and any other attention-getting devices the desperate young hopefuls could dream up. If he wasn't busy, George glanced at them and occasionally set one aside to look at further. Usually he was busy, and his secretary put them, unsorted except for rough alphabetization, into a bin labeled optimistically "To be filed."

"Yeah, but look what she clipped to her photo," George persisted. He held up a black lace garter.

"Better sign her up, then," said Nick. "German dialects are always in demand."

George hung the garter on his ear, tossed the photo onto the stack he'd already checked, and rummaged on through the pile. "God, what a business," he lamented. "All these hopeful kids."

"They won't be hopeful long."

"Yeah? Some of them turn into hopeful middle-aged bald guys."

"Not hopeful. Masochistic. Speaking of which, I'd better be on my way." Nick put down his stack and stood up. "Have to see if the powers at Black Rock think I'm talented enough to die in a fiery car crash."

"Yeah, I hope they take you off the streets," grumbled George. "Keep you from wasting all my time looking for résumés of somebody who's already dead."

"By the time you get around to us, it's a wonder we aren't all dead."

"Yeah, most of you audition that way," retorted George, picking up another photo. "God, this is about the tenth résumé this Bartlett kid has left. I ought to take him on. He'll keep after the jobs. Not like you, wasting your time playing policeman."

"Okay, okay, I'm going. Ready to die ignominiously in flames just to earn you a fat commission." In fact, Nick worked fairly steadily by the standards of a profession in which more than ninety percent of even union members were usually unemployed.

"Yeah." George flipped through a last pile of photographs. "That pretty well finishes the B's anyway. I'll call Russell and ask if this kid was maybe enrolled in a class there. But if he was an actor, he wasn't trying very hard."

"Maybe he just heard the truth about you and decided to shop elsewhere for an agent."

"Get out of here, ingrate!" George threw the garter at him. Nick shot it back slingshot style and ducked out the door before more lethal missives could follow.

Waiting for the subway that would take him to the CBS audition, Nick wondered about Dennis Burns. He was intrigued by the young man who, like himself, had lost a father and had hoped to make a name for himself in the theatre. Clearly, he was not a very active actor. He must have put in an appearance at some cattle calls, since the volatile Curt had accepted Nick's lie about meeting Dennis at one of them. But he was not a member of Equity, had not been cast in any of the dozens of nonunion productions Nick and George had skimmed over, and had not even left his photo with a reasonably well-known agent. Whatever the big job was, it didn't have much to do with acting.

Some kind of con game? A lot of criminals in this city

might like a clean-cut kid from Winston as a front. Or drugs? His father had been a doctor, right? Was that what he'd left with Curt—drugs? Was that why Curt was half-expecting the mob? Well, there just wasn't enough information yet to draw any conclusions. And right now, Nick had to concentrate on becoming a criminal himself, a criminal whose life would end in a flaming car. He turned his mind to the upcoming audition.

By late afternoon, the pounding in Len's head had considerably eased. Dumb move, drinking so much. He hadn't done that since college, on the day he'd faced up to the fact that he was not an artist. What was he having to face up to now? Nancy leaving, of course. The abortion question. Their future. The fact that a joyous and carefree love sometimes had painful consequences. She'd said: I'm not a person who hurts people. And he'd made soothing noises and started talking about money. Not smart, in retrospect, but dammit, money was important too. Some hurts it could soften.

Despite his dulled state he'd managed to get some work done. He'd given his apartment-building proposal to Joyce, with a brief explanation, and she'd promised to look at it when she could. She'd had a busy day, calling lawyers and bankers and appraisers to make sure everything would be set for the million-dollar Feldheim closing scheduled for the next day, in addition to her usual rounds of appointments. Len had shown a couple of buildings and was now making up a list of owners in an improving district where Banks Realty had recently sold four apartment buildings with commercial street floors. He had suggested to Joyce that they send letters with news about the prices and sales to these owners. "If they know we can sell in that area, they'll call us when they're ready to sell."

"Actually, they'll call their brothers-in-law," Joyce informed him. "But you're right, Len, we may get a listing or two from people who don't have relatives in real estate."

"And one listing would pay for the mailing, right?"

Joyce smiled. "Go ahead."

That had taken him several hours. But now, finishing the list of addresses so that Renata could type them tomorrow, he began to think himself capable of facing

Nancy with greater success than the previous night. She'd call tonight, surely. Or even stop by.

Joyce came out of her private office and over to his desk. "I looked over your proposal, Len."

"Oh. Thanks. What did you think?"

"I'd like to do it. We have a meeting Thursday afternoon. I'll bring it up."

"Thanks, Joyce! That's great!"

"I can't promise anything. But I'll tell them it seems worth a try."

"It'll work out, I know. All I need is a little help getting started."

Joyce smiled, approving of his optimism. "I'll tell them. Right now, I need the key to show that co-op tonight." She opened the lock box, and looked around as the door opened. "Hello, Arthur!"

"Joyce, honey, you did it!" Arthur Lund skipped across the room to hug her. "I came straight over from the office to thank you! Loretta is so excited!"

Joyce returned his embrace, smiling. "I appreciate it, Arthur, but Len here is the one to thank."

"Oh, I thanked him when he brought my copy of the contract over," said Lund, nevertheless turning to crush Len's hand in his own. "But I wanted to ask if there's anything else I should do."

"Not until closing," said Joyce.

"It's in the lawyers' hands now," Len explained. "We just wait around for them to summon us."

"Shouldn't I have the place cleaned or anything?"

"It looked fine when I was there," said Joyce. "Len, did the police make any kind of mess that should be cleaned up?"

"No. If anything, it's better dusted now than ever. Of course, there's Mrs. Northrup's place. But even that was neat the last time I saw it."

"She wouldn't let you in to clean it anyway," said Joyce.

"Well, okay," said Lund. "I just don't want this deal to fall through for any reason."

"It shouldn't," said Joyce. "You're holding the mortgage yourself, so a bank can't mess things up. And if there is anything that needs adjustment, the lawyers will tell us."

"Nick and Maggie won't back out," said Len. "They're

enthusiastic about the place. I was surprised, frankly, with that body up there, but—"

"Oh! Don't remind me!" exclaimed Lund. "I thought right then it was all over for that house."

"So did I. We were lucky," said Joyce. "But really, Arthur, there's nothing else you have to do until closing. Your lawyer will tell you what to bring—tax bills, utilities, and so forth. Keys. Checkbook."

"Oh, I've had those bills ready for a long time. I update them every month," said Lund. "Well, okay, thanks. Let me know if you think of anything I can do."

"Sure. But basically, just take it easy."

Lund went out again, a happy, if nervous, man. Joyce shook her head, amused. "Ever notice how the little sales take more time? Someone like Feldheim can decided millions of dollars in a few minutes, while Arthur frets for months over a few thousand."

"A few thousand seem like a lot from down here," said Renata.

"Besides," said Len, "these people may bring us a big deal tomorrow."

"Not someone who thinks as small as Lund. Taking out short-term loans for months and then finally dropping the price to where it should have been in the first place."

"Well, Nick O'Connor then. Suppose he gets cast in a big hit like *Kojak*."

Joyce laughed. "Optimism, Len. You're right." She locked the keys away and went back into her own office.

Len turned back to his list of addresses. There were nearly sixty different owners in the blocks he'd selected. Karen Weld and Fred Stein finished and left by five, but Len decided to complete the list before he went. No Nancy to hurry home to anyway.

The phone rang. "For you, Len," said Renata.

"Len? Glad I caught you. It's Maggie. I wondered if it would be possible to get the measurements of the kitchen on Garfield Place. We want to make plans and get materials ordered so we can start work as soon as it's ours."

"Sure. I have rough measurements already."

"No, we'll need exact numbers for the kitchen. Would Lund let us come back?"

"I don't see why not. He was just here asking if there was anything he could do. When do you want to go over?"

"Tonight, tomorrow night. The sooner the better."

"Let me see what I can set up. Shall I call you right back?"

"I'm still at the office."

Len dialed Julia Northrup's number, but there was no answer. Well, that might not be necessary anyway, if Maggie just wanted to see the kitchen on the first floor. He unlocked the key box and looked through it, and then again, more thoroughly. The little amber tag was nowhere to be seen. Lund's keys were gone.

Where were they? He'd returned them himself last week. Hadn't he? He tried to think. The police! Brugioni had left them on Mrs. Northrup's bookcase for him. So he must have brought them back here. And he didn't think anyone had been back to the house since. Fred? Had Lund himself taken them back? Well, they'd turn up. He called Maggie.

"We'll have to wait until tomorrow," he told her.

"Fine. I'll plan on that."

"Well, even that may not be certain. I wasn't able to reach Mrs. Northrup. Do you want to see her place too?"

"No. Just the parlor floor. Does that mean we can go tonight?"

"Well, the keys aren't here at the moment. Tomorrow would be better."

"Okay. Shall I come over after work? About this time? I've got a lunch meeting so I can't manage anything earlier."

"Sure. That'll be fine."

"How's Nancy doing?"

"Well, you know. As well as can be expected. Every time we bring it up, she gets upset and runs out."

"God, yes, I remember. Where does she run?"

"To go paint, usually. Or—somewhere."

"Somewhere?"

"Yeah."

"Len, what's wrong?"

"Nothing. It's just that this time she took her clothes. But she'll be back."

"Mmm. Yes, I think so too. Just have a little patience."

"I know."

"Do you know where she went?"

"She's got a couple of good friends at Bianchi's. Painters. Probably one of them."

"Yes. I wish I could help her."

"So do I."

"You can, Len. Just get it through to her somehow that you care."

You don't care, Nancy had said. Did she really believe that? Len said, "I'm trying."

"Good luck. I'll see you tomorrow."

Len hung up to find Joyce, car keys in hand, looking at him severely. "Nancy?" she asked. "Is that who you were talking about?"

"Um, yes."

"She's moved out?"

"No, not really. She'll be back."

Joyce turned abruptly back into her office and a moment later Len's proposal landed in front of him. "You'll have to rework it," she said tersely.

"What?"

"I can't recommend a project that involves the money and talent of someone who may not be in on the project."

"But she will! This is only temporary, Joyce!"

"Maybe so. But as a businesswoman, I can't bet on it. I was edgy before, but I figured at least there wouldn't be children to mess things up. But you see, you don't have a contract with her. Not even marriage. Bring something with her legal signature, or else rework the proposal so it involves you alone."

"Yes. I see. Okay." Len could feel the flush rising through his skin. Joyce's tone humiliated him.

"I'd still like you to bring it to the board meeting. But it has to be a truly viable proposal."

"Yes, I see." Part of him realized that the advice was well-meant.

Joyce regarded him sadly. "I don't understand you young people sometimes. You and Nancy seem more married than ninety percent of our married friends."

"She really will be back." His certainty surprised him.

"Well, I'm not preaching. Just explaining economic reality." She tapped his proposal with a manicured fingernail. "Give it another try, okay? I'll need it by Thursday morning. We meet at two. You should plan to come too, if the revised proposal looks okay to me."

"Okay. Thanks, Joyce." Len tucked the papers into his briefcase and watched her leave. Damn.

"It'll be okay, Len," soothed Renata. She was looking rather down at the mouth today too.

"Yeah, I know."

"Spat with Nancy?"

"Not really. She's just under some pressure. Needed a little vacation."

"I know how she feels."

"Yeah." He was thumbing through the directory. "Here. I've got two more addresses to add to this list, and it'll be done. Think you'll have time to type them the next couple of days?"

"I think so. Joyce gave me all this stuff for the Feldheim closing and the Wednesday meeting, but addresses are easy to squeeze in."

"You're terrific, Renata."

"Yeah, spread the word, why don't you?"

"I always do. Want me to spread it anyplace in particular?" She looked around the office, dissatisfied. "No. This is as good a job as I'm likely to get. And Joyce isn't bad. Gives me raises along with all the extra work. Listen, Len, this project you were just talking about with her. Is that a personal loan?"

"Not exactly. There's a building that would secure part of it, and a chunk of my own money. If I blow it she'd lose some but I'd lose more." He slid the last addresses onto her desk and stood to leave.

"A building, huh?" Renata looked glum. "I don't have a building. She probably wouldn't just give me a loan."

"A little one, she might. She knows you'd pay it back."

"Yeah. Well, forget it. It's not important. See you tomorrow, Len." She turned back to the Feldheim papers.

Once on the street, Len changed his mind about going home and decided to get a hamburger first. He pulled out his proposal and looked it over as he munched. Subtracting Nancy's savings would hurt, but not as much as subtracting her talents in the renovation. Len had a good eye but not her ability to find the perfect audacious combination that lifted a space from pleasant to exciting. At home she had painted the walls a warm shade of off-white, the mantel a cool shade. Both looked dingy until she hung one of her big paintings over the mantel and suddenly the entire space resolved into a humming chord of harmony. Still, it was hard to put a dollar value on talent; and Joyce's investors would look only at the numbers.

Maybe he should get it over with. Taking Nancy out of this proposal would hurt. Why prolong the agony? He paid for his burger and went back to the office.

It was already darkened and locked. But not empty. As he turned the key and stepped inside, he heard an indrawn breath. Len fumbled for the light switch and the room sprang from its shadows.

Renata was closing the lock box.

"Hi. What wicked things are you up to in the dark?" he teased.

She gave him a weak smile. "Hi. I was just—well, I was leaving, and forgot something. Did you forget something too?"

He dropped his proposal on his desk. "No, just decided to come back to finish some papers. Listen, are you okay?" Looking at her now, he saw that she was pale, the eyes behind the hornrims hollow.

"Yeah, sure. Everything's groovy."

But he was disturbed. He walked over to her, fastened the lock box, and led her to her own chair. "Sit down a minute and rest. You want a glass of water?"

"Everything's okay."

"I don't think so." He pushed aside the newspaper clippings and scissors on the edge of her desk and sat on it, hand on her shoulder. "You are scared, and sad, and poking around in the dark. What's wrong? Is it your brother?"

"Oh, God, Len!" She buried her face against his knee as the sobs burst out. "I don't know what to do!"

"Hey, I'm sorry. I didn't mean to upset you." He felt clumsy and thoughtless. Couldn't do anything right.

"No, no, it's not your fault. You're right, it's Tony."

"Do you want to talk about it?"

"You know that scene last week? That fight he was in?"

"Yeah, where he got his leg broken."

"Yes. Well, a lot of kids got hurt. And one of them was Leone's son."

Len whistled. Leone was reputedly a capo, with hit men at his beck and call. "Leone's hassling Tony?"

"No, he doesn't know! Nobody knows except Tony's

friend Paul. But Paul says he'll tell if Tony doesn't pay him off." She spoke in little bursts, in the rhythm of weeping.

"Some friend!"

"Leone's offered a reward for information. They know the boy was hit with a wine bottle." Unbidden, Dennis Burns's image swam into Len's mind. "But Paul is the only one who knows it was Tony. I mean, it was a freaky mistake. He was fighting on the Leone kid's side."

"So Leone is hunting down the other side. Unless Paul tells."

"God, my crazy brother! This has really shaken him up, Len. But what if we can't get the money?"

"You were asking about a loan from Joyce."

"It's a thousand dollars, Len! To match Leone's offer. I mean, Joyce would want to know why. I can't tell her."

"Yeah, I see what you mean."

"God, Len, you know my grandfather disappeared. Probably mob. And my mom swore she'd shake loose for Tony and me. Sent me to college two years, army for Tony when he's old enough. But he can't seem to get it together!"

"Look, Renata, what does all this have to do with the lock box?"

Red-nosed, she gave him a frightened glance and murmured, "Len, I'm at the end of my rope!"

"What were you doing?"

"I thought—well, you know, some of the places we show have nice things, and people have moved out—and Tony needs the money so much!"

Len shook his head. "Renata, I don't know what the answer is. But I know that's not it."

"I couldn't think of anything else. Do you have any money, Len?"

"I'm pretty much a have-not like you," he said. The edge of the desk was sharp but he stayed there. He didn't want to seem to be withdrawing. "Listen, Renata, can Tony go away?"

"Away?"

"Do you have friends or relatives in another state?"

"Some cousins in Iowa. But Tony won't want to split from his friends."

"His so-called friend Paul won't stop with the thousand bucks, you know."

"Yeah. I've thought that."

"Well, I just think you ought to talk it over with Tony before you destroy everything you and your mom have been working so hard for."

"Yeah." She pulled another tissue from her bag. "Tony's so freaking stupid! But, you know, he's my brother."

"He'll be okay," said Len, wishing he could believe it. "He's young. He'll straighten out."

"I know. But he always turns out to be in heavier than he tells me." She stood up, tightened the belt of her coat, and picked up her bag. "I'll talk to him again, Len. Please don't tell Joyce."

"Of course not."

"Or anyone else."

"None of this happened," Len promised.

"Thanks." With a last watery smile, she left.

Len took out his proposal, but found he had no heart for it anymore. Maybe tomorrow. He left it in his desk drawer and went home.

The bottle of Scotch, uncapped, was still on the nightstand. He put the top on and took it back to the kitchen, along with the dirty glass, and looked around. A mess. If she came, it might help if it looked less like skid row. He made himself some coffee and sipped it while he picked up the kitchen, then straightened the bed and gathered up the scattered clothes and newspapers. There. No traces of his binge. Jag. Spree. Orgy. All those cheerful rollicking words, nothing of the desperation of the reality.

Poor Renata. He and Nancy weren't the only ones with troubles. That brother of hers was a real headache. He wondered idly which keys she'd been taking.

Or returning, he realized suddenly. She could have been putting them back.

Quit thinking things like that, Len Trager. Haven't you got problems enough?

He turned on the TV and tried determinedly to concentrate on a bad sitcom. Once, just in case, he called Mrs. Northrup again, but she was still out. Or drunk again. Not that he was any shining example. He decided to keep the line clear so that Nancy could call.

She didn't.

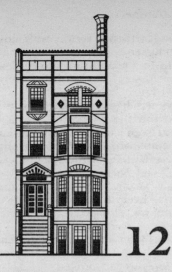

12

Julia's drooping eyelids felt gritty.

Eight-thirty, she thought, though she could hardly make out the numbers on her watch. Tuesday night.

Twenty-four hours she'd been here, sawing at the thick oak door with her pitiful little tool. Twenty-four hours of filthy clothes, grimy hair, aching muscles, the latrine-like stench in the near dark. A sob ratcheted up through her dry throat. Her knees throbbed with pain, and she was desperately sleepy.

She'd stayed awake late last night in the vain hope that she could weaken the wood around the hinge enough to kick her way out. And now, though closer to that goal, it was clear that she'd need hours more to rasp her way through to the last screw.

She felt guilty about Pauline's begonias. Poor things, they'd be getting thirsty too.

But she'd probably do better if she got some sleep. Maybe she could wake up early tomorrow.

She checked her blouse pocket. His hair was still there. Carefully, she dropped the screw in next to it. Then she curled up, fetuslike, pressed against the rigid walls of the oaken prison. A cruel womb, dry and rigid. No life-giving fluids to buoy her up. Strange location you've chosen for

141

your second childhood, Mrs. Northrup. Well, yes, Sonny, but it was handy to home, you see.

Julia whispered good night to Vic and slid into restless sleep.

Past Yonkers, a flood of violets had swept through the tender grasses. It was dusk, but the energy of the new season was palpable in the air. Even along the rails, among cinders and two centuries' worth of buildings and trash, the green tides of spring were lapping higher.

"May's newfangled mirth," said Nick.

"Yeah." Pensive, Maggie was gazing out the grimy window of the commuter train. "Everything is newfangled right now. Everything is changing. Flowers, leaves, home, job, baby."

He nodded. "The end of this year will be a lot different from the beginning."

"Yes. It's scary." Her blue eyes were troubled.

"Mm-hmm. Are you scared of anything in particular?"

"All of it. I want to be the best mother. The best wife. The best statistician. The best business partner for Dan. It seems such a big job."

He took her hand. "Oh, you can do all that stuff. But thank God you aren't aiming to be the best housekeeper. Then I'd know you were in trouble."

She laughed. "True. I don't need any lessons from Mrs. Northrup in how to trash an apartment."

"No *Ladies' Home Journal* award in our future."

She smiled absentmindedly. "Nick, you have to change jobs so often. Is it still frightening?"

"Always. Each one could be the last."

"You aren't used to it? I mean, more than at the beginning?"

"Not really. But I've learned to cope with my feelings. Learned to channel the fear and despair into productive directions."

"Wish I could. I'm glad they liked you today."

"Yeah, this hiatus was relatively painless."

"But this is the first time I've changed jobs. And Dan is a friend too. I mean, now that he's arranged this deal on the computer, it suddenly seems real. We'll have to borrow so much just to get started! And there are the mortgage payments on the brownstone, and the baby, and even Mrs.

Northrup , bless her sour old heart. All of a sudden other people really depend on me."

Nick remembered his first wife: committed actor, intelligent woman, guilty child. Without her dependence, would he ever have matured enough to cope with his erratic profession? He said, "That can be a source of strength too, you know."

"I guess so." She frowned. "But I have these crazy worries. You know, about the baby. Will it be healthy?"

"Most likely. You know the statistics," he chided gently.

"With my head," she admitted. "But I want this baby so much. And I'm just not worthy. I mean, Christ, the gall it takes, to assume responsibility for another human being! I can sense God up there, cackling, the lightning bolt already poised. And then I think, why should He care? And that's even worse." She tried to smile, but the shadow of loss hung in her eyes. "Anyway, it scares me."

"I'm supposed to say, pooh! Silly! What ridiculous fears!" He kissed her fingertips. "They are ridiculous, of course. But I have them too."

"You do?"

"Old Good-time Nick a father? Are you kidding? Fathers are solid. Young. Earn salaries. Mow lawns. Fathers trudge stoically down the road to being grandfathers. Me a grandfather? What am I getting into? It's like admitting I'm mortal. And fathers know what to do with a kid. I don't. I'll probably drop it or stick pins in it. I'm an oaf. So surfeit-swell'd, so old, and so profane."

"And so ridiculous!" She squeezed his hand, comforted.

He shrugged. "I know that with my head. Like you. But all those worries are there. We'll hurt the baby, or the baby will hurt us. Ugly Lear: 'If she must teem, create her child of spleen, that it may live, and be athwart disnatur'd torment to her!'"

"You're saying people have always had these worries. And have muddled through." She stirred the hair on the back of his hand with her fingertip. "And so will we."

"Yes. We will too. But it's true, the newfangled can be pretty terrifying."

Outside, apple trees dotted the Westchester hills, pink-and-white celebrations in the dusk. This was a green area of estates, the wide-scattered houses shielded from the railroad lines by woods and hedges. Nick glanced at his watch. "Just think how much these people have to pay to be so far from work."

"Tree fetishists," said Maggie, with the condescension of the country-born New Yorker. "I just hope there are a few people still awake when we get there."

"Do you think they'll know Dennis Burns is dead?"

"Probably not. The Brooklyn police don't seem to know his background yet. And Curt and Amy aren't talking much about it. We had to trick her into admitting what she did. It'll take Brugioni a while to slog through channels. He'll have to do it the hard way."

Remembering the little revolver, Nick said, "I wouldn't call Curt the easy way."

"Well, you know these Westchester toughs. The city ain't safe."

Nick eyed the three carefully coiffed matrons in pastel wool who were passing them in a puff of Chanel, headed for the smoking car. Each looked like a careful copy of Pat Nixon. "Yeah. Hard cases, all right."

He and Maggie got off two stops later. More violets, more new leaves, a compact village center surrounded by more wooded subdivisions. They found a phone book in a drugstore.

"No Dennis Burns. No Dr. Burns," reported Maggie. "The library is on Front Street."

They were lucky—it wouldn't be closing for another hour and a half. Last year's directory yielded a Dr. C. K. Burns, obstetrician, at an address not far away. They strolled through twilight smells of earth and new leaves to look at it.

It was an early-nineteenth-century house, white clapboard, near the little downtown. The yew bushes around the foundation were ragged, the windows dark. A large brown-and-yellow sign advised that the building was For Sale, and to Call Winston Realty Now! They did.

"Just here for an hour," Nick told the young woman who answered. "I've been thinking about moving out of Manhattan. Tired of the rush. A colleague told me Dr. Burns's place might be available."

"Oh, yes! Do you want to see it, Dr. Connery?"

"What are they asking?"

"Well, it does, um, need a little modernization. So they're only asking seventy thousand."

"Yes, let's take a look. Meet you there in twenty minutes."

Maggie frowned at his turtleneck and jeans as he hung up. "You don't look much like a doctor, love."

"But you look like a doctor's wife."

"Well, we're halfway there. Buy me a drink."

There was one bar. Crowded. Maggie hung up her trench coat, quickly downed her 7-Up, and headed for the women's room. Pregnancy had reduced her capacity. Had also made her fussy about diet and drinking and exercise. A health book personified. But not a prude. Nick smiled at his scotch, remembering last night's madeleine-scented frolic from sofa to hearth rug to bed. Living with Maggie was a festival.

By the time he'd paid the tab, she was waiting for him by the coat rack. "We'd better hurry," he said.

"I know. Here." She was already in her trench coat, holding one out for him.

He shrugged into it and they went out into the spring air. He could button it, just barely, if he didn't inhale. "Nick the sausage," he grumbled.

"It was the biggest one there. Don't complain, Doc, it's a Burberry."

"Within which rift imprison'd, I do painfully remain."

She grinned. "Let's go, Ariel. Thou shalt ere long be free."

The woman who met them at the doctor's office was in her twenties, with a nice figure marginally too rounded for her miniskirt. Straight dark hair swung at shoulder length. "I'm Jill Marden," she informed them brightly. "Sorry it's not daytime. It's hard to appreciate this lovely old house at night."

"Well, let's see the inside. That's where I'd work," said Nick, into his role. Brusque, clinical, no bedside manner when office-hunting.

"Of course, Dr. Connery." She was already unlocking the front door. "Though you understand it will need a lot of modernization. He was an old-fashioned doctor, I'm told."

They followed her into a pleasantly proportioned hall that smelled of dust and closed windows. Dim shadows on the colonial wallpaper showed where long-gone chairs and tables had stood against the walls.

"This was the waiting room," said Jill.

"Did he leave any equipment?" asked Nick. Maggie was poking into a built-in cupboard—empty—and glancing at the reception counter, also empty.

"Only the old X-ray machine," said Jill apologetically. "The family sold most of his things. Will you be needing—"

"Probably wouldn't have been very up-to-date equipment anyway," said Nick. "My colleague said there was a financial problem. Alcohol, he thought."

"Yes, I'm afraid so." Seeing that the Burns family secret was out, Jill became more forthcoming. "He really did fail those last ten years. My mother says he was a fine doctor at first, excellent reputation, but then his drinking got the upper hand. Word gets around and after the Collins affair, people stopped going to him, even though they hushed it up."

"Collins." Maggie's convincing frown covered her fishing expedition. "That was the woman who died in childbirth?"

"Oh, no! That was Mrs. Briggs. An aneuryism, my mother said. Unavoidable. Mrs. Collins was different. She was supposed to be having a routine hysterectomy but Dr. Burns was so shaky he severed a spinal nerve. She sued, of course, and the hospital dropped him. Insurance trouble too."

"Must have been hard for him to make a living," said Nick dispassionately. But he was thinking sympathetically of young Denny at that fragile age when good opinion was of life-or-death importance. A drunken father, sued for crippling a woman—that would be tough. They were wandering through empty labs, examination rooms, bathrooms, all done in a 1950's version of modern. After the spring air it was closetlike.

"He ended up doing exams for insurance companies, and not many of those. No obstetrics, of course," Jill informed them.

"Hard on the family, too. Weren't there children?" asked Maggie.

"Just one boy. He wasn't bad, just a little trouble once for running a car into a tree. Not a bad kid. Did a lot of school plays. Look, I forgot to ask, are you an obstetrician too?"

"Yes," said Nick. "The layout of this place is good. But I was hoping for something larger, or that at least could be expanded. In my field it's helpful to have a partner."

"Hard to get a vacation in, or even dinner," explained Maggie, with a conspiratorial woman-to-woman grin. "Babies don't arrive by appointment. I'd love for him to have a partner."

"I know what you mean, Mrs. Connery." Jill smiled back. "You know, I bet it would be possible to expand toward the back. Let's look."

It was a relief to get out into the twilight breeze again. They dutifully admired the small graveled parking lot and traded suggestions about possible expansion plans. "It would take quite an investment, though," said Nick. "Do you think they'd come down on the price any?"

"They're ready to negotiate," Jill assured him. "Mrs. Burns sold her house already and is back with her family in Pennsylvania. The boy graduated from high school and went to try to find work in the city. They're eager to sell. It's a shame. I was away at college, but my mother says it was a rough few years for them, at the end. He started out a very popular doctor."

"Well, if they'll be reasonable on the price, I may be back in touch," said Nick. "We're looking at a number of locations here in Westchester, of course. But this is a definite possibility. Thanks for showing us around."

"Here's my card. Keep in touch," said Jill.

As soon as her car was out of sight Nick eased out of the trench coat gratefully. "Enough!" he said. "As a doctor I'd have to advise myself to go on a diet."

"You looked okay."

"Nah. It smothers up my beauty from the world."

She grinned. "What next, beautiful?"

"No records left in that office," said Nick. "The widow's in Pennsylvania. We don't even know Amy's maiden name or Curt's last name. What does that leave?"

"High school," decided Maggie. "Let's see if we can build on Amy's story about the big role. Might even be a good turn for her."

She returned the Burberry to the bar coat rack while Nick located the high school on the library map. It was a long hike. Once, they paused for Maggie to sweep her hair sideways and to unbutton her blouse halfway to her navel. As they arrived, a little after nine, lights on the playing field were clicking off. A cluster of boisterous boys with baseball gloves and bats came into the parking lot.

Nick had looped Maggie's red scarf loosely around his turtleneck in what he hoped was a fifties bohemian fashion. The artist as lowlife and tough. "Where's the theatre, fellas?"

"Theatre?" A couple of the boys stopped and stared at him.

"The high school theatre."

A third boy, acne-infested, joined them. "They're working in the cafeteria."

"And where is that, darling?" asked Maggie, as husky-voiced and heavy-lidded as the most clichéd soap-opera actress-vamp.

"Around the corner. Big glass doors about halfway along."

"Thanks, darling!" She kissed the astonished youngster on his pimply cheek, took Nick's arm, and swept around the corner. Behind them they could hear jeering echoes of "Thanks, darling!" as his teammates ragged the lucky informant.

The glass doors opened into a big low-ceilinged space, lights at the far end. Nick's throat caught. Nighttime cafeteria smells of stale food covered by disinfectant and young sweat. Long tables and cheap chairs in the semi-darkness. A little raised and curtained platform under the lights. It was so like his own high school stage. The earnest girls moving chairs back down from the platform to the main floor were like the first stage crews he had known. The loud-voiced and cocky pair talking to a mascaraed blond with Rapunzel-like hair to her waist were like the first actors he'd known. But had he ever been so young? With so much swagger, so much naiveté, so many pimples, so much hair?

Maggie's quick worried glance roused him to the realization that someone had asked if they could help. She was stepping forward, still the husky-voiced vamp of the parking lot. "We're looking for someone named Burns," she said.

"Nobody here named that," said a young woman in hornrims. "And we're just trying to wind up here. About to go home."

Nick pulled himself together. "Dennis Burns," he said. "We were told he graduated from here."

"Hey, man, that was years ago!" A tall young fellow with

brown curls dismissed the question. "He graduated when I was a freshman!"

"Right. And where is he now, darling?" asked Maggie.

A bored silence; these sophisticated facades were not as easily breached as the young ballplayers'. "His dad died, didn't he?" asked one of the stage crew at last.

"Like, why do you want to know, anyway?" A gawky youth, skinny as bamboo and edging toward belligerence, shifted a clipboard to his other hip.

Nick knew these kids, knew how to reach them. "Because I'm a casting director in Manhattan," he said, and suddenly the silence was no longer bored. "Dennis Burns auditioned for me. And when I tried to call the phone number he gave me, it had been disconnected."

"A casting director!" Rapunzel's black-rimmed gaze had locked on him, full of undying devotion, and of speculative hope. Five other pairs of previously contemptuous young eyes were fixed on him too. Nick the Messiah. Nick the fraud.

Disgusted with the game, he pushed ahead. "The only clue we have is this high school."

The young woman in hornrims stood up. "I'm Stella Barrett. Drama teacher here." Pleasant humorous mouth, straight brown hair, looked maybe two months older than her students. She held out her hand.

"Claude Nicholas," improvised Nick as he shook hands. "And this is my assistant, the actress Zelda Cocker." Maggie shot him an amused and resentful look.

"Glad to meet you, Mr. Nicholas, Ms. Cocker. Now, who is it you're looking for? Though I'm afraid I'm new this year."

"Dennis Burns," repeated the sultry Zelda Cocker. "For a part in a show."

The previously disdainful young people were swarming around them now. "You mean Dennis is going to get cast? Far out!" exclaimed Curly. "You mean, like Broadway?"

"Maybe even that someday. If we can find him."

The atmosphere was heavy with eagerness and desire to please. Information crystallized from it like drops of dew.

"His dad died."

"His mom like moved away. Probably Brooklyn. They came from Flatbush."

"Naw, not Brooklyn. She went to Pennsylvania. New Jersey, maybe."

"Isn't he the guy that used to hang out with that redhead?"

"Amy Hale, yeah. She's still around."

"My sister's friends with her. She lives over on Vinegar Hill. But Dennis went to New York." That was the bamboo-thin lad with the clipboard, veneer of belligerence melted away now.

"Well, if he's in New York, he's damn hard to get hold of," said Nick, wishing it were not so true.

Bamboo said, "My sister even said Amy is in the city now visiting him. But see, he doesn't have like a place of his own there."

"Damn right he doesn't, " said Nick. "No phone either. Is he staying at a hotel or the Y or something?"

"No. He's thick with a guy named Curt Pritchard. Split for the city right after graduation. Don't know where he hangs out."

"Around Twentieth Street, I think," said a husky boy. "Or Nineteenth."

"Wherever," said Curly. "I think Dennis would crash with him."

"So how do I get in touch with him, if you don't have an address and his phone is disconnected?"

"Curt's mother remarried," volunteered Husky. "They moved somewhere. Albany, maybe. My mom probably has her address from Christmas. I could find Curt's address and phone for you in a couple days."

"Jesus! You think I came out here to the boonies for fun? You think producers sit twiddling their thumbs while we chase down kids who disconnect their phones and take the day off? This kid Burns is front-runner for this part, okay, or I wouldn't be here looking for him now. But there are two hundred others who tried out for it, and one hundred of them are just about as good. If I don't find him tonight, that's it. Kaput. He's out of a job!"

"Look for him in a bar, like his dad," said Husky darkly.

"Shut up! He's okay."

"Smashed up that car, didn't he?"

"Yeah, and you never scraped a fender?"

Nick broke in, a heavy-handed referee. "Okay, people, is

that all you can think of? We'll get back to the city, if that's where you think he is."

"Look, man, that's all I know," protested Curly.

Rapunzel blurted, "Please, Mr. Nicholas, before you go, could you watch me do a scene?"

Nick glanced at her, and suddenly the blonded hair and black-rimmed eyes and youthful dewiness no longer concealed her raw hunger to perform. The recognition was like a blow: his successful friends, his failed friends, his dead wife, he himself had all begun like this; in a stale cafeteria they made believe was a theatre, with a batch of other green kids they made believe were actors. And with a savage passion to act that was not make-believe at all. A passion that gnawed away reason, spawned idiotic and necessary self-delusion, corroded lives. He could see his young self, stripped to the bones, in those pleading, predatory eyes.

So he said, "Hell, no! I'm not here to watch scenes!"

Their teacher stiffened. "Excuse me, Mr. Nicholas, but they've tried very hard to be helpful. Couldn't you take just a couple of minutes to return the favor?"

"It's no favor!" Nick exploded. Maggie's astonished eyes turned to him. He jabbed a finger at the blond. "I know what little Rapunzel here is thinking. And Curly, and Husky, and all the rest of you. You're thinking fate has chosen you to be a star. If you're on the right stool at the right soda fountain, a casting director will descend from the heavens and discover you. And here I am, descended from the heavens! Ergo, I must be here to discover your great talent, right? No, ma'am, doesn't work that way. It doesn't happen. It's a myth."

He looked around at his audience: astonished, hurt, slack-mouthed. Only in Maggie's eyes did he see the quick reflection of comprehension. He went on. "Myth Number Two: if you really want it, all obstacles will fall before you. Someone will notice your burning desire, your bone-deep need, and give you a chance. Right? Wrong! There are thousands and thousands of good, talented, trained actors in New York, all burning with the desire to act, all needing to act. Thousands more in LA, and all across the country. Actors who really want it. And they aren't acting! Do you understand? They have all the qualifications, all the talent, all the desire. And they aren't acting! So what makes you think you can?"

There were tears of anger in the blond's dark-edged eyes. "Look, I get your drift, you can lay off now!"

Nick the brute. They were only in high school. But he couldn't forget the distorted young face of Dennis Burns, who had followed the myth to death in an alien place. He said tiredly, "No, you haven't got the drift. That dream of being a star, of applause, of being the instrument that transmits a gift of something universal to humanity— that's a tough dream. Doesn't dissolve in a few tears."

Rapunzel nodded violently, her eyes blazing. "Yeah, well, it's tougher than you! I'll do anything to become a star!"

"Ah, yes. Myth Number Three. You aren't the only kid who's ready to sell her virtue for a part."

"Mr. Nicholas!" Stella Barrett was pale.

"You say you'll do anything," said Nick, ignoring her. Dennis Burns too had been ready to do anything. "Do you mean it? Really? Do you have any idea what you have to do?"

Rapunzel met his eyes, glare for glare, gutsier than he'd thought. "Whatever it is, I'll do it!"

"I'll tell you, then. First, you train. Train your voice. Train your body. Train your mind. Study mime and dance and singing and philosophy. Study people. Next you get a marketable skill. Cabbie license, bookkeeping, whatever. Anything that you can do in odd hours. Third, you make rounds. Knock on hundreds of doors. Leave your picture. Smile at secretaries. For years. Because your big chance, if it comes, won't come from the clouds. It'll come maybe the hundredth time you smile at a casting director and ask if anything's happening." God, he sounded preachy. The Billy Graham of greasepaint. But it had to be said. He shrugged. "And if that sounds like a lot of work, well, it is. But if you're really ready to do anything, that's what you have to do."

They were silent, sullen, wanting to disbelieve him. Nick started to turn away, but glanced back at Rapunzel. "As for seeing your scene, sure, I'll be glad to. In New York. After you've graduated. After you've studied voice and dance and scene analysis and literature and psychology. But you'll have to get in line behind the two thousand others who got there first." He strode out.

They crossed the parking lot and turned down the long road that led back toward the station, toward their faraway home. Beside him, Maggie murmured, "Cruel to be kind."

"Yeah. Probably sounded like Moses to them. Thou shalt not dream. But I felt—I don't know. Responsible."

"I know. I was starting to get qualms too. It seemed a good idea at first, because of Amy. We turn up with a story that gives her some evidence that Dennis was a good actor. Gives her something to hold on to. That seemed kind. But seeing how those kids reacted, how personally they took it—" She shook her head. "*Si jeunesse savait.*"

"Yeah. We were contributing to the myths. I just couldn't leave it there."

"You think anyone will listen?"

"If even one of them does, I've saved years of squalor and anguish."

"Would *you* have listened, Nick?"

"Jesus, of course not! I mean, fate chose me to be an actor, right? And I *really* wanted it. And I was willing to do anything. How could I miss?"

Pleased, she took his arm fondly. "I see."

"Besides, young blood doth not obey an old decree."

She chuckled. "Know what, love? You're going to be a damn good dad."

13

Julia didn't so much wake Wednesday morning as come to. She sat up slowly, in a dry haze of aches and needs. She had to work, to do something. What was it? It was so hard to think. She had a good mind, her papa had always said. You don't belong in Brooklyn, you belong at the Algonquin Round Table. You don't belong in Brooklyn, said Vic Jr. too. But he meant it, he wanted her to move away. But she'd stay here, she had decided. She remembered that she had decided. But what else was she trying to remember? Something she had to do. Water Pauline's begonias. They were thirsty. And work. *Work is the province of cattle.* But even so, she had to work. Where was she? Shouldn't she get out of this place so she could work? Get out, yes, that was the first thing.

She pushed on the dark door, and the sharp pain in her fingers cleared her head. The hinge. That's what she was working on. With a screw, wasn't it? Where was the screw? She hunted around slowly, groping all the corners of her prison, and finally found the screw in her blouse pocket. She pulled it out and fingered it. That was it, she remembered now, that was what she had to do. That was her work. *The province of cattle.* But she was so tired. She needed rest. *Rest's for a clam in a shell.* So she'd better work.

After a while she noticed that there was a problem.

154

What? Why wouldn't her mind work? Concentrate. Oh, not a problem, really. She'd finished the hinge, that was all. Three screws exposed, she could feel their lengths with her torn fingertips. Her throat burned. She tried to make her sluggish mind focus. What came next? Oh, yes. Push. So she could water the thirsty plants. But when she tried, the door wouldn't move. She pushed again, and pain shot through her cramped body.

Okay, Teach, concentrate.

Four attachments. Hinge low, hinge high, bolt high, latch low. Right. The low hinge was loosened now. The other three made a sturdy triangle. So she should remove another one. Which one? Latch or hinge? Not bolt, that was in the middle. Latch or hinge, latch or hinge?

Exercise. Maybe that would clear her aching head. She remembered yesterday, a couple of times, stretching her legs. Standing up, bent at the hips, swinging her arms. That would help.

She mustered her failing strength, forced her stiff knees under her, straightened up to kneel erect—and blacked out.

When she came to again, there were flies. Where was she? Why flies? A fly lit on her cheek and she brushed it away, annoyed. She'd been going to stand up, why was she crumpled down here? Okay, slowly now. More cautious this time, she raised her head, her shoulders, leaned back dizzily against the wall of the cabinet. Pretty soon the dizziness eased, and she pulled her aching legs forward. She'd forgotten to put on her skirt. Oh, yes, her skirt, she remembered. And flies. That's why the flies were here. Ugh. But that wasn't the big problem, was it? The big problem was getting out. Concentrate, Julia. Hinge low, hinge high, bolt high, latch low. Something good had happened. What? Oh, yes—the hinge was loose! The low hinge. Her heart seemed caught in her constricted throat. She had to work on the high hinge. But she'd have to raise herself to do it, and that had made her black out.

How about the latch, then? It was low. *Concentrate*. Why not the latch? There was a reason why not. *Concentrate*. Oh, yes, too much wood. It took a long time even for a hinge. The latch was all the way on the outside. It was a normal sort of latch, she remembered. An image swam into her head. A beveled catch. The kind that was bad for

front doors because plastic cards could open them. If you
had plastic cards. She should have planned ahead, applied
for a credit card. Your passport to the world. Julia giggled,
but no laughter came out, only harsh rattles, and she
stopped because it sounded so scary. She didn't have any
credit cards. Nothing stiff and slim. Just a screw, her
blouse, her torn skirt, her loafers, and her undies. Nothing stiff.

Her loafers.

Carefully, Julia removed one shoe, and probed inside
gingerly with scabbed fingertips. Yes. Maybe. She scrab-
bled around in the shoe, finally found a loose place. It was
hard work. She tore a fingernail, and from time to time
she couldn't remember what she was doing. Finally, after a
long time, she managed to peel off a piece of the insole
lining, a precious, irregular piece of tough fabric stiff with
glue. Bewildered, she clutched the piece in her bleeding
fingers.

Why had she wanted it? Why? She knew it was of value.
She had three things of value. Hair. Screw. Insole lining.
Three be the things I shall have till . . .

They were kept in her pocket. She reached in, checked.
Hair. Screw. Now insole lining. She tucked it in too. In a
minute she would remember why it was valuable. Concentrate, dammit, old woman!

After a while, miraculously, she did. She pulled out the
insole lining. The screw fell out too. She found it, returned
it to her pocket. Had the hair fallen out? No, there it was.
Hair, screw. And insole lining. Yes. The insole lining was
her credit card, that's what she was doing. She was going
to break in. No, break out. Slip the card through the latch.
Light now seeped through the crack around the door. She
found the latch, and laboriously jiggled the piece of lining
toward it. Resistance. Gently now. Concentrate. Strong
spring in that latch. There. There, it was done! The catch
was pressed back, the insole lining was caught between it
and the strikeplate.

Now what?

Think!

Hinge low, hinge high, bolt high, latch low.

The low hinge was loose. The latch was open, sort of.

That left, let's see, high hinge and high bolt. Yes, time to
push the door again. Work, Teach. *Province of cattle.*

She pressed against the door. Blackness swirled behind her eyes. She rested, pressed again. A little movement. Not much. Not enough.

She was too weak. She couldn't push hard enough now. She'd never get out. No, no, that was wrong. She'd have to take out the upper hinge too.

But first maybe she'd better rest a little.

She leaned back, checked her pocket for her things. Screw, yes. Hair, yes. Insole. Where was the insole? Had she lost it? She groped around, worried, hearing her breath rasp in the darkness, realizing dimly that she was fading out again, until finally she remembered that the lining was already in the latch. Good. Hey, Teach, old thing, two down. Get that last hinge and you're all set. Things are looking up. Hurray.

But first, she decided, she'd just take a little nap.

> *And work is the province of cattle,*
> *And rest's for a clam in a shell,*
> *So I'm thinking of throwing the battle—*
> *Will you kindly direct me to . . .*

Julia slept.

"Nance?"

"Len!"

"I'm sorry to call you at work, Nance." He stood at the phone at the rear of the coffeehouse, not wanting Joyce or anyone to overhear. A teenage boy with a mane of strawberry-blond hair and tattered, flared dungarees waited impatiently for him to conclude a conversation he hadn't yet begun, staring at him with fierce eyes. "But couldn't we meet for dinner? I want to see you so much."

"I don't know, Len—"

"Please. It'll just be an hour or so. I want to see you."

"God, Len."

"At Rossini's, okay? That's close. Just for a little while, Nance."

"Oh, hell, why not? Six-thirty."

"Six-thirty. Great! I just want to see you."

"I already said okay. Okay?"

"Okay."

"Bye." She hung up abruptly. Len replaced the receiver and found he'd been sweating. He turned and strode away, avoiding the teenager's accusing stare. Damn, how could a person get so dependent on another person? In running away, she had kidnapped his hopes and his future. Her power over him infuriated him. Why had he let himself be tethered to her this way? What obscure urges would cause a man to let his independence slip away, and not even notice until it was too late?

And why did he feel so much happier now than before she had given him that grudging consent?

Damn.

He had several commercial buildings on Seventh Avenue and Flatbush to show to a new prospect that afternoon. Maybe now he could face up to reworking his apartment proposal too. Joyce needed it first thing tomorrow. He walked briskly back to the office, weaving his way through the noontime bustle of the streets.

Renata was leaving for lunch as he turned into the block. She'd been hollow-eyed but composed and efficient all morning. He paused to greet her. "How's it going, Renata? Didn't have a chance to ask, with our Wednesday meeting this morning."

She shrugged and adjusted her miniskirt. "Who knows? Joyce advanced me enough for a Greyhound ticket to Iowa. I gave it to my brother and told him it was up to him."

"Good."

"Maybe. I don't know. But he did take the ticket."

"Good luck."

"Yeah, we could use some." Her eyes behind the hornrimmed glasses blinked and she pushed past him, her platform shoes clopping on the pavement.

Fred Stein was alone in the office, pawing disinterestedly at some papers. Joyce was at the Feldheim closing and the other two had lunch appointments. "How're you doing, Fred?" asked Len.

No answer, just a rustle. Len glanced over at him. Fred was staring stonily at the papers on his desk.

"Is there a problem?"

The bright eyes darted a glance at him. "Renata told me you were thinking of getting a building of your own. With Joyce's help."

Oh, God, so that was it. Len said, "Well, Gordon and Joyce said it might be a good idea."

"Jesus!" Fred slammed a fist down onto the desktop. "I

hand you your future on a silver platter, and you trot it straight over to sell to Joyce!"

"Fred, for God's sake! I told you from the beginning I couldn't antagonize her! I asked in a general way. She said, do it now."

"Look, she's no good, Len! Makes promises, turns right around and does something else!"

"Joyce has always been completely square with me."

"Yeah, that's what I thought at the beginning!" Angry, Fred looked foolish, a little chattering creature. His strengths were amiability and solid preparation, not forcefulness. "But after you came—"

Stung, Len swung around to face him. "What?"

"Look, it can't be a secret! Joyce comes to me, says take care of this kid—he's wet behind the ears. So I do. And then instead of funneling some big stuff to me, she takes what I used to get and gives half to you!"

"Fred, it wasn't that way! This office was understaffed. Losing sales. That's why they took me on."

"Understaffed? Are you kidding? With the bottom falling out? All the big developers leaving the city? Okay, so Joyce is still solvent, but people working closer to the edge are failing in all five boroughs."

"We've all got work. Are you—jealous?"

"Of course I'm jealous! Jesus, kid, if it hadn't been for you, if Joyce had come through, I wouldn't be—well, hell, you didn't mean to, I guess. But watch out."

"That loan—the one that's due soon. Is that the problem?"

Fred refused to meet his eyes. "I expected enough work to pay it off by now, yes. And instead she hires you and siphons it away!"

"Can't you reschedule the payments? Sometimes banks—"

"This isn't a bank," said Fred, and then seemed to regret it.

Len felt a chill. Renata's terrified face swam into his mind. "Jesus, Fred! Are you in trouble?"

"No, no, no. Not that bad." A little evasive smile twitched Fred's face. "Or maybe worse."

"Worse?"

He hesitated before he said, "My nephew. My sister loaned me her boy's college money. He graduates from high school next month. You can't reschedule that."

"Jesus." Len was dismayed. He poked his toe at the leg

of Stein's desk. "Would it help—I mean, maybe I could do a sketch or two for you after work? Get you started with the doctors."

Fred sighed. "Not good enough. But I understand, you've got your future to think of, too. Getting your own kids through college someday." Bitter, he looked back at his papers, his face twisted.

Len, dismissed, could think of nothing to say.

Julia was dancing. Dancing on the greensward, with Vic. She could hear water, a fountain playing. She had on her nicest white sprigged frock, with a low pink sash that kept her from looking too hippy. She looked pretty. Winsome. They were in Central Park, and Abe Lincoln was watching, his eyes kind, and sassy old Caroline Sweeney O'Rourke, and Fred-Law. Not young Fred-Law, of course, but the older, wiser Fred-Law, bearded and leaning on his cane. Band music floated across the lawn, and she and Vic and the other couples danced and danced. *I'll be young and lusty among the roaring dead.*

She was thirsty, though. Dancing made her thirsty. So thirsty. She tried to tell Vic that she needed a drink, but her voice didn't work and her lips cracked. Not pretty. And the music was suddenly shrill. There was a fly on her face. She brushed at it and woke up.

The phone. The phone was ringing.

Well, let it. She was too tired to answer. No law that said you had to answer the phone.

But there was something she was supposed to do. The hinge. Oh, hell. The upper hinge.

Dratted phone. How could she concentrate?

The screw. She patted the pocket. Yes, there it was. All she had to do was get up to where the hinge was, take the screw from her pocket, and scratch with it until the hinge was loose.

Slowly, inch by inch, Julia raised herself. When the dizziness came, she lowered her head until it cleared. Visions, some dark, some lovely, pressed in and fell back. At last, kneeling erect, she found the place where the hinge blocked the crack of light. She pulled the screw from her pocket and began, tediously, to scrape at the hard wood. Just this one to go. Come on, Teach, keep at it.

How much time passed before she heard the doorbell?

Someone coming to see her? Who? Vic? It didn't matter. She must yell, shriek. "Help! Police! Help!" But the words made no noise. They rasped out in a harsh whisper. The doorbell repeated. She tried again. But after that there was only the quiet, broken by her rattling breath.

The effort had exhausted her. She was too tired to work on the hinge anymore. It would just have to wait until she felt better. She sagged back down into the corner. Maybe she would let that dream come again. It had been so nice, dancing on the greensward. Maybe this time Vic would bring her some mint tea.

"Hi, Len. Hope I'm not too early."

"Oh, hi, Maggie! No, this'll be fine. But I didn't expect you till after five."

"I went in early this morning and asked my boss if I could cut out a little early this afternoon. It's a pretty flexible job as long as you have continual brilliant insights."

Len laughed. "Yes. That takes you a long way in my job, too." He glanced at his desk. Everything done except for his own apartment proposal. He had roughed out the figures, swallowed a bit at the size of the loan he now had to request, found a couple of corners to cut, and decided to go ahead. But the proposal was still just a few pages of scribbles and dramatic-looking arrows pointing to unlabeled numbers. An hour should do it, though. He'd come back and copy it tonight after he had dinner with Nancy.

He shut the figures into his desk and turned to the key box. The Lund keys were still gone. Damn, he should have checked earlier, but with all the showings, he'd forgotten.

"Renata," he called, "have you seen the keys to the Lund place?"

She laid down the big silver scissors she was using to cut out the day's ads for the scrapbook and frowned. "No. Aren't they in the box?"

"They've got to be there," said Joyce, who had been pouring herself some coffee. She came over.

"Did Lund pick them up, maybe?" asked Len.

"Not while I was here," said Renata.

"Fred? Have you seen them?" Len asked Fred, who was on the phone. Without lowering the receiver from his ear, Fred opened his desk drawer, sorted through a few keys, and shook his head.

Maggie was watching with frank impatience. Joyce, who hated to appear less than competent in a client's eyes, frowned at Len. "Did you take them home yourself?"

"Home? No. I never take keys home."

"None of us do. But you were the last to have them, and it was a rather upsetting day."

Maggie said, "Brugioni had them at the house. But I remember him getting them out for you."

"Well, I'll check." She was right, Len thought; but he couldn't remember what he'd done with them. "The question is what to do now."

"Does it have to be today, Miss Ryan?" asked Joyce. Surprisingly, there was an edge in her voice.

"No, but I prefer it. How about Lund? Would he have keys?"

"He might not mind," said Len hopefully. "Just yesterday he was offering to help if he could. We could drive by his office. It's close."

"I'll call him if you want," said Joyce.

"Let's just stop by." Maggie was already half out the door. Len grabbed his umbrella and followed. It wasn't raining, but the humid May day was threatening. They hurried out to the car.

"His office isn't far," said Len, turning toward Flatbush.

"Did you ever manage to reach Mrs. Northrup?" asked Maggie, settling into the passenger seat.

"No, but I didn't try very hard. You said you didn't have to see that part of the house."

"I don't. It's just that I had something else to tell her, and I haven't been able to reach her either. Did she say anything about going away?"

"No, but I doubt she'd tell me anyway."

"True. We're neither one of us on her preferred list."

"What are you planning on doing in the kitchen?"

"New range and countertop. And paint."

"You'll probably want to paint a lot of the rooms."

"Yes. Kitchen, bedrooms first. And tear out that old paneling."

Babies needed preparation. Len murmured, "Makes sense."

"Len, stop!" They were still two blocks from Lund's office, but Maggie was jerking up the hand brake, grabbing the door handle, jumping out. Startled, Len watched

her dodge oncoming traffic to the sidewalk to confront a
short man with thin dark hair.

Arthur Lund, hurrying away from his office.

Double-parked, Len got out and joined them.

"Oh, yes, Joyce called," Lund was saying nervously. "I
was just on my way to your office. Guess I misunderstood."

"Glad we caught you," Len said, confused by the crackle
of tension in the air. "Could we borrow your keys? Our set
seems to be out, and Miss Ryan needs to measure the
rooms."

Lund hesitated. "But what happened to *your* keys? Did
the police take them?"

"They had them," admitted Len, "and I was in such a
state of shock I wasn't keeping track very well."

Lund was still reluctant. "But listen, there's old Mrs.
Northrup. You don't plan to go in her apartment, do you?"

Maggie shook her head. "No. And even if I did, I'd ask
her permission first."

"But—" Lund caught himself. "So you won't be seeing
her?"

"Not that we know of."

"Well, okay then." Lund selected a ring of keys and
handed them to Len. "Trager, you'll be personally responsible for them?"

"Of course. In fact, if you want, I can drop them by
your home tonight."

"Fine."

"Okay. We'd better get moving." Maggie started over to
the car, but Lund pulled anxiously on Len's sleeve.

"Trager?" he whispered pleadingly. "Don't let her talk to
the old lady. It could all fall through."

"Don't worry, Mr. Lund. We won't have to talk to her.
But I don't think it will fall through. They want the place,
and they're committed. Legally. Money down."

"I know, but—well, be careful. Tell her we'll clean it
again if she wants. Anything she wants. This deal can't fall
though!"

"It'll be okay. Don't worry."

Len escaped back to his car, and they rejoined the heavy
rush-hour traffic. It was well after five when they arrived
back at Garfield. Len said, "I have a six-thirty appointment back in the Village."

"It won't take us long. See, I have a sketch already. Just have to fill in the numbers."

"You're all set, then."

They parked a few spaces away from Lund's brownstone. Len was surprised at its air of serenity, as though in its eighty years it had become used to human foibles. Maggie ran down the two steps to ring the bell of the basement apartment.

"I thought you weren't going in there!" Len objected.

"I just want to tell her about something. It should only take a second," Maggie told him placidly.

But seconds went by, and minutes, and there was no answer to her repeated rings. She moved over to the bay window of the apartment. The drapes were drawn but she peered shamelessly through a crack where they didn't quite meet.

"Do you see her?" asked Len. Maybe Mrs. Northrup was in one of her alcoholic fogs. Maybe Lund was right. After all, when they'd visited before, she'd tidied up for some screwy reason. Would the sight of Mrs. Northrup, stewed again, make Maggie change her mind?

"No, I don't see her," said Maggie slowly. "But there's a coffee mug on the bookshelf next to the door. And something's wrong with the door chain. It's just dangling from the door—Len, let's go in."

"She's probably just out with a friend—"

Maggie, exasperated, said, "All right, if you insist. But I just remembered I wanted to measure the laundry room too."

"The laundry room? But—"

"It shares pipes with the kitchen over it, right?"

Reluctantly, he unlocked the door to the basement hall and then dropped the keys back into his jacket pocket. Nothing seemed amiss—the uncarpeted steps up to the locked landing door off the first-floor hall above, the darkened laundry-room door at the far end of this hall, Mrs. Northrup's door closed solidly. It was silent inside. No gospel music today, thank God. Maggie had hurried to the door and was turning the knob. "It's locked," she said.

'Of course it is. And we can't go in there without her permission. It's illegal."

"Is it a deadbolt?"

"Yes. We can't go in. On top of everything else, we promised Mr. Lund."

"Len, I'm worried about her! I know you think she's just an alcoholic old woman. But even if she is, we should check."

"Well, we can look again when we're finished," he temporized. "She's probably just taking a nap, or out visiting a friend. Maybe she'll answer next time we ring. Let's get the measurements done."

He walked past her decisively, but at the laundry-room door realized that she had not followed. He turned and saw that the door to Mrs. Northrup's apartment was ajar and Maggie nowhere to be seen. In disbelief, he reached into his pocket for the keys. They were gone.

Len sprinted back to the apartment door and yelled, "Dammit, Maggie, it's illegal! And her son is a lawyer!"

"I'll confess that it's all my fault." She was searching the room hastily, opening closet doors. "Do you smell something?"

"It always smells in there."

"No, this is different." She disappeared through the little passageway that led to the kitchen. Len hesitated, then, despairing, followed her in. Joyce would fault him whatever he did, but maybe he could prevent worse damage. Mrs. Northrup's apartment was neat, he saw, except for three coffee cups. But Maggie was right, there was a stench.

Maggie, heading for the bathroom door with a quick glance at the empty kitchen, paused. She was looking at a jumble of mops and buckets strewn in the corner of the kitchen, and at the cabinet door, where a torn piece of dirty cardboard was stuck between latch and frame. A fly landed on it and crawled into the crack. Swiftly, she bounded across the room and lifted the top bolt. The door sagged as she jerked it open.

A withered apparition of filthy, stringy hair and cracked lips blinked out at them, brushed away a fly, and made a harsh noise.

"Hair?" repeated Maggie.

"Pocket," rasped the apparition, slowly swinging bloodless legs over the edge of the opening. It started to straighten up, clutching at its breast, then pitched forward onto the floor.

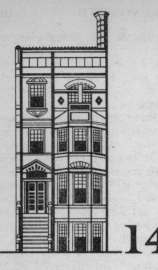

14

"God, I've never seen her this bad!" exclaimed Len, batting at a fly that came whining from the smelly cabinet toward his face.

Maggie had scooped up the limp, filthy old woman and was striding out. "Hospital," she said.

"She's just drunk again, isn't she?" Unable to keep the hopeful note from his voice, he hurried after.

"No." Maggie kicked the wrought-iron gate under the stoop and shoved it open. "Will you get your goddamn car? Or do I have to lug her all the way to the emergency room like a sack of potatoes?"

Emergency room. Len galloped to his car, urgency warring with disbelief, and opened the door for them. Maggie folded herself into the back seat with her thin burden across her lap. Well, at least they were no longer trespassing, thought Len morosely, though he wasn't sure if kidnapping was a preferable charge.

The hospital was five blocks away. He pulled into the emergency lane, took the smelly old woman from Maggie's arms, and carried her in. Maggie darted ahead to speak to the crisply unflappable admissions nurse.

"Heart attack?"

"No. Dehydration."

"You're sure?"

"She's had nothing to eat or drink since Monday night."

"Nothing?"

"Locked in a closet."

"Sure it's not heart?"

"That's what it'll turn into if you don't get a move on! And listen, her son is a lawyer!"

"Yeah, yeah, she's waited three days already, you say." But she turned a starched white back and summoned other people, who took Mrs. Northrup from Len's arms, checking her pulse and pressing her fingertips as they deftly wheeled her away to the treatment area. One eye on the proceedings, Maggie was giving the nurse information: Mrs. Northrup's name, age, address.

"No, I'm not the next of kin," she said. "Len, do you know who her son is?"

"No. Never met him."

"Where does he live?"

"Once she mentioned New Jersey."

"Check this directory, okay?" Not bothering to ask the well-ironed nurse this time, Maggie pounced on a book by the telephone on the desk and handed it back to Len. "It's Jersey. Should say 'attorney' or 'Esquire' after his name."

Len thumbed through several pages before he found a Northrup. "Victor Jr.?" He looked up to suggest.

"That's the one." Maggie gave the name to the nurse and assured her that he would take care of payment. The nurse, still skeptical, shrugged philosophically; obviously she had seen many worse cases of indigence in her career.

When the nurse ran out of questions, Maggie called the police from the booth. "Pass it on to Lieutenant Brugioni," she added to the officer who took the information. "Yes, we'll wait here." Only then did she turn back to Len.

"What the hell happened to her?" Len struggled to keep the exasperation from his voice. "How do you know so much about it?"

"Let's sit down." They found a scuffed bench. "I don't know what happened exactly. But she's been locked in that little pantry since Monday night."

"How—"

"I visited her Monday night, and I left that coffee mug on the bookcase by the door myself. She would have cleaned it up."

"Are you kidding?"

"No. She's a neat person, except when it suits her to be otherwise."

"You saw her *Monday* night?"

"To tell her we were buying the house. She was perfectly healthy then."

"You're sure?"

"Yes. And tonight, the chain on her door had been forced. It was okay Monday. Had to undo it myself when I left. But the main deadbolt lock hadn't been tampered with."

"Maybe she tore off the chain herself. She's an odd lady."

"Oh, sure, you can make up other theories. We don't know how she got locked in that cabinet either. Maybe the door blew shut when she was in there and that top bolt dropped down to trap her. But it's also possible that someone broke in and locked her in there."

"You mean the murderer came back? But she'd been living there alone for a week—no, longer than that, after the murder was committed."

"Oh, I know. She'll tell us about it when she comes to, I imagine. Assuming those dolts in there are treating her for dehydration and not heart attack." Maggie shot a surly look at the admissions nurse, who smiled back serenely. "Anyway, maybe she really did lock herself in that dumbwaiter. But there are things that make me wonder. One, that chain. Two, the keys missing from your office."

"But I probably took them home by mistake!" Len's mind balked at following the implications of Maggie's words.

"You can check. Three, her basic good sense. And four—"

"Good sense! Mrs. Northrup?"

But Len was interrupted by a uniformed policeman who came in and jocularly began to take down their story. Len cringed as Maggie unblushingly admitted to picking his pocket and entering the Northrup apartment without permission. Finally, to Len's utter bafflement, she pulled a small clump of hair from her pocket.

"These were in her blouse pocket," she explained. "She said 'Hair—pocket' before she blacked out. It's important. She'd even scratched it into the cabinet. 'Hair in pocket.'"

"Graffiti everywhere," observed the cop cheerfully. "Think it means anything?"

"My guess is it belongs to whoever locked her in there. Maybe we can ask her soon. But I'm certain it's important."

"All right." He slipped the hair carefully into a plastic bag.

Len, in turn, had to answer some questions, then Brugioni arrived and they had to go through it all again. The lieutenant called across to the nurse, "Can we talk to Mrs. Northrup?"

"Just a minute." She made a call. A harassed young doctor appeared shortly.

"No," she said simply to the lieutenant's question. "She's still unconscious. Even if she were awake, she'd probably be incoherent. Tomorrow sometime is the earliest we can hope for."

"Isn't it just hypovolemic shock?" demanded Maggie.

The doctor's eyebrows lifted, appraising Maggie. "Yes," she told Maggie, "most likely."

"When I had it, it only took a couple of hours to come out of it."

The doctor shrugged. "Maybe you weren't as dehydrated. And you're younger. With someone her age, we have to go slowly with the IV's or it can cause pulmonary edema and stress the heart."

"I see."

"But"—the doctor turned back to the lieutenant—"if she responds well, she could be back to normal soon. She's basically healthy, aside from the dehydration."

"Well, all right. Tomorrow, then." Brugioni sighed and nodded at Len and Maggie. "You two can go on home now. I'll let you know if we need anything else."

They walked back slowly to the car. Len unlocked it and asked, "Can I drop you off somewhere?"

"Well—" Maggie looked at her watch, and a look of dismay crossed her face. "Len! Your appointment!"

Len checked his own watch. Seven o'clock. "Oh, Jesus Christ!" He pounded his fist on the top of the car.

"It was important?"

"Nance. I got her to agree to have dinner."

"Shit! Well, get the hell over there! I'll catch the IND." She practically shoved him into the car.

Len got the hell over there, but Nancy was gone.

"Did she leave a message?" he asked the headwaiter.

"Nope. The lady waited twenty, thirty minutes, then left."

"Hell!"

"Can we do anything for you?"

"No. Yes. I want a Scotch." Len sat down in the bar to pull himself together. What the hell should he do now?

He knew where she was. She'd be down the block, at the studio.

He was not supposed to bother her at the studio. Her painting time was sacred, and had its own rhythms. Interrupting her was probably the worst thing he could do, now that she so desperately needed the peace and fulfillment it brought her. It would be the worst thing he could do to their relationship.

Or would it?

He ordered another Scotch.

She would be furious at him. He'd better explain. Get through to her that you care, Maggie had said. And Maggie had been through this herself.

He paid for the drinks and quickly, before his courage failed him, hurried down the street and up the stairs to the studio.

Two or three people were spaced around the huge room amidst the untidy clutter of easels, canvases, paintboxes, storage cabinets. They were all silent, concentrating, oblivious to the traffic noises that rumbled through the metal-framed windows. Nancy had moved her easel to a corner of the room, and, in profile to Len, was focused intently on her canvas. She had on a smudged blue smock, and there was a smear of black paint on her cheek.

Len went closer and cleared his throat. "Nance, I care. I really do."

Her head jerked around. Her trance was broken. Pain twisted her face. He hurried on. "It was old Mrs. Northrup. We were at Lund's place and she collapsed. I had to help take her to the hospital."

"I see."

"It was life or death."

"I see." She lowered her brush and looked back at her canvas, dully.

Len edged around behind her to see what she was painting. She saw him move and stepped forward to jerk the big canvas from its easel and lean it, face hidden, against the wall. But Len had already seen.

"God, Nance! God!" He was staggered by the ugly image he had glimpsed. The big blackened canvas. The little area, sharply bordered, that had been worked and reworked in smears of brown and gray, tight little twists laid on top of each other, scrubbed out, laid on again. There was one break in the border, a tiny one, and through it one of the little gray twists surged, thinned as it leaped across the canvas, and ended in a puddle of red and dead brown. Tormented, hopeless, it bored into his heart.

"You weren't supposed to see!" There was a little catch in Nancy's voice. She thrust her brush into the solvent and ran to the door.

Frantic, he followed and caught her on the landing outside the studio door. "God, Nance! That's how I feel too!"

"How could you? *You* have your own life." She was backed against the stained wall, the bare bulb above turning her hair to an aureole.

"You mean my job? My scrambling around trying to distract myself with an apartment project? That's just another little gray twist, Nance. Another twist in the same trap."

"But I don't know what you want! You won't tell me!"

"I don't know what I want, either. What do *you* want?"

Nancy looked down at the worn staircase, shrugged one narrow shoulder. "I don't know, Len. Except I want this whole thing to go away."

"Yes. Me too."

"But don't you have any feeling, one way or the other?"

"God, hundreds of feelings! Both ways! Nance, I don't— I'm sorry. I'm no good at explaining. I can't paint. But if I could, I swear to you, it would look like that." He shook his head. "I care about you, about what you decide. *You're* the important one. Why are we talking about me?"

"Because I need to know how you feel."

"But I don't know!"

"Hundreds of feelings, you said. Tell me some."

"God, Nance!"

"Please."

Her urgent tone forced her need upon him. Len struggled for the words. "Well—I feel confused. Sad. Happy. Betrayed."

"Betrayed?"

"Not by you, dammit! Betrayed by that four-percent failure rate. By the goddamn doctor. By fate. By love. By something. I feel angry."

"I feel angry. At my body. At you."

"At me?"

"Yes. Aren't you angry at me?"

"Angry at you?"

"Yes." Her eyes were intent on his.

"No, Nance, of course not! It's not your fault! Why should I—oh, hell. Yes! Yes, somewhere in those hundreds of feelings I'm angry at—not you, really. At your power over me. I want to be free."

"To be free?"

"But I want to be a father too. All at the same time." He kicked at the iron balustrade. "I'm angry because this decision is so important to my life and it isn't mine to make. And I'm not ready to make it anyway! I feel helpless. I feel guilty."

"But it's not your fault!"

"You asked for feelings, right? Well, these are feelings!" Len was wound up, heedless of her now, letting everything out in a rush. "I feel sorry for myself. For you. For the baby. No matter what happens, I feel sorry for all of us. I feel like an adult, and like a kid. I feel helpless. I feel powerful. I feel virile."

"Virile!" Nancy shook her head with a little unbelieving laugh. "Len! Our whole life is collapsing and you feel virile! And so do—"

Oh, God, he'd gone too far. The Scotch. He never should have had those drinks. He said stiffly, "Nance, I'm sorry, I'm no help to you. You were right. I shouldn't have come." Ignoring her protest, he turned abruptly with what dignity he had left and clattered down the stairs. Damn, why hadn't he shut up? Why had he spewed out all that pointless stuff to a woman already as tormented as Nancy was? God, why had she stayed with him this long?

He drove three blocks, saw a bar, and with sudden decision, parked. She'd never come home now. With despair and doggedness, he began to lay in the Scotch.

* * *

Someone was knocking.

Len raised his throbbing head and blinked. Rain on a windshield. He seemed to be in the car. And the someone knocking was a cop.

"Hey, pal, better move on. Can't park here in the daytime."

"Yes, of course." Len fumbled in his pocket, then saw the ignition key lying on the floor of the car. There had been some problem with it last night, he remembered vaguely. Something about it not fitting very well, so he couldn't start the car.

It fit now. He got the car moving sedately down the street, though any movement made his head throb furiously. The rain thudded on the roof. After a block or so he remembered to turn on the wipers. What time was it? Seven o'clock. He was due at the office in an hour and a half. And he was supposed to have that proposal ready for Joyce first thing. Damn, he'd meant to go back and finish it last night. And something else too. What? Oh, keys. Lund's keys. He'd promised to return Lund's keys last night. He groped in his pocket with little hope. Yes, they were gone. Did Maggie still have them? He'd better remind her right away, and get them back to Lund.

Well, one thing was clear. He didn't have time to go home. Not that he much wanted to anyway, now that he'd lost Nancy. Joyce had been right in saying not to count on her. Damn, why had he said all that garbage? Why had he been stupid enough to interrupt her work? What an ugly, ugly vision that had been. And right on target. That was the other reason he had said too much, he realized. The glimpse of Nancy's torment somehow had implied permission to express his own. That painting had had none of the taut beauty of her other pictures, none of the vigor and color that created harmony in their very tension. No harmony now. None. For either of them.

His head throbbed.

Better go through the motions, though. Back to the office now. She was well rid of him, but even so, his responsibility wasn't over. Child support, if she needed it. If she'd accept it. Just in case. So he'd copy over the figures, leave them for Joyce, call Maggie about the keys, arrange to get them back to Lund at his office. Find a place to shave. Buy some coffee. Renata wouldn't be in for another hour and a half to brew the office supply.

This early there was a parking space in front of the café. He ran through the downpour to get a black coffee and bagel to go, then dodged past the plate-glass window into the inadequate shelter of the Joyce Banks office doorway. He had trouble with the familiar lock as he juggled keys and food, hunched over to lessen the impact of the blowing rain. Finally he twisted the key hard the wrong way and then back. The door opened.

Strange to be here so early, without even Renata to greet him. The office seemed mysterious. Odd. But it was all the same. Stein's desk immaculate. Renata's still holding the scrapbook and scissors and phone books. His own with a couple of telephone notes and books of mortgage-rate tables. He pulled his proposal from his drawer and sat down at his desk. His trouser legs and shoes were unpleasantly soggy. Doggedly, he concentrated on copying the figures.

God, he was asking for a lot of money. How could he ask Joyce and her partners for that much? Especially with a head like his today. Right now, if he had any money, he sure wouldn't invest it in Len Trager.

Still. He read over the proposal carefully, clarified two points, checked all the arithmetic again with his calculator, and glumly decided it wouldn't get any better by being stared at. He'd leave it for Joyce, get another coffee, and phone Maggie to arrange to get Lund's keys back. She'd probably quiz him about Nancy too, dammit. He wouldn't want Joyce to walk in on that conversation. Better call Maggie when he got to the coffee shop.

He picked up the proposal, paper-clipped the pages, and took it into Joyce's office. His head was definitely not in good shape; standing up set it to pulsing again. There was already an open manila folder on Joyce's usually immaculate desk, he saw. Stapled to it was what looked like a medical record. Douglas somebody's record. But he read no further. As he reached the desk, the floor creaked behind him. He started to look around but something hard smacked into the turning angle of his jaw.

The world contracted to a pinprick and then went black.

15

Julia opened her eyes to a white fluorescent glare. Light. She hadn't seen light for days. *I shall come back*, said Parker, *from cool Eternity, a mild and most bewildered little shade*. Well, Julia certainly didn't feel mild. Bewildered, yes. There was a sense of constriction. Her left arm, she saw, was wrapped, tubes running in the elbow. Her right wrist was held by a young black woman, looking at her watch. She wore a crisp white dress. A nurse.

"We've got a nice pulse this morning," said the nurse approvingly.

"Have we really?" asked Julia. By golly, her voice was working again.

"Very nice. Dr. Malley will be pleased. She may even decide to take us off the IV soon."

The nurse's watch had an expansion band. Julia pulled it deftly from the dark wrist and looked at it. Six-twenty.

"Here, honey, let's not do that!"

Julia handed it back sweetly. "We just took it off our arm for a minute."

"Don't get too smart, honeybunch." The nurse, pushing it back onto her wrist, was amused. "You're already down for lethargy and confusion."

"We'll write us down for loony, is that it?"

"That's it."

175

"Is it Wednesday?"

"Thursday morning."

Time like an ever-rolling stream. Julia asked, "May I have a glass of water?"

"Not until the doctor sees you. We're monitoring your fluids and blood pressure very closely."

"Are we really?"

"Different kind of we." The nurse gave her a mock-sour look. "You have two notes there on your table if you're up to reading them. Dr. Malley will be in soon, and if you cut the sass she may let you have some breakfast."

Breakfast! Julia had a delicious swimming vision of orange juice, coffee, tea, pancakes, bacon, Danishes, more coffee, sausage, blueberry muffins. More orange juice, fresh-squeezed. More coffee. But as the nurse walked on to the next bed, Julia sighed. This was a hospital. Canned orange juice. Hard curds of scrambled eggs. A dry piece of toast. And the coffee, if any, would be stale. Better think about something else. She rolled over a little, carefully, and picked up the notes from the table with her free hand.

"Dear Mother: I waited all night but the M.D. said you needed your sleep. I have a couple of important meetings but will check hourly and come see you in the afternoon. You'll come home with us, of course. Love, Vic." Phooey. Had Vic Jr. found her? She tried to remember. She remembered the little dumbwaiter car. Hours of scratching in the dark. Getting weak in the head. Dancing with Vic—that wasn't real. Not in the sense she was interested in now. Was Vic Jr. there? She couldn't remember. There was an image, fleeting, of a blaze of light, and Maggie, of trying to give Maggie something, and then nothing at all. Was that a dream like the dancing? Probably. Probably Vic Jr. had found her. Phooey. Hard enough to argue with him when things were going well. Now that someone had tried to murder her, he'd get her into Jersey as fast as he could get her declared incompetent. Lethargy and confusion already, the nurse had said.

Maybe he was right. Her present condition didn't look much like the results of competence.

The second note surprised her. "I gave the hair to the police. Bonesy." And then two phone numbers, one la-

beled "work." Now there was a satisfying note. Maybe that
fleeting image was not a dream.

So. Nothing to do now but lie here and wait for the
doctor. And think.

Why had he attacked her? After all this time, why now?
What had changed?

He hadn't known she had access to the rest of the
house, for one thing. He'd found her searching. Then he
had attacked.

Because he didn't want her to find something? What?
Or because he thought she'd found it already?

Maybe it was something he thought she knew. Something damaging. Did she know something she didn't know
she knew? But then, why hadn't he attacked until he
found her searching?

Julia had the frustrating feeling that she was missing the
main point. Viewing it from the wrong perspective, somehow. She needed a fresh point of view. But who could she
trust? Vic Jr., never. Jean was too far away. So was Pauline,
for that matter, at the moment. Ruth? Ellie? Too conven-
tional. They'd just urge her to tell the police. Benny? He'd
keep quiet, but the poor boy was too dumb to be of much
help. Maggie?

Maggie.

If Maggie was planning on evicting her, she'd love to get
her hands on this information. But Julia had new evidence now. The hair. Not enough to get a conviction,
maybe. But something.

And there was the slim chance that Maggie was telling
the truth, and didn't really want to evict her. She seemed
genuinely interested in finding the murderer. Seemed
sincere in upholding their promise to Amy not to tell the
police about her, or about Curt's existence. Maybe this
would be a good test. See if she kept her promises.
Because if she was lying about not evicting Julia, then it
didn't make much difference what she did about this
information, did it?

Keeping a watchful eye on her tube-infested arm, Julia
sat up. Ugly hospital gown. She probably looked a fright.
Looked like lethargy and confusion. Well, fight that battle
when it came. She picked up Maggie's note, swung her
bare legs over the side of the bed, paused for a moment to
make sure she wasn't dizzy, then stood. The IV unit had

four little wheels. She pushed it to the next bed. An old woman lay there, asleep. She had a paperback book and a few coins on her table. Julia borrowed a dime and pushed her IV to the door. The hallway was empty and, yes, there was a phone, not too far away. "Heel, Fido," she muttered to the IV, and walked it along. A strange breed of dog you keep, Mrs. Northrup. Yes, Sonny, but it's very quiet and doesn't shed much. She dropped her borrowed coin into the slot and dialed the home number on Maggie's note.

"Hello?" Nick, a sleepy mumble. Poor pet, it was barely six o'clock.

"Julia Northrup here. May I speak to Maggie?"

"Of course." Bless him, not even a moment of hesitation. And a second later, Maggie's voice. "Hello, Mrs. Northrup."

"I want to talk to you. Privately. Now."

"Okay. I'll come over before work. You're still in the hospital?"

"Yes. Don't bring the cops."

"Wouldn't dream of it!"

"I'll try to be in the lounge. But there's a nurse hammering on this booth this very minute, ordering me back to bed. Listen, was it you who found me?"

"Len Trager and I."

It was difficult to say the words, but Julia managed: "Well. Thanks."

"You'll probably have to do it for me someday. I get into scrapes too."

"Yes, I imagine you do."

"About twenty minutes, then. Oh, shit, it's raining. Make that thirty."

That was quick enough. Julia meekly allowed the clucking nurse to trundle her and the IV back to bed. Dr. Malley came, proved to be a presentable young female, said the IV could come out and that she could have breakfast, but she wanted to keep checking her fluids for a few hours. Julia got her permission to sit up in bed; the doctor seemed pleased at how chipper she had become.

She'd barely finished her orange juice—canned, as predicted—when Maggie arrived, trench coat dripping.

"Well, I told them all you needed was a little liquid," Maggie said with satisfaction. She put down her briefcase and umbrella and dropped the wet coat over the back of a chair. Her dress was a summery blue. "They wanted to treat you for a heart attack."

"Would the food have been any better?" grumbled Julia, poking at her square of dried scrambled eggs.

"Next time I'll check the menus before I sign you in."

Julia looked up into the amused blue eyes and decided to take the plunge. She said, "Maggie, he may try to kill me again."

Maggie sat down, alert and unsurprised. "Who? Why?"

"You have to promise not to tell the police."

"Why not?"

"Telling the police is dangerous for me too."

"Then why tell me?"

"Well, I thought I knew what was going on, but I can't figure out why I was attacked. I need a fresh view of the situation."

"I see. Well, I can promise this much. I won't tell the police or anyone else unless you seem to be in danger again. When I know more we can decide how best to protect you."

"That's only half a promise," Julia argued.

"Best I can do."

"You think I need a nursemaid," complained Julia. But she was privately relieved: if Maggie was going to be this sticky about the wording of the promise, it indicated her intention to take it seriously. Julia added slowly, "I have to admit, it wasn't good in that closet."

"No."

"I kept thinking about Vic. And about how I was supposed to water Pauline's begonias. How thirsty they'd be—" Julia trailed off. She blew her nose into the paper napkin.

Maggie rescued her with a change of subject. "How in the world did you get that hinge off from inside?"

"Scratched it off with a screw."

"God. You're one tough woman."

"Sure. I'm the Teach."

"How did you get trapped, Teach?"

Julia munched on her eggs and toast between sentences. "You see, I'd fixed up the dumbwaiter so I could get to the top floor."

"I noticed it had new ropes. But it's walled off on all the upper floors. I looked."

"The middle floors are walled off. On the top floor there's only that thin paneling. I rigged it with hinges to open like a door. And I replaced the old ropes and counterweights and made myself a private elevator."

Unlike Vic Jr., Maggie didn't scold. Instead she chortled in delight. "Teach, I want to grow up to be just like you!"

"Don't look now, Bonesy," snorted Julia, "but I think you already have."

"Heaven help us both."

"Yes. So I used the contraption to check out the house after all the other tenants got driven out. Artie Lund was doing so many mean tricks to get me to leave, you see."

"Yes. Sensible to keep an eye on him."

"Anyway, that Wednesday, the day before you first came to look at the house, I went up to see what that plumber had done in the morning. I found the body."

"And didn't report it?"

"Nope. I had reasons. I didn't get much sleep that night, thinking about it up there. But I couldn't report it. It would have been playing into Artie's hands." She scrutinized Maggie's face for skepticism, but the young woman appeared to understand.

"Because you think he arranged to have it brought there?"

"Or maybe even did it himself, though I didn't think so then."

"Why do you think he was involved?"

"Because he's tried every other way to get rid of me."

"He thought a body would scare you away?"

"I think he'd know better than that. No, he wanted to get me arrested."

"How?"

"Planting evidence that I did it. That's why I was so sure I wasn't really in danger. I thought if he were really a murderer he could have killed me long since. But he didn't, because he knew that if I died he'd be the suspect. That body scared me, because it showed he at least knew a murderer, but I still didn't think he'd do it to *me*."

"I see."

"And then Monday you said you were buying the house. With me still in it, you claimed."

"That's right."

"You didn't make the offer contingent on me being out?"

Maggie reached into her briefcase and handed Julia a document. It was lengthy but clear: the Sellers, Arthur and Loretta Lund, had no obligation to deliver the building vacant. Julia squinted at the signatures and corrections. It was an original. She handed it back to Maggie. "So now there's no reason for him to get rid of me!"

"Then why the attack?"

"That's the question, all right." Julia pushed her breakfast tray away and rearranged the lap of her shapeless gown. "I wondered if maybe Artie might have killed that young man himself, and maybe dropped something and came back to look for it. Did he think I found it? Did he think I'd seen something in the part of the house he'd locked me out of? Why attack me?"

"What about Amy's visit? Could she have told you something?"

"I wondered about that too—maybe Curt was Artie's accomplice. But I don't think so. The reason is that I heard him searching for about an hour after he'd locked me up."

"Mm. We may be able to check that. Nick found Curt."

"He did?" Julia sat straight up in her excitement. "What does he know?"

"He won't tell much. He's a very sad, suspicious kid who's lost his best friend. I asked Nick to try to get him to come here this morning. Maybe if he sees another victim —"

"You invited men here to see me like this?" Julia plucked at the gown in dismay.

"Come off it, Teach! Compared to the first time we saw you, you look like Princess Grace," Maggie reminded her tartly. "Anyway, right now why don't you tell me exactly what happened after Amy and I left."

Julia described it—her hunt, and her failure to find anything; Artie's furtive approach via the kitchen porch; the way she'd been tricked as Artie ran up the back stairs while she waited cautiously on the front ones; how she was tied while he ran down to lock the dumbwaiter exit to her kitchen; the struggle and her prize handful of hair; her horror as she heard the first counterweight fall; jamming in the screws and hearing the second fall.

"So you could have been killed when the whole dumb-waiter dropped into the cellar?"

"I was only one floor up at that point. I might have escaped with a few broken bones."

"'Escaped' is not the word, Teach."

"No."

Their eyes met, gravely. Then Maggie said, "What did he do next?"

"He rummaged around for a while. In my apartment and on the stairs. I could hear him opening drawers, moving things, even washing up."

"Everything looked tidy when I got there. Apparently the plan was to make it look as though you had locked yourself in there by mistake."

"I thought so. The ransacking sounded pretty discreet."

"What happened next?"

"The door closed. He went away. I'd been very quiet. Didn't want him to know I wasn't unconscious in the cellar. He banged on the door once but didn't open it, dammit."

"I bet you were ready for him."

"He'd be here today instead of me!"

"I believe you."

"He left by the kitchen-porch door again. Did you notice that the building at the corner has a little yard behind it? Well, they leave the gate unlocked sometimes. And of course Artie won't fix the break in our fence. So he probably got in and out that way too."

"I see. Any idea what he was looking for?"

"No. I'd think everything that could be found had been found. I don't think he found it either. He just ran out of places to look. Not as thorough as Brugioni and me."

"Okay. Now, you said you didn't see him at first. Only the doorknobs moving. Did you see him while you were fighting?"

"Let me think. No. No, I guess he didn't know that I already knew it was him. He made sure I didn't see him. Shielded himself with that cloth thing that he tied around me."

"Did he say anything?"

"No. He grunted once, that's all."

"But you're still sure it was Artie Lund?"

"Well, it's obvious, isn't it?" The question astonished

Julia. "Who else would want to get rid of me? And he was about the right height, and soft and pudgy, and had dark hair."

"Yes. The hair was dark and short," said Maggie. "Okay. Next question. What evidence did he plant the day he left the body? And where did you hide it?"

Julia had hoped it wouldn't come to this. Her lips tightened stubbornly.

"You want a fresh perspective," Maggie argued patiently, "but you won't let me see the whole scene."

Fastidiously, without looking up, Julia brushed a crumb from her lap. "One Thanksgiving my Grandpa Sweeney let it slip that he hated turnips. Next Thanksgiving, and every one after, my Aunt Kitty brought turnips, though she never had before. And she had a lot less to gain than you."

For an instant there was such a depth of hurt in Maggie's eyes that Julia was ashamed. This woman had saved her life, had proved companionable, had passed every test of trustworthiness that Julia had been able to devise. But Maggie recovered, shrugged. "You're right. Trusting is one of the hardest things for me too. Were you a Sweeney, then, Julia S. Northrup?"

"Poor branch. Grandpa Sweeney was Cornelius Sweeney's younger brother. So when Vic went into a wheelchair after his first stroke, and we needed a cheap ground-floor apartment, the family came through. Caroline Sweeney O'Rourke was already in her eighties, so I kept an eye on her too." Julia realized she was talking too much, avoiding the real subject. She made herself stop babbling, fidgeted a moment with the unlovely hem of her gown, and said, "Do you really think it would help if I told you? It probably has nothing to do with the attack."

"Probably not. On the other hand, it was something he left behind to implicate you, right? And he planted it someplace between the body and your apartment for the police to find. But you haven't been arrested, or even questioned very hard. So now he knows something went wrong. Maybe the police didn't find it. He might have been hunting for it, wondering why they missed it."

"You'd have to be blind to miss it. He left it right on the banister. Stuck on a splinter, as though I'd stupidly dropped it as I hurried down after strangling that poor young boy.

Artie's not too bright—how was I supposed to hold the kid still while I killed him?"

"You bashed him first with his own Chianti bottle," Maggie reminded her. "But what was stuck on a splinter?"

Julia took a deep breath. It was like being a little girl again, eight years old, running timidly up to the edge of the foaming sea at Coney Island, drawn and yet repelled by the boundless possibilities and boundless danger.

At eight, she had closed her eyes and jumped in.

At sixty-eight, too, she closed her eyes as she said, "The weapon. Nylon support hose. It's so obvious, it had to be to frame me! I don't wear the dratted things anyway, but I'd never convince the police. Support hose naturally go with crazy old ladies in basements."

"I see."

"So I hid them, hoping the police would get some other evidence pointing to Artie. I guess they didn't."

"They searched your apartment."

"Yes, I figured they would. So I stuck them in a McDonald's bag and hid them in a trash basket by my grocery store until the police had finished. Then I brought them home."

"Why not just let them be thrown away?"

"I thought about it. But I figured once they had Artie accused, there might be some tie-in with him. You know, his wife's size or something. Evidence."

"I see. And you don't think Artie found them in his Monday-night search?"

"I was listening for the right kind of noise. It didn't come."

"I see." Maggie nudged back her blue cuff to check her watch. "Seven o'clock. I don't have to be at work until nine. Would it be okay if I went to your apartment and looked it over? See if I can tell what he was searching for?"

"I imagine you'd like to see the weapon too."

"Well, if you could bring yourself to tell me—"

"I could. I will. I shall," said the ex-schoolmarm. "It's still in the McDonald's bag, at the bottom of the sugar canister."

"Thanks." With a pleased grin to acknowledge Julia's gift of trust, Maggie stood, brisk in the summery dress.

Julia said gruffly, "You're not really a bag of bones, you

know. You're attractive enough. I imagine your Nick finds ample delights."

A flash of surprise and gratitude in the intelligent eyes. Maggie said, "I bet your Vic did too."

They smiled at each other across the chasm of years. Julia nodded. "Yes, we managed to keep each other warm. Be careful now."

"Okay."

"I mean it. What if Artie comes back?"

"No problem." Maggie was shrugging back into her wet coat. "He can't get in this time. I have his keys."

"Um—one other thing. I keep thinking about those thirsty begonias."

"Consider them watered. See you in—oh, Nick! You got here!"

Julia smoothed her hair and swiftly adjusted the sheet around her knees as Nick, damp, ushered in a neat, dark-haired young man in a bright yellow slicker. Nick smiled at the two women. "Hi. Mrs. Northrup, Maggie, I'd like you to meet Curt Pritchard. Dennis Burns's friend."

Curt and Julia inspected each other. Curt went straight to the point. "You were attacked too?"

"Yes. Probably because I know something about your friend's death." Julia met Curt's eyes squarely. "Unfortunately, I don't know what I know, so I can't help much."

Curt jerked a thumb at Nick. "Yeah, he said we could compare notes. But I'm not showing anybody the stuff he left."

"Understood," said Nick.

"What happened to you?" the boy asked Julia.

"I was locked in a closet and left to die. Whoever it was searched my apartment afterward."

"He didn't hit you?" Curt sounded disappointed. As bad as my grandson, Julia thought, looking for the blatant signs of evil: blood, broken bones. Hours of thirst and darkness were not dramatic enough for young males.

She hastened to reassure him. "Oh, yes, he slugged me to get me into the closet. I've got a big bruise on my ribs."

"But he didn't like strangle you?"

"No. Didn't want it to seem connected to your friend's death, I think. Which makes me think it was."

"You're right." Curt nodded.

"Can you tell me why your friend was in the house?"

Curt glanced at Nick, then back at Julia. "All I know is he was meeting someone. A woman. Not a young one."

"And not me."

"Yeah, I wondered—but you were really hurt."

"Yes. Can you tell me anything else about the meeting?"

"No. He didn't tell me where. The only other thing was that she asked him to go disguised. So he put on an old wig he had saved from a play he'd been in."

"A wig!" Julia slapped the mattress in her excitement. "That's why I couldn't remember him! I saw him go into the house, Curt. Nine o'clock on Wednesday."

"Yeah, that would be about right. He split at eight-thirty."

"I thought he was a plumber. And I always go out for groceries about then. So I was out of the house when it must have happened. You don't know why he was meeting this person?"

"No." Curt hesitated. Julia was reminded of a fifth-grader trying to decide if giving the teacher the information she'd asked for really constituted ratting on a friend. She put on the look of friendly expectancy that had won over many a child in the past. Curt looked into her eyes and said, "His dad left him some old medical records from his days in Brooklyn. I don't know why they were special. Denny made copies and told me to take care of them."

"Medical records? Not drugs?"

"Drugs?" Curt laughed. "Nah. Only drug Denny's old man used was alcohol. A real boozer."

"What did the records say?"

"I don't understand the language much. I did look up the names in the Brooklyn phone book but they don't seem to live here anymore. So I don't know what Denny was into. It's freaky."

"Maybe Mrs. Northrup would recognize the names. She's lived in Brooklyn a long time," Nick suggested.

Curt looked at Julia skeptically. "You know people from Flatbush?"

"Sure. Some," said Julia. "Who?"

"Let me think. Um, Rosalind Williams, the Hepburn sisters, Douglas F. Kilmer, Rock—um, Rock Martin. Oh, and Natalie Kelly."

Julia shook her head sadly. "No, guess not. How about Lund? Arthur, or Loretta?"

"No. Oh, screw this, I knew it wouldn't work! Let's split."

The boy wiped his forehead angrily with one hand and turned away.

"It's slow sometimes, Curt, but we've got to try," Nick soothed.

"We were really tight, Denny and me. God, I want to throttle the guy that did it!"

"So do I," said Julia.

"Curt, do you think it had to do with something else?" Maggie asked. "His work as a waiter? An audition?"

Curt shook his head. "I wondered that. But he didn't open up much about the job, except to complain about customers ripping him off. He was like ashamed of that job."

"How about auditions?" Nick asked.

"Well, he worked at that. Left his résumé all over and went to cattle calls when he could."

"Really? I asked an agent and he hadn't heard of Dennis Burns."

"Well, agents always ignore you." Curt's voice was bitter. "Anyway, his stage name was George Day. Said his dad suggested it, and laughed. Private joke, I guess."

"Well, that explains why I couldn't find him."

"Listen, I've got to split." Curt turned back to Julia. "Let's trade phone numbers, okay? And share anything that comes up? But no police. I think I can find out more if the guy isn't scared."

"I'll share," promised Julia, "and I don't want the police around either. But I've got to protect myself too." She scribbled her number into his notebook and tore off the page with his.

Maggie had been looking dreamily out the viewless window. "Dr. Burns suggested George Day for Dennis. Fill in the blanks." Her head snapped around and her wide-eyed gaze caught Nick's. Julia could sense something crackling between them.

"Robert Mead?" asked Nick.

"Donald Nickleby. Wow!" She pounced on her umbrella and briefcase, eyes alight. "Look, I'm going to go check Julia's place, and then go see if anyone is at the real-estate office yet. Curt, if you'd get those records and join me there, we may find another piece of the puzzle."

"You putting me on?" Curt looked as bewildered as Julia felt.

"Come on, I'll explain on the way," said Nick.

They all disappeared in a puff of excitement, but Maggie stuck her head back in after a moment. "I called Brugioni. You don't have to tell him a thing, Teach, but you might think about how to convince him that you need police protection. That Doberman of a nurse out there is no match for determined types like Nick and me. And our murderer is a determined type, and may hear that you're out and functioning." She disappeared again.

Puzzling over their words, Julia drank another glass of water before light began to glimmer. But before she could work out how she fit into it, Lieutenant Brugioni poked his nose around the door, looking disgusted. "How are you feeling, Mrs. Northrup?"

"Much better, thanks. Come on in. Hello, Sergeant Cleary."

Cleary's pink Irish face beamed at her, but Brugioni was complaining, "The nurses were supposed to let me know when you woke up. How did Miss Ryan know you were up?"

"I phoned her. Woke her up. Thought she might have noticed something when she dragged me out of that closet. I'm curious, Lieutenant."

"Yes, we all are." He pulled up the chair and sat, adjusting his damp trench coat. Cleary, notebook out, tried in vain to make himself inconspicuous against the white wall. "Now, would you like to tell us about how you got into this situation?"

Omitting Artie's name and the evidence he had planted, and scrupulously avoiding Curt's not-for-police-ears story, Julia described the attack again. Brugioni quirked an eyebrow when she mentioned her dumbwaiter access to the upper floors, but seemed more interested in another aspect of her story.

"Yes," she answered him, "I just grabbed and somehow caught his hair, and then he shoved me into the dumb-waiter car."

"Was there anything strange about his hair?"

"Strange?"

"Was there anything strange about pulling it out?"

"How would I know?" Julia was becoming exasperated.

"What can I compare it with? I don't go around regularly yanking out people's hair, Lieutenant. Only on special occasions. Christmas, Easter, and whenever someone tries to murder me."

"Yes, I'm sorry." Chastised but persistent, Brugioni rephrased his question. "I wondered if it came out easily, if there was resistance, that sort of thing."

"Well, his head sort of followed my hand a few inches as I pulled, then he jerked away. Is that what you mean?"

"Yes." Brugioni glanced at Cleary. They both seemed pleased.

"Why are you so curious about it?"

"Well, the lab looked at the hair, Mrs. Northrup. And it's modacrylic."

"What?"

"It was from a wig."

"That wig again!"

"Again?"

"I haven't had a chance to tell you. I remembered where I saw Dennis Burns. He was the workman going into the building at nine o'clock Wednesday morning. He was wearing a black wig. That's why I couldn't place him."

"I see."

"So the killer must have taken the boy's wig, and then worn it when he attacked me!" Julia gave a little bounce of excitement on the mattress.

Brugioni smiled wanly. "Perhaps. That still doesn't tell us who it is."

"It tells us one thing," Julia insisted.

"What?"

"The killer doesn't have thick black hair." Artie's was thin.

"Perhaps." Brugioni nodded. "Now, is there anything you want to add?"

Julia hesitated. She hadn't accused Artie directly. Her case against him was too intimately tied to the evidence he'd planted against her—evidence that Brugioni might decide to take at face value, especially now that he knew about her elevator. No, she couldn't accuse Artie or she'd be in real trouble. She thought wistfully of mentioning Amy and Curt. That would give Brugioni another angle, a lead that might reveal a connection between Artie and the victim. But she'd promised them. And in all her years of teaching and mothering, she'd never broken a promise to a child. She said slowly, "I don't think so, Lieutenant."

"Well, if it's all right with you, I'll take a look around your apartment. And—what are you doing here, Miss Ryan?"

Maggie, dripping wet and looking very serious, was standing in the doorway. "I told Mrs. Northrup I'd fetch her handbag."

"Hey, Maggie, guess what?" Julia enthused. "The hair was from a wig! The killer took Denny's wig and wore it when he attacked me!"

Maggie did not look pleased. "That seals it," she said. "It's not the one we talked about."

"But—"

"Nobody's trying to frame you, Teach. It's for real."

"Frame you?" interrupted Brugioni. "What do you mean?"

"Nothing!" Julia glared at Maggie. "We just wondered, since I live in the house, if the killer might try to make me a suspect. Nothing specific."

Maggie crossed the room to the bed and dropped Julia's handbag beside her. "It's up to you, Teach. I won't make your decisions for you. But there are other possibilities. I'm going now to start checking them out."

A sense of dread lay heavy in Julia's stomach. She ignored it. "Well, keep us posted," she said cheerfully.

"Of course. Oh, one other thing. Don't worry about the begonias, they hadn't dried out at all."

Julia felt her eyes filling. Angry at her own weakness, she drew up her knees under the sheet and rested her face against them. Didn't want the young folks to see her sniveling.

"Things will look better tomorrow, Teach," said Maggie gently, her hand light on Julia's shoulder.

Julia shrugged it off, swiped at her eyes with the ugly sleeve of her gown, and glared at this clear-sighted, disruptive young woman who seemed to read her so easily. She snapped, "'So long as I have yesterday, go take your damned tomorrow!' Now scram, Bonesy, I've got a lot more to tell the lieutenant."

Obediently, Maggie scrammed.

16

This was a hell of a hangover.

Len opened his eyes. Light splintered his head and he closed them again. Hadn't he done this already this morning? A cop, hammering on the car—

He wasn't in his car now. His head was floating somewhere. A memory tugged at him: his proposal. He was working on the proposal. At the office, right? In Joyce's inner office. He tried opening his eyes again, just a slit. Yes. Here was the flecked carpet, itchy against his face. That was Joyce's radiator, unabashedly Victorian under its thick wrap of layered paint. And his proposal—his proposal! Where was it? He raised his head and saw it, pages fanned out, by his left hand. The coffeepot lay beside it. Why? He squinted at it. What was it doing on the carpet?

For that matter, what was Len Trager doing on the carpet?

A familiar voice knifed into his consciousness. "Is Len here?"

"Len? No—ah—"

Len mumbled, "Nance!" He sat up, brain throbbing, and squinted through the door into the main office.

Nancy was running toward him, her raincoat dripping. "Len! What's happened?" She dropped to her knees beside him.

191

"I don't know. My head—I hit my head somehow." His tongue was too thick.

"Let me see." Her gentle fingers brushed through his hair, probing delicately. Beyond her he could see Joyce frowning at them. "You'll do," Nancy decided. "A little bump is all."

"Why are you here?" Len enunciated carefully.

"I waited for you at home. All night."

"You were home?"

"You ran away so fast! By the time I cleaned up enough to follow you, you'd disappeared. So I waited at home."

"God, Nance! I was out getting drunk."

"So I see."

The quick smile in her eyes helped clear his head. He said, "I thought you'd never want to see me again, after what I said."

"After what you said, you'll never get rid of me! But, Len"—there was real concern in her voice—"what happened here?"

He dragged his amazed eyes from her and struggled to make sense of the scene. "I was here early. Someone must have broken in. Everything was normal when I got here to finish my proposal. No, wait, the lock gave me trouble. So maybe he was already here, hiding in Joyce's office. He must have hit me with the coffeepot and then escaped while I was unconscious. Did you see anyone? Did you, Joyce?"

"Not in here," said Joyce. "And only that old wino outside." Her eyes were wary, fixed on Len.

Nancy rose slowly to her feet. "Len?" she asked. "Were you unconscious very long?"

He blinked at his watch. "No," he said, surprised. "It's just now a quarter to eight. Maybe ten minutes since I checked the time."

"Ten minutes!" Nancy turned to Joyce. "Did you phone for a doctor?"

"No. The door was unlocked when I arrived. I was—ah—checking to see if someone had broken in."

"And poor Len lying here!" Nancy's indignation was swelling into flush-faced anger. She stepped accusingly through the office door toward Joyce.

"Nance, be reasonable!" protested Len, stumbling to his feet and clutching the desk for support. "She thought

someone had broken in. She probably didn't even see
me—" He trailed off. Next to him, draped across Joyce's
desk chair, were her damp raincoat and her big handbag.
The medical record that had been on the desk was gone.
He looked back at Joyce, and suddenly his skin seemed to
tighten.

"No one broke in, Len!" Rage roughened Nancy's voice.
"She knocked you out herself!"

Joyce was studying Len, tenseness about her eyes. "Not
true. Maybe he stumbled and hit his head. Nancy, Len and
I have some business to discuss. Would you wait outside
for a moment?"

Len, still hazy, struggled to keep the anger and fear
down in his stomach. He leaned against the frame of the
door to the main office. Through the plate-glass window
he could see a couple of people half-hidden by umbrellas,
scurrying beetle-like past the building. Across the street a
bag lady adjusted the plastic trash bag that covered her
hair and nestled herself mournfully into a doorway.

Nancy was shaking her head, following Joyce toward
Renata's desk. "No. How can you ask me to leave him
now?"

"I must talk to him. It's vital!"

"At best, you didn't help him. At worst, you knocked
him out!" Nancy insisted.

"Nancy, please." An edge of desperation colored Joyce's
words. She reached out a hand in nervous appeal to
Nancy, took her wrist, and wrenched it up behind her
back. Nancy gave a little cry. Unbelieving, Len saw the
sudden flash of Renata's big scissors in Joyce's hand. His
body went rigid. The cruel points rested on Nancy's
throat.

"I hate to do it this way, but I must talk terms with Len!
And people will be here soon," said Joyce. "We'd better go
for a drive."

"What do you want me to do?" Len's tongue seemed
unbearably thick. Nancy stood stiff with fear, unre-
sisting. The ice-bright blades gleamed at the hollow
of her throat.

"Bring my handbag. Nancy will carry it."

There was no choice. He went to her inner office and
picked up the bag from the desk chair. He had to keep
Nancy safe, concentrate on doing what Joyce wanted. But

his head was pulsing with pain and with questions: Why? Why was Joyce threatening Nancy? Had she in fact hit him? Was she insane? Or was there a reason? What terms did she mean? Her bag was gaping open, and he caught a glimpse of the medical record inside as he closed the flap and turned back to Joyce. "Here it is."

"Stand five feet away from us and hand it to Nancy. That's right. We'll take your car, it's right outside. You drive, we'll sit in the back seat, and we'll work something out. Really, I think you're getting greedy."

"Greedy?"

"To try to claim I attacked you, on top of everything else!" Joyce shifted the scissors to Nancy's back. "But first, get rid of her."

"Get rid—oh." Len followed her gaze and saw Maggie Ryan outside the door, closing her umbrella.

"Hello, everyone," Maggie caroled cheerfully as she stepped inside and set her umbrella to drip next to the others by the door.

"Hello, Miss Ryan." Joyce smiled, warm and businesslike except for the set of her eyes.

"Hi." Len was amazed that his voice didn't crack. "What can we do for you?"

"I'm glad to find you all here so early. Especially on a day like this." She glanced out the window.

"We aren't really open for another hour," said Joyce. A faint thread of desperation ran through her tone. "In fact, we were just leaving."

"Just a couple of questions. I have to get to work too." Maggie was standing with her back to the door, looking brightly from one to the other. A puddle was forming below her dripping coat.

"Sure, if they're quick," said Len. Joyce's mouth tightened. He had to get rid of Maggie somehow.

"Let me just find something." Maggie unsnapped her briefcase. "Where are you going so early? Nothing much is open."

"It's, ah, a special appointment at my decorator's," Joyce improvised smoothly. "I need some advice from an artist, and Nancy has such excellent taste."

"Oh, I know." Maggie smiled. "Len brags about her."

Len's mouth was dry with anxiety. "Well, we do have to—"

"Here they are!" Triumphantly, Maggie pulled a set of keys from her briefcase. "Len, in all the excitement, I forgot to return Mr. Lund's keys last night. And you were in such a rush to get back to Nancy, because you were late."

"Thank you." Len snatched the keys. "Now, would you excuse us?" If she'd only get out of the way! Joyce was so tense, so unstable. The hand holding the scissors at Nancy's back was trembling.

But Maggie stood fast. She had put down her briefcase and was unaccountably unbuttoning her coat. "I hope you weren't too hard on Len for being late, Nancy. Did he explain what happened?"

"Yes." Nancy didn't nod or gesture, and Len could sense the strain that went into keeping her voice level. "About finding Mrs. Northrup and rescuing her."

"Yes. It was such a shock!" Maggie was gushing. Why was she so thickheaded today?

Joyce shoved Nancy toward the door. "Excuse me, Miss Ryan, we're leaving."

"You'll need your raincoat, Mrs. Banks!" Maggie was half out of her own. But at last Maggie was stepping aside, turning to look at them as she did. Len, relieved that Joyce was no longer being antagonized, still felt a pang to see Nancy approaching the door.

"Open it, Nancy," urged Joyce. Nancy bent away from her slightly to put down the handbag so she would have a hand free to reach for the handle.

Then Len saw that Maggie was stepping between them, her arm snapping up below Joyce's to knock the scissors up. Endangering Nancy.

"Do what she says, dammit!" He dove across the room to tackle Maggie around the waist, to jerk her away. She ignored him, concentrated completely on the weapon. The scissors raked against Maggie's cheek as Len dragged her off balance and Joyce turned on her, but she managed to seize Joyce's wrist. Then something heavy slammed painfully into Len's head as Maggie writhed out of her raincoat and free of his grasp.

"Whose side are you on, idiot!" he heard someone—Nancy—demand. She had struck him with the handbag.

On all fours, Len shook his head, woozy from the blow and from his hangover. He saw his hand still gripping

Maggie's wet, rumpled raincoat. The important thing, he realized, was that Nancy was free. Time to get her away from here.

Except that Joyce and Maggie were blocking the door. Joyce, grunting, was pounding furiously on Maggie's back with her left hand, clawing at her hair, her eyes. Gone was the carefully manicured businesswoman; instead Len could glimpse the fabled Olympic contender, raging for the win as though her life depended on it. But Maggie ignored her, focusing on the scissors. Both her hands were still clenched on Joyce's right wrist, keeping the glinting blades at bay.

Joyce went suddenly still. "Look, this is ridiculous," she gasped. "I'm an old woman. I quit."

Maggie didn't release her. "I don't know what the problem is, Mrs. Banks. I don't want to hurt you. I'm being as ladylike as possible. But you have to drop the scissors."

"All right." The fingers of her right hand loosened and Maggie relaxed to take the scissors. But with a flick of her left hand, Joyce snatched them, pulled back, drove the points at the younger woman. Maggie lurched violently away, stumbled over Renata's chair. The points gashed the blue dress.

Nancy screamed, "Joyce, stop it! She's pregnant!"

Wrong move. Awkward and off balance, Maggie was wrestling with the overturned chair, desperately trying to right herself. And Joyce twisted Nancy's words into a recipe for victory. She leaned slowly over Maggie's struggling form, drew back the scissors, and aimed straight for the unprotected belly.

Aghast, Len tried to stand up. But it was Nancy, swinging the handbag, who clipped Joyce behind the knees. The stab went wide. Maggie, still off balance, slapped wildly at the scissors hand and seized it again, wrenching Joyce down. They skidded back across the chair together, flailing.

But now Maggie too abandoned all restraint. She fought with a hailstorm of fists, knees, teeth. Wild as a street punk, yet coldly efficient, she snapped Joyce's finger back until the other woman screamed in pain. The scissors fell. Maggie drove a savage elbow between Joyce's breasts and she screamed again. By the time Len had reached his feet, Maggie had a knee on Joyce's abdomen. She snatched up the scissors and nudged them into the hollow of Joyce's throat. A trickle of red oozed onto the designer collar.

"It's all right, Len," Maggie panted, not looking around. The scratch on her cheek was bright. Joyce lay rigid, unmoving. "Mrs. Banks and I have reached an understanding. We're both going to be ladylike now. Call Mrs. Northrup's number. Brugioni should be there."

Len turned to Nancy. She was leaning white-faced against Stein's desk, Joyce's big bag still dangling from her hand. She gave him a trembly smile. "I'll be okay. Call him."

He picked up the phone. Be right there, said Brugioni's deep voice.

"Now," said Maggie, still focused on Joyce, "would someone please tell me what's going on?"

"I don't know." Len's pulse was jackhammering in his temples, as though he'd been the one fighting. He forced his thoughts into coherence. "I came in early to work on my proposal. There was some problem with the lock, I remember. Maybe it was unlocked already. I came in and everything was normal. But when I went into Joyce's office to leave my work on her desk, someone hit me. I think with the coffeepot. I blacked out for a few minutes. When I came to, Nancy and Joyce were here."

"Joyce hit him," Nancy declared, "and then threatened me with the scissors."

"Mrs. Banks?" Maggie's voice was courteous, but when Joyce tried to shift beneath her, the scissors prodded her throat and Maggie's bony knee ground into her stomach again. Joyce grunted. "Mrs. Banks?" Maggie repeated. "What were you doing?"

Joyce spoke through her teeth to keep her chin from jostling the scissors against her throat. "I was checking to see if anyone had taken anything. The door was unlocked. I did not hit Len."

"That's what she said before." Nancy was scornful. "You saw what she did to me! And you!"

"I was trying to work something out with Len!"

"Work something out?" asked Maggie. But when Joyce remained silent, she said, "We'll come back to that. Len, do you think she hit you?"

"I think she was here already. With that weather out there I would have noticed if someone came in, even if I wasn't looking. And someone sure hit me." He touched the tender place behind his ear and winced. "And some-one moved the medical record. It was on Joyce's desk, and now—"

"Are you insane?" Joyce spat at him.

"It was there!"

"Len, don't." Joyce lay rigid on the floor, still wary of the scissors and of Maggie's immobilizing knee, yet she seemed more afraid of Len. "I'll meet your terms!"

"My terms? Why do you keep talking about—"

"Freeze! And drop those scissors!"

The uniformed officer came bursting through the door into a combat crouch, gun leveled at Maggie. His black rain gear rivered water into the soggy carpet.

Maggie didn't take her eyes from Joyce. "Len, is it a real cop?"

"Yes." Len could see the patrol car outside, the second officer approaching the door. "Real gun too."

"Okay." She rose slowly and tossed the scissors across the room away from Joyce before lifting her hands. The second policeman briskly patted her down and then turned to help Joyce to her feet.

"Are you all right, ma'am?"

"For the most part." Joyce could not hide the sly triumph in her glance at Maggie. "Thank God you came, Officer! This woman ambushed me!" She stood erect, though pale. Len could see the marks of teeth on her arm, and she cradled her right hand in her left.

"Let's have everyone's name," demanded the second policeman coldly.

Lieutenant Brugioni, with Cleary on his heels, pushed open the door. "Hello, Steve," he rumbled, raising an eyebrow at the gun. "What's going on?"

"Young lady here was attacking this older lady with the scissors."

"And why was that, Miss Ryan?" Sounding mildly intrigued, Brugioni motioned to Cleary, who promptly pulled out his notebook.

"Because she attacked Nancy Selden." Hands still held high, Maggie gestured at Nancy with her chin.

Brugioni's flat intelligent eyes inspected Nancy. "Glad to meet you, Miss Selden. I'm Lieutenant Brugioni. And why did Mrs. Banks attack you?"

Joyce stirred, indignant. "I didn't attack her. I just wanted to talk to them."

"Mm. Difference of opinion here. What do you say, Steve?"

"Young lady was attacking the other lady."

"Why don't we start at the beginning? Who was here first?"

Len licked his lips. "Joyce, I think. I arrived a bit after seven. The door was unlocked already. I did some work at my desk, then took it into Joyce's office. I started to put it on her desk and then someone clobbered me, I think with the coffeepot."

"And I think he stumbled and hit his head on the desk," declared Joyce. "He was here first."

Len stared at her, trying to untangle the workings of the mind behind the pale tense mask of her face. "Then why is the coffeepot on the floor in there?" he demanded, but she only shrugged. "Anyway," he continued stubbornly, "when I came to a few minutes later, Joyce was here, and Nancy too." He went through the familiar story once again. Nancy chimed in with her observations, but Joyce shook her head.

"Mrs. Banks, you don't agree?" asked Brugioni.

"When I arrived, Mr. Trager was already here, unconscious. The important thing is that Miss Ryan attacked me." She started to gesture with her right hand but halted, smothering a wince.

Brugioni's appraising glance was full of sympathy. This was not going right at all, Len thought. He protested, "But it was Joyce who attacked us!"

"That's not what the officer saw."

"She knocked me out! Threatened Nancy with those scissors!" Even as he said it, Len realized how unlikely it sounded: well-groomed, businesslike, rich Joyce Banks doing all that? Even mussed by Maggie's pummeling, Joyce retained her formidable dignity. But Maggie was studying her, eyes narrowed, and Len understood that the battle between those two was not finished yet.

"Those are ridiculous accusations!" Joyce declared.

"We'll see," Maggie said quietly. "Here come the men in the white hats. I hope."

A neat, dark-haired young man in a bright yellow slicker entered. Behind him, Len saw Nick swiftly take in the scene: his wife with bloodied cheek, torn dress, hands high before a policeman's gun. At a nod from Maggie, he asked unbelievingly, "In front of everybody?"

"You bet!" said Maggie vehemently.

Nick turned his attention back to the young man, who was pulling a thin bundle of manila folders from under his slicker and asking, "How is this supposed to help?"

"Check the names on the records Denny left," Nick instructed him. "You'll see the name is right."

"Joyce Banks?" said the young man dubiously. He shuffled through the folders, stopped at one, and whistled softly through his teeth. "Son of a gun."

"She's also Mrs. Gordon Banks."

The young man's face came to life. "Jesus! Well, Denny always said a couple of these folders would set him up for life. But I don't—"

"Just a minute," interrupted Brugioni. "*Who* are *you*?"

"Curt Pritchard. I was real close to Dennis Burns."

"And you know something about his death?"

"Not much. A week ago Tuesday night he got a call. He was supposed to like meet somebody the next morning. He told me to take care of these folders for him. And he said he was supposed to go like disguised. He put on a black wig and preened around in it a little, joking. And early the next morning he grabbed the wig and the bottle of wine and went off. He was like feeling good, you know? And he never came back."

Brugioni nodded at the folders. "What are they?"

"Denny's dad was a gynecologist. These are copies of some medical records he kept. Denny took the originals."

"This is ridiculous!" Joyce lunged toward Curt. But Maggie, hands still held high, gazing attentively out the window as though the answer to her problems lay somewhere in the rain-swept streets, stuck out a lanky leg and neatly snagged Joyce's ankle. Joyce stumbled to her knees. Cleary helped her back to the chair.

"Hey, settle down," said Brugioni to both of them; then, "Go on, Mr. Pritchard."

"He was going to like sell the originals back to people. But I don't know why. Like what is this crap?" He tapped the top folder. "Fibroadenoma 1950, tubal ligation 1951, fibroadenoma 1953, endometrial biopsy 1960, Rubin test 1961—what does all that mean?"

"This is ridiculous!" Joyce exclaimed. She was poised taut on the edge of her chair, held back only by Cleary's proximity. "Lieutenant, I need medical attention. Why don't you arrest this young woman for assaulting me and find out about the young man's problem later? It couldn't have anything to do—" She trailed off at the malevolent triumph in Maggie's eyes.

"I've got a glimmer, Lieutenant," Maggie announced. "Len, that party was the Bankses'—what? Fifteenth anniversary?"

"Yes." Len was mystified.

Nick was frowning at Maggie in consternation. "What about that meeting?" he asked her.

With an impatient shake of her head, she continued, "So they married in, let's see, 1957."

Joyce was looking at Maggie in terror. Len saw that somehow Maggie—hands still raised before the gun—had won. Joyce whispered, "Please!"

But Maggie's frosty gaze was implacable. "You think you're the only one who can hit below the belt? No, ma'am!" she said. Len saw Nick's eyes narrow in appalled comprehension. Maggie turned to Brugioni. "Joyce was sterilized in 1951, Lieutenant. And married Gordon Banks six years later."

"Wait a minute," said Len. This couldn't be right. "They wanted kids! That can't be Joyce on that record. Gordon said he probably wouldn't have married again at all, but he wanted kids!"

"Right!" said Nick.

Len shook his head doggedly. "You're trying to say it's blackmail. Well, it can't be that. Gordon said Joyce was disappointed when her doctor couldn't find anything wrong to treat. They did tests. And the doctor's name wasn't Burns. It was Dr.—not Dr. Gable. Clark, that's it. Dr. Clark."

"Yeah," said Curt. "Dr. Clark Burns. Denny's dad."

"Dr. Clark Burns?" repeated Len stupidly.

"Right," said Nick scornfully. "The Rex Morgan of Flatbush. Joyce's dear old doctor. And Denny's noble dad."

"Put your hands down, Miss Ryan. And you, put that gun away," said Brugioni irritably. Maggie moved around to stand behind Nick and Curt, peering at the folders. "I'll take that," Brugioni snapped, jerking the top one from

Curt's hands and inspecting it. "So Dennis Burns was going to blackmail her? Because she didn't want her husband to know about this?"

"See, his dad started it," explained Curt. "When his practice started falling apart, he really needed money bad so he went back to his old records from Brooklyn. Found some people who like didn't want to have things about them known. He'd been picking up a little money for years that way. Denny didn't approve, really. But when he found out what a bitch it is to get work acting—well, he wanted to do well for Amy, you see."

Brugioni looked up from the folder. "But this record is labeled Douglas F. Kilmer."

Nick said, "Celebrity fill-in-the-blanks. Douglas F. is Douglas Fairbanks, so you get Banks in the blank. And Kilmer is—"

"Joyce." Brugioni nodded. "I've been to school too." He glanced at Curt. "You say Dennis took the originals of these with him?"

Len said, "The original of that one is in Joyce's handbag."

"What?"

"It was on her desk when I went into her office," Len said. "Douglas F. Kilmer. When I came to, it was gone. Then I saw it in her bag." He indicated the handbag that Nancy still held. She opened it and pulled out the folder. Brugioni glanced from it to Curt's copy, then turned to Joyce.

"Do you want to say anything? You have the right to remain silent."

Joyce raised her head. Len was astonished to see tears streaking her usually flawless makeup. Nick glanced at Maggie in consternation. Joyce said dully, "The only reason to remain silent is gone now."

"You want to call your lawyer?"

In her grief she didn't seem to comprehend. "If only—is there any way to keep it from Gordon?"

"I'm sorry, Mrs. Banks." Brugioni's deep voice was surprisingly gentle. "Do you want a lawyer?"

"No, why? I'll try to explain." Slumped in Renata's chair, knees together, hands clasped. Her streaked face and bloody collar gave her the air of an unfortunate schoolgirl called before the principal for some mischief or other. "It was because of my sister Jeanne. We were swimmers, you know."

"Olympic-class," murmured Maggie.

"Yes. We beat most of the medalists, at one time or another. We worked so hard. She was a year younger but we were like twins. We trained together, long, long days. Happy days. We promised each other we would win the Olympics and then become very, very rich." She blinked down at her damaged hand. "And then—well, swimmers aren't necessarily puritans, you know. I'm not even sure who the boy was. But something went terribly wrong—you wouldn't understand!" she hurled angrily at Maggie.

"I'm trying," Maggie said.

Joyce studied her a moment, perhaps found the hint of compassion she was searching for. She went on, "We were training hard that spring. And suddenly one day she got a bad cramp. At first we thought it was a muscle or something. But it got worse. She was pale. She said, 'Joyce, this is it. You'd better go on and win for me too.' And by the time the ambulance got there she was so far into shock they couldn't save her."

"What happened?" Nancy's voice was very small.

"Ectopic pregnancy. Ruptured and killed her."

Nancy bit her lower lip. Len cupped her hand in both of his and saw that Nick had gripped Maggie's too.

Brugioni cleared his throat. "This was a long time ago, Mrs. Banks."

She said, "I couldn't train anymore, of course. Couldn't concentrate. That was the end of the Olympics. Best I could do was a bronze in one event. But one thing I vowed: I couldn't let it happen to me. I had goals to fulfill for both of us now. So when I heard about a nearby doctor who did—things—for people, I went to him and had myself sterilized. Then I set out to win the world for Jeanne."

"You did it, too," said Maggie, softly.

"Pretty near. Head to head with men, and I won. On their grounds. Because they couldn't hurt me the way they'd hurt Jeanne. You're very foolish, you know," she added to Maggie.

Maggie's lips tightened. She crossed her arms and stared out into the rain. The others were silent, watching Joyce. Len could imagine her as a young woman, flinging herself into the business world with all the competitive hunger of a fine athlete joining with the vengeful thwarted rage of a grieving sister.

"Well, I accomplished a lot. But not what Jeanne and I had dreamed. And then Gordon happened along. He liked my looks, and I could use his wealth. So I thought, 'Hey, Jeanne, we've won.'"

"And that's why you married him?" asked Maggie, still gazing out the window. "As a sort of trophy to prove you'd defeated the male gender?"

"Listen, things were not that easy in the fifties! It's easier now. In the fifties you'd have been home in an apron, young lady. You'd have been defeated!"

"I doubt that." Nick stepped in hastily, heading off Maggie's retort. "But in fact your marriage lasted."

"Gordon is a good business partner. We speak the same language, in a way. He understands what I'm trying to do."

"Except that no children came."

"Yes. I couldn't get him past that. Gordon just doesn't give up easily. He insisted on the Rubin test and those other ghastly fertility things. So I hurried back to Dr. Burns and offered money if he'd cooperate. He smiled and took it. Did the tests and reported to Gordon that the problem was beyond scientific comprehension, just happened that way sometimes. When Gordon finally accepted the story I thought it was all over." A bitter smile twisted her lips. "A few months later I got my first letter from the good doctor. He wanted to move to Westchester, he said, and needed a little help with his mortgage payments. So all that started."

"Look, I still don't understand," Maggie said. "You didn't care about your marriage except economically. Why didn't you quietly get some assets transferred to your control and then tell your husband about it? Get back at the blackmailer by exposing him? Get back at your husband for being the same sex as the guy who ruined Jeanne?"

"I thought of that, of course." Hands clasped in her lap, Joyce looked up at Maggie. "But the strangest thing had happened. It—well, the closest way to describe it might be to say that after all those years Gordon had become my best friend. It was funny. I really cared about him. I didn't want him to be hurt."

Len thought of Gordon Banks in his lush penthouse garden, mourning for his unconceived heirs, and suddenly felt sickened by what lay ahead for the sharp old man.

Brugioni said, "What about Dennis Burns?"

"I didn't even know that the doctor had died. But a couple of months ago I got a note from Dennis. Introducing himself and giving a new address. And quadrupling the size of the payments."

"Ah," said Brugioni. Cleary was scribbling rapidly in his book. "So you asked to meet him?"

"Meet him?" Joyce seemed puzzled.

"To work out more reasonable payments, maybe?"

She frowned at Brugioni, then with quick wariness at Len and Maggie. "So that's it—no, I never met him. I could afford what he was asking. And just a couple of weeks after the first payoff to him, you told me he was the one who'd been killed. So again I thought it was over."

Brugioni exchanged a sharp glance with Cleary. "You're saying you didn't meet him?"

"I didn't meet him. Ever."

"Even so, Mrs. Banks, you'll understand that we'll have to take you in for questioning."

"Questioning? You think that—" Joyce shook her head in weary disbelief. "It makes no difference now. But, Lieutenant, this is ridiculous. Last weekend someone called me. Used the same words Dennis Burns used. It was like hearing a ghost. It told me to unlock the office at six-thirty this morning and leave a money order for ten thousand dollars on a desk, and I'd get my medical file back. I wasn't to return before seven-forty-five. Well, I followed instructions. One does. When I arrived at a quarter to eight the money was gone and the folder was there. But Len was still lying there because he'd somehow knocked himself out. Don't you see? *He's* the blackmailer! And where could he have gotten that folder? Only from Dennis Burns!"

"Joyce, you're crazy!" Len was stunned by the vicious accusation. "You're making this up! You got that folder when you met Burns!"

Joyce's eyes flared open. "Do you want me to say 'uncle'? Doesn't Gordon have enough to bear?" She turned to Brugioni in desperate appeal. "Look, Lieutenant, I don't

kill people! My God, why don't you charge Len? Not me!
You might as well charge Sergeant Cleary, or that bag lady
out there! Not me! I don't kill people!"

"You tried to stab me, and now you're trying to convince
us that you don't kill people?" demanded Maggie.

"I wouldn't have—look, I had to arrange terms with a
blackmailer! Len was about to ruin everything I'd done for
Jeanne, and for Gordon—" She slumped back into the
chair, a hand hiding her ravaged face.

"Well, now, Mrs. Banks—" Brugioni rumbled uncom-
fortably.

Maggie seemed suddenly weary. "Oh, hell, enough of
this. Lieutenant, excuse me, better not arrest her. Joyce
Banks didn't murder Dennis Burns."

"What do you mean?" squawked Len. "You just heard
her *admit* how he was blackmailing her! How she'd be
better off without him! And, my God, you *saw* her attack
Nancy! And attack you too!"

"Oh, yes, that's all true," Maggie agreed. "I'm not saying
she's nice. She packs a mean pair of scissors when she's
upset, and if she ever tries it with me again I'll kick her
face in. But she's right about one thing." She jerked a
thumb toward the rain-streaked window. "That bag lady
did it."

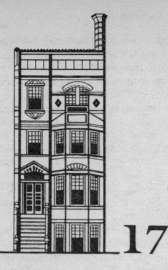

17

"Miss Ryan, you've been very helpful, but this is no time for joking!" Exasperation laced Brugioni's deep tone.

"Well, shouldn't you at least talk to her? She was out there before I arrived. She must have seen whoever came in and out."

"We can talk to her later."

"It's wet out there. It's an act of charity to bring her in."

"Maybe so, but we have to go over Mrs. Banks's statement very carefully. We'd better get started."

"Still, you don't want to go arresting Mrs. Gordon Banks until you've checked everything pretty damn carefully," Maggie pointed out.

Brugioni looked pained. He stared out at the sluicing rain and sighed. "Go haul her in, Steve. Let's see if she can throw any light on the comings and goings here."

It took some convincing and considerable gesticulating, but the officer succeeded at last in coaxing the old woman to the shelter of the office. She halted just inside the doorway, clutching a bundle wrapped in torn plastic and blinking blearily at them. A tattered sweater and soaked sneakers clothed her stocky body, and a black plastic trash bag hooded her head and shoulders.

"You must be glad to get out of that rain," said Maggie warmly. "Here, I'll take your cape." Before the woman could react, Maggie had whisked off the plastic and draped it over the puddling umbrellas.

"My cape," murmured the old woman uneasily. Her mouth made little smacking movements that reminded Len of a guppy.

"It'll be fine," Brugioni reassured her. "Look, dear, what's your name?"

"Sukie."

"Have you been out there long?" Brugioni spoke slowly, as if to a child.

"Dunno. All night."

"And did you see people coming into this office?"

"Yeah. Sure."

"Who?"

Almost as if reciting, she chanted, "Young guy first. Then tall blond lady. Then little blond lady. Then brunette."

Len tried to remember if he had seen her in her doorway shelter when he arrived. No, but then he was busy balancing the bagel and coffee, and trying to unlock a door that Joyce had already unlocked. He could have missed her. Face it, he could have missed King Kong.

"Then"—the ruined old face puckered and the lips smacked—"there was a fight. Then lots of cops. See?" She bestowed a gappy grin on the officers. The one called Steve grinned back.

Maggie took advantage of her distraction to yank the bundle from her arms. "Here, put this down. Nick will guard it for you."

"No! No!" Panicked, the old woman lunged forward, but Maggie evaded her grimy hands and flipped the parcel behind her back to Nick, who fielded it neatly.

"Miss Ryan, this isn't necessary!" exclaimed Brugioni.

"Look, Lieutenant," said Maggie, pointing to the old woman's legs. "Support hose." Brugioni opened his mouth to protest. "And look at her sweater. Len, whose sweater is this?"

Len inspected the ragged garment, pilling and unraveling, sloppily darned with darker yarn, and recognition dawned. "My God!"

"That's the one Mrs. Northrup wears!" exclaimed Joyce, again sitting upright, at attention.

"Good to see you two agreeing," said Maggie. "This

sweater was still under Mrs. Northrup's vanity table as late as Monday night. Saw it myself."

Brugioni studied the old woman carefully. "Sukie, can you tell us where you got your sweater?"

She looked at him vacantly. "Trash can."

"Where?"

"Dunno. Over on Garfield."

"Good answer," Maggie admitted. "Now let's get down to business, Mrs. McGuire. Curt, read off the record for the Hepburn sisters."

The old woman's face decomposed into a look of disbelief and then panic. She tucked her chin into Mrs. Northrup's unspeakable sweater and whirled to charge at the door like a football lineman. Cleary, the nearest, grabbed the handle, but it was all he could do to hold it closed against her furious attack.

Curt said, "Hepburn sisters. Sisters means—Andrews Sisters, right? No, wait, you said McGuire. McGuire Sisters!"

"Go on," Maggie nodded.

"It says, born 1943."

"She's older than that," said Nick, frowning dubiously at the old woman, now slumped against the doorjamb.

"It's her daughter Audrey's record," explained Maggie.

"Born 1943," repeated Curt. "In 1958, gonorrhea . . . 1959, diaphragm . . . 1959, trichomoniasis . . . 1960, gonorrhea. God, that's a lot of VD, isn't it?"

"Especially for the fifties," said Maggie. "Especially for someone in high school at the time. Especially for someone who's now married to a religious fundamentalist."

"McGuire," said Brugioni thoughtfully, looking down at the crumpled old woman. "When I met you, you were wearing glasses and a sweatshirt. Cleary, wasn't Mrs. Northrup just telling us about her friend Pauline McGuire?"

Cleary thumbed back through his notebook. "Yes. Went on and on. She said, let's see, her friend Pauline McGuire was in Utah visiting her daughter, Audrey."

The bag lady had gone ashen. She was still slumped against the door blocked by Cleary, but her face had turned slowly toward Brugioni. She licked her lips. "Northrup?" she asked hoarsely. "You—talked to her?"

"Teach has been renovated. Good as new, and chattering away to the detectives and me," Maggie informed her.

"Go on, Sergeant," said Brugioni.

"She mentioned Audrey's husband was paying Mrs. McGuire's rent. Said Audrey's husband thought Audrey was pure as the driven snow. And, let's see, the only other thing was that she was supposed to water Mrs. McGuire's plants because they dried out daily, and they hadn't been watered since Sunday."

"And were they dried out, Sergeant?" asked Maggie.

Cleary said, "I didn't look. Thought she was just rambling on."

"I looked," Brugioni admitted. "The soil was moist. You're suggesting that Mrs. McGuire has been in Mrs. Northrup's apartment?"

Maggie shrugged. "Motive. Sweater. Begonias. False alibi."

Len was looking back and forth between Joyce and the old woman. "I don't know what to believe!" he said.

"Len, think a minute," said Maggie impatiently. "Dennis Burns was killed before ten or so Wednesday morning, right, Lieutenant?"

"That's what the medical examiner says."

"And he was seen alive by Curt at eight-thirty and by Mrs. Northrup at nine. Well, Len, where was Joyce between nine and ten Wednesday morning?"

Len tried not to look stupid. "Here," he said sheepishly. "At our regular Wednesday meeting. Joyce, we alibi each other."

But Joyce was rising slowly from her chair, eyes locked on Maggie in unbelieving anguish. "You knew! You knew all along that I didn't kill him! And you made him read that—that—Why did you do it?"

Maggie's bony fingers smoothed the front of her slashed skirt. "I'm not real good at turning the other cheek," she explained, and Joyce's eyes fell.

Brugioni cleared his throat. "Mrs. McGuire, do you want to tell us about it?"

The old woman huddled in the doorway, shaking her head, clutching the frayed edges of the sweater. She was silent.

"You'll need a lawyer," said Maggie. "But it's easy enough to see what happened. Your daughter had a wild, promiscuous adolescence. You did your best, found a doctor who would treat VD and prescribe birth control for unmarried girls. Not easy to find such doctors in the fifties, and you ended up where Joyce did. At last Audrey found Jesus and also found a priggish young fellow with a good head for business. He's an ideal son-in-law—when you were evicted he came up with the extra rent that you needed to stay in this neighborhood. The only problem was that Dr. Burns threatened to send him the record of Audrey's wild oats. You had to pay him to keep quiet. To keep her renovated reputation clean. Right so far?"

"I want a lawyer."

"Right. Then young Dennis inherited the records. And asked you to quadruple the payments."

"He was a pig, a drunken young hippie! He didn't care about breaking up families, about people getting thrown out of their homes! He had no understanding! I had to protect my family!"

"Hey, hang on a minute, that's pretty heavy!" exclaimed Curt. Nick murmured something to him, and he subsided.

"Did you try to explain to him?" Maggie asked the old woman.

"Yes, he laughed at me. Said I'd find a way. I shouldn't say any more." Her dark eyes squinted fearfully at Brugioni.

"That's okay, we know. You visited Mrs. Northrup last Tuesday and when you went up to tell the plumbers to quiet down so that your meeting could continue, you got the idea of meeting Dennis privately. You rigged the kitchen door to stay unlocked, then called Dennis that night and told him to come disguised early the next morning. Mrs. Northrup saw him arrive by the front door. You must have come out of the back of your building, across the broken fence, and in the kitchen door. Then you unlocked the front door for Dennis. You met him upstairs so you wouldn't be overheard if Teach came back early from her errands. But he wouldn't listen to reason. You got the bottle somehow—"

"I finally told him I'd get the money for him, and he laughed and handed me that bottle, said we should drink on it. I took it, and then, when he looked out the window—" She stopped and studied her sodden sneakers. "It had just been a fantasy, but—"

"Yes. I understand."

"He fell down. And I was frightened but then—he looked dead, and I thought, I'm free! Just like my fantasy. Free!"

"That's what I thought when I heard he was dead," Joyce murmured.

"But then he moaned a little," Pauline McGuire continued. "So I couldn't let him live. Audrey was trying so hard, everything was finally going right—And then I was really afraid. I took his I.D. and the folders, and his wig, and the hose, and ran away out the kitchen door. But on my way out I dropped the pantyhose somehow. And I couldn't get back in to look for them. It was an awful night."

"Next day was Thursday," Maggie said. "We found the body. You came around as soon as the police arrived."

"I had to know what was happening. And I wanted to look for the hose, but I didn't see them and couldn't hunt very thoroughly."

"But you had good luck," said Nick. "Because when the lieutenant gave back Len's keys, he just dropped them on the bookcase by the door. You managed to palm them because Len was as distracted as the rest of us."

"God, that was stupid of me!" Len exclaimed.

"Should have handed them to you directly." Brugioni looked discomfited too.

"So, as soon as you could, you came back to hunt for the lost weapon," Maggie continued. "But just when you were beginning to hope that they'd been permanently lost, because the police weren't asking about them specifically, you decided to attack Mrs. Northrup. Did you know she'd found them?"

"She said she knew something about the weapon."

"But she thought Mr. Lund had left the hose to frame her. How was she a danger to you?"

"She's smart," said Mrs. McGuire simply. "She would have figured it out."

"She did figure it out," said Brugioni. "Why else would she tell us so much about you?"

"Yes, see? And when I found her searching the building on her own, I knew I had to do something." She gave a sudden sob.

Brugioni looked longingly at the tattered plastic-wrapped bundle that Nick had placed on Len's desk. "We'll need to question you, Mrs. McGuire. May we look in your package?"

"No! I want a lawyer."

There was a crash. "Whoops," said Nick blandly, "clumsy of me."

The contents of the bundle had spilled onto Len's desk. Glasses, a sweatshirt, half a dozen manila folders with the now-familiar medical records stapled to them, a set of keys with an amber tag, a wet black wig.

Joyce stared at the medical records. "Those are the originals!" she exclaimed. "That means—you're the blackmailer, not Len! You called me last weekend! You took my money this morning!"

"And you were still here when Len arrived." Nancy stepped forward so indignantly that Len touched her arm lightly to calm her. "You panicked, and hit him! Just like you hit Dennis!"

"I want a lawyer," repeated Pauline McGuire, hiding her face.

"Mrs. McGuire, I would like to warn you . . ." Brugioni began to recite the Miranda warning in a flat voice.

They took her away in the squad car. Curt and Joyce were asked to make statements immediately. The rain was abating as they watched them go. Maggie looked at her watch and sank into Renata's chair. "God! Not even eight-thirty! What a morning!"

Len reached shyly for Nancy's hand. "You feel like going to work?"

"Sure. But, Len, what does this do to you? To your job?"

"Well, it may be a little hard to go on working with Joyce." He was surprised at his own equanimity. Last week this problem would have set him floundering. Now he was no longer envisioning his life as Joyce's salesman, but as his own boss. He said, "It's a complication, sure. But I've got a damn good proposal. If it doesn't work out with her, I'll show it to Fred and his doctors."

At the door Nick gave a last fatherly wave to the departing Curt and turned back into the office. "Maggie! What's wrong?"

Len looked at her too. Slouched in the chair, the scissors slash still red on her cheek, she looked vacant, gazing luminously into the distance as though stunned. Nick reached her in two strides. "What's wrong?" he repeated.

"Nothing's wrong." She focused in on him, smiled a little. "Everything's right." She took his hand and placed it carefully on the blue fabric across her belly. In a second his face became rapt too, and the two remained entranced, oblivious, in intense communion with the first flutters of the quickening life within her.

Nancy's hand tightened in Len's. "I don't know about now," she said softly, "but we ought to have kids someday."

"Yeah. I don't know about now either. But it's time we started talking about it. Come on, I'll walk you to work."

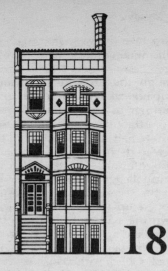

18

Nick pulled out his keys as he turned into Garfield Place. The cool November air had an edge that promised colder things to come. Never-resting time leads summer on to hideous winter. As he approached the steps he saw a well-bundled Julia Northrup emerging from her door under the stoop.

"Hi, Teach!"

"You bastard!" She eyed him severely. "Saw you go up in flames on TV last night. And good riddance!"

"Hey, you hated me! Good!"

"I just hope Vic Jr. didn't watch. He'd try to rescue me out from under your roof again."

"Any dutiful son would. What's that you're carrying?"

"Just arrived. I'm taking it over to show Ellie." With a bashfulness that Nick found winning, Julia held out the little book. Leafy trees, an impish Victorian boy. *Fred-Law Grows Up*.

"Congratulations!" Nick bent to enclose her in an exuberant hug. "I'll send champagne!"

"You still think I'm a wino at heart," she grumbled, pleased.

"Who are you going to write about next?"

"I'm tired of men. Thought I'd do Sarah Bernhardt."

"I'm honored."

"You blasted Irishmen always take things so personally," Julia sniffed, and marched off. Smiling, Nick went up the steps to unlock his own door.

Inside was disaster. Through the arch to the living room, two-by-fours and old paneling lay splintered and jumbled across the floor. Peelings of stripped wallpaper curled down like stalactites from the ceiling above Maggie's hastily abandoned stepladder. It had looked like this for weeks. The Vietnam approach to decorating, Maggie had said, bemused. Destroy the place in order to save it.

But he'd gotten the kitchen installed, though not painted; and two of the bedrooms on the second floor were clean and freshly white. Nick scooped up the glad little black dog that was scrambling down the stairs on short legs to meet him, informed her that she was not much of a housekeeper, and carried her upstairs. A neat stack of papers labeled "Grant Proposal: Check with Dan" sat next to Maggie's briefcase on the hall table. Nick put down the dog and leaned against the doorframe of the smaller bedroom.

Maggie was sitting on the rug, wearing blue jeans and nothing else, and crooning softly, something Irish. When she saw him her eyes smiled at him, but she didn't stop singing. Nestled against her breast, a drowsy infant suckled sporadically as it drifted into the last stages of euphoric slumber.

She finished the song and removed the sleepy little mouth from her nipple experimentally. Opaque dark eyes twitched open. Maggie stood up, smoothly, and held the limp happy baby upright against her shoulder. It belched with total commitment. She smiled proudly.

"Sarah stinks," she announced to Nick. "I'd better change her before I take my stuff to the office."

"I'll do it," he said, holding out his arms.

There was the familiar hesitation, just an instant. She was always reluctant to give her up. She'd even made a scene in the delivery room, when, exhausted and bloody, she'd punched and bitten the nurse who had tried unsuccessfully to take Sarah away from her to be dried and examined. But, more reasonable now with Nick, Maggie handed him the baby. "Try not to wake her too much."

"Right." He gazed down at the scrap of satisfied humanity drowsing in the crook of his arm. Maggie smiled and went into the other bedroom to dress.

Nick removed the diaper, cleaned the fat little bottom, and slipped on the fresh clothing. Fleetingly, his daughter awoke and looked at him stupidly, her fists momentarily churning before the enormous eyes closed again. He was in awe of her. Tiny tough little creature, full of fierce instincts for feeding and digesting, learning and sleeping, growing and loving. Right now sleep was in the ascendant. He laid her in the crib on her stomach. Her head turned sideways, the tender mouth opened, the breathing became regular and contented. His hairy hand could cover her whole back. He tucked a cotton blanket around her gently.

Maggie was watching him from the door, grinning at his foolish primal pride in the small greedy animal he had helped create. "Do you feel like a dad, love?"

"Maybe." His finger brushed a wispy curl. "I feel connected. To her, to you. To the future. To the past, my own parents. To the renovation of the whole damn human race."

"Yes." His words had made her sad. "It's too bad when that connection is betrayed. Too bad it can't always be like this."

He thought of Dennis Burns's warped inheritance from an alcoholic father, of Joyce Banks's dishonest marriage, of Pauline McGuire's twisted attempt to protect her child, and put a grateful arm around Maggie. "Yes. But then few things in life are like this."

"Yes." She bowed her head onto his shoulder. "Very, very few."

P. M. Carlson is the author of four previous Maggie Ryan mysteries: AUDITION FOR MURDER, MURDER IS ACADEMIC, MURDER IS PATHOLOGICAL, and REHERSAL FOR MURDER. Her newest Maggie Ryan novel, MURDER IN THE DOG DAYS, will be coming from Bantam in January of 1991. Carlson has a Ph.D. in Psychology and, like Maggie Ryan, she lives in a Victorian house in Brooklyn that she has renovated.

If you enjoyed Maggie Ryan in
MURDER UNRENOVATED,
you will enjoy
P. M. Carlson's next mystery,
<u>MURDER IN THE DOG DAYS</u>
also starring Maggie Ryan and
her husband Nick.

▽

Turn the page
for an exciting preview
of the suspensful new
P. M. Carlson mystery,

MURDER IN THE DOG DAYS

∇

The big graying air-conditioner in the window of the so-called city room of the Mosby *Sun-Dispatch* groaned piteously. Olivia Kerr scribbled a last correction into a pre-release story about the filming of *All the President's Men,* leaned back in her chair, and stared at the machine suspiciously. For ten days it had been laboring, with only partial success, to convert the polluted ninety-eight degree Virginia haze outdoors into livable air. "When that thing goes on strike," Olivia declared, pointing at it accusingly with a freckled finger, "I do too."

Nate Rosen switched off his tape recorder, peered around the edge of his cubicle and nodded. His thin, mournful face looked longer every day as his hair receded a bit further. "I'll be right on your heels," he agreed, with a worried glance at the suffering air conditioner.

"This heat wave is a killer."

"Not a metaphor," he informed her, tapping the page he was working on. "Guy up in New York got shot in a fight over a fire hydrant. And he's the third this weekend."

"God. I wish I could say I can't understand people

fighting over trivial stuff like that. But right now I can," said Olivia. "I'm glad I'm off to the beach."

Nate raised his eyebrows. "Aren't you afraid you'll get freckled?"

"Hey, one more crack like that and I'll ask you if you aren't worried about getting bald."

"Don't rub it in, O cruel maid," grumbled Nate, turning back to his keyboard.

Olivia pulled the barrette from her humidity-frizzed hair. In romantic moods Jerry called it chestnut-colored. Of course he'd also been known to point out that it matched the stain in the sink. The lout. The only possible response had been to whack him with a pillow. Olivia grinned to herself. The resulting pillow fight had quickly turned bawdy. Very bawdy. With Jerry romantic moods came in a lot of different flavors.

She twisted her hair up away from the nape of her neck and clipped the barrette across it. Then she stood, tossed the strap of her bag over her shoulder, and went to look out the window. Jerry wasn't down there yet. Today only a few people had ventured out, shuffling sweaty and exhausted along the sidewalk through the unmoving pool of sultry, half-toxic air.

The door of the managing editor's office opened and a round woman arrayed in black came out, smiling and nodding behind her. She hadn't been smiling when she went in. Edgerton had smoothed some more feathers. Well, that's one of the things editors did. Olivia looked out the window for Jerry again.

"Hey, Liv!"

Damn. "Yeah?" she answered, turning reluctantly from the window.

Edgerton was pudgy, moist-lipped, imperious. "Wire service just sent in some more on the Joanne Little trial. Work it into the story." A yellow page from a legal pad dangled from his plump outstretched hand.

Olivia's conscience told her she'd better not bolt for the door. Damn conscience. Doing the rewrites on the Little story and writing the associated features was her chance to break out of the women's pages. True, Edgerton had given her the assignment with the assumption that it was a feminist issue. But it had already grown beyond that. She crossed the room to take the paper. "What is this?" she asked, trying to decipher Edgerton's uninhibited scrawl.

"Kunstler just got out of jail. Had a few choice words about Judge Hobgood." Edgerton puffed the information at her close range, blanketing her with coffee breath.

Olivia stepped back, wondering how he'd got the woman in black to look so happy. Maybe she had an olfactory problem. "I'll bet he did." Why couldn't they keep Kunstler locked up until she'd left for the day? She hurried back to her cubicle and grabbed her copy of the story. What a circus this case had turned into! Joanne Little admitted stabbing her jailer with an ice pick; the trial was meant to determine whether or not she had done it in self-defense when he tried to rape her. But the spicy ingredients of race, sex, and Southern justice had turned it into a national extravaganza. Joanne Little's defense team played to the visiting reporters with relish. This morning they had attempted to add the famed New York lawyer William Kunstler to the team, but Kunstler had promptly insulted the judge and been jailed instead.

"You should have made a run for it," said Nate when Edgerton was safely back in his office.

"Nah. This is the best story he's ever let me handle." She cranked paper into her typewriter. "Biggest thing he ever gave me before was Ann Lander's divorce."

"What about Patty Hearst?"

"Dale Colby had that while it was hot. He didn't assign it to me until it was dead. But if they ever find her I'll be set."

"So what? Good stories don't pay any better, and the hours are worse. Don't know why you bother."

"You want to know why?" Olivia squinted at Edgerton's scrawled notes. "Because when they make the movie, I want Robert Redford to play *me*." She ignored Nate's snort and settled down to type.

In fact, she decided grudgingly, Edgerton was right. This new quote made the story better. Kunstler, upon being released, had said about the judge, "I think the man is determined to see this woman convicted by any means necessary, in violation of his oath as well as the Constitution, and that constitutes in my mind a criminal act." Nice. Manipulative, of course; Kunstler knew what newshounds wanted. So all over America, people like Olivia were putting it into the papers and TV news, maybe publicizing the very real difficulties of black women in the South, maybe just publicizing Kunstler. Every now and then Olivia wondered uneasily if it was Joanne Little or North Carolina that was really on trial. But what the hell, North Carolina had never even ratified the constitutional amendment giving women the vote. Olivia typed in the quote. Take that, North Carolina.

Beyond the wheezing of the air-conditioner, she became aware of music somewhere outside. Sixties music, guitar, and the sweet blended harmonies of Peter, Paul and Mary singing "Puff, the Magic Dragon." Then her attention was distracted by the opening door. A thickset man with a pink complexion, curly brown hair and loosened necktie shoved in. He held the limp jacket of his light summer suit tossed back over his shoulder. "Hey, Edgerton!" he yelled.

Edgerton stuck his head out of his door. "Hi, Leon. What can I do for you?"

"Get that bastard reporter off my back! That asshole Colby!" the chunky newcomer demanded.

"Colby again? Okay, okay, simmer down. Too hot today to get steamed up. Come on in and tell me the problem." Edgerton, with a scowl at the music drifting in the window, gestured the thickset man into his office and closed the door.

Olivia picked up her revised story and tossed it onto the big central table. Nate was standing at the window now, gazing out with amused eyes. "Who's that?" Olivia whispered to him, jerking her thumb at the closed door.

"Edgy's visitor? That's Leon Moffatt. Colby should

tread lightly. The widow Resler didn't look too happy either."

"The plane crash story?"

"That's the one. Moffatt's father went down in it." Nate pushed the current issue of the *Sun-Dispatch* toward her. Dale Colby's report was on the bottom of the front page, reporting the latest information about a small chartered plane leased to Congressman Knox last January. Olivia skimmed it. She could see why Moffatt and Mrs. Resler were upset. Without actual libel, Dale implied that the survivors of the five victims were better off now than before the crash. Including the Congressman's office. Thin ice there, Dale. But knowing him, she was sure he had plenty to back up his statements. A very careful reporter.

Nate added, "Listen, you're going to the beach with the Colbys today, right? You might just breathe a word in his ear."

"Okay." She picked up her shoulder bag.

"And tell me, Liv, isn't that the love of your life down there now?"

Olivia joined him at the window. "Oh, Jesus Christ."

It was Jerry Ryan all right. Even from the second floor there was no mistaking that lanky build, those black curls. He was standing between his sister Maggie, also lanky and curly-haired, and her brawny, balding husband Nick. With amazing energy for such an oppressive day they were belting out the song about the magic dragon. Olivia giggled. "God, can't turn my back a minute!"

"Pretty good imitation," Nate observed. It was true; Nick was accompanying them expertly with his guitar, and all three were warbling away with gusto. Before them, unaffected by the exhausting sultriness, a tiny girl not yet three was dancing. The heat-wearied passersby forgot their discomfort for a moment to smile at her and at the singers.

Olivia sprinted for the door. "Listen, Nate, when Edgy comes out tell him the story's there on the table. See you tomorrow!" She escaped and ran downstairs.

The heat hit her like a wall when she opened the front door. She was dripping by the time she reached them. They had started on "Blowin' in the Wind." She caught Jerry's eye but he only winked and held up a cautioning hand. "How many times must the cannonballs fly?" he sang. Her little niece, still dancing, was trying to sing too. "Answer blowin' inna wind!" she chirped. Olivia had to smile. She hadn't heard little kids singing those songs for years. It was a whole different age now. No Peter, Paul, and Mary. No Woodstock. No peace marches. All gone. Except maybe for Maggie. Pregnant again, Jerry's sister was recycling an old red maternity T-shirt emblazoned with a peace sign. And recycling the old songs too. Nostalgia time.

The handful of listeners applauded heartily when they finished. Jerry took a sweeping bow and loped over to Olivia. "Hiya, Livid. Aren't we great?"

She tried to contain her smile. "You're a bigger ham than Nick is! And you don't even have the excuse of being an actor."

"Listen, the instant the MD business starts to drag I'll be off like a shot! I mean, this is *fun!* Besides, the Maggot was wearing her peace shirt. How could I resist?"

"Yeah, it's all my fault." Maggie, leading her little daughter, rejoined her brother with a grin. Her eyes with the same laughing jay-blue of Jerry's. "Kid sisters are always to blame. Are you a kid sister, Liv?"

"No, thank God."

"Some people have all the luck. Hey, how's Joanne Little doing?"

"She'll win hands down if her lawyers don't clown around once too often. And speaking of clowning around, are you guys finished? Ready to go pick up the Colbys?"

"Hey, look!" Maggie's husband called gleefully. Nick O'Connor was a big, bald, pleasantly homely man who periodically appeared in TV commercials selling beer or paper towels. Olivia was sorry she hadn't been able to see him in any plays, but they'd all been in New York Right now he was picking coins from the open case where he was about to stow the guitar. He jingled them jubilantly in his hand. "We made seven bucks!"

"Wowee!" Jerry scooped up small Sarah, grabbed Maggie's hand, and capered over to inspect the haul. "We should have left the guitar case right next to the sidewalk!"

Olivia shook her head, got out her keys, and climbed into the driver's seat of the Ford passenger van parked a few steps further up the street. She turned on the air conditioner and tapped the horn. Within seconds the others piled in, still jabbering excitedly about the commercial future of their little quartet.

Dale Colby lived in the Sandford subdivision, a set of nearly identical one-story ranch houses grouped around a small park. A century ago it had been woods and farms traversed by Union soldiers in search of the confederate army. What they'd found was Mosby's irregular cavalry band, who struck and then melted back into their home woods in the best guerrilla tradition. Today the area had a reputation for low prices and good schools, no trace of its bloody past.

Olivia pulled into the driveway behind the Pinto. Donna Colby, a neat, worried-looking blonde, opened the front door for them. "Oh—please come in. Sit down a minute," she said. "Dale's on the phone. He's—well, he's not feeling too well today." She waved them into the immaculate living room with a flutter of her hand.

Olivia said, "Donna, do you remember Jerry? And this is his sister Maggie Ryan. Her husband Nick O'Connor. And this is Sarah."

Donna smiled brightly at their greetings. "Glad to meet you. This is Tina, with the Barbie dolls. Say hello, Tina."

A girl about nine was sitting on the hearth. She looked up and said, "Hi!" She exchanged a solemn glance with Sarah, who trotted over to inspect the dolls. At another nervous wave from Donna, the two men sat in the wing chairs.

Donna continued, "And Josie, with the book. Josie, put your feet down!"

A twelve-year-old girl on the pink-flowered sofa sullenly removed her sandaled feet from the cushions.

Maggie glanced at the book and murmured to the girl, "My favorite character is Gollum. Who's yours, my preciousss?"

Surprised hazel eyes flicked up. Olivia saw the touch of interest before defiance returned. "The Nazgûl," Josie declared.

"Right! The Ringwraiths!" exclaimed Maggie approvingly, perching on the arm of the sofa. "I always wanted to be able to fly too. I still want to be an astronaut."

"Really?"

"Sure. As long as I can still have a hobbit hole. Maybe on the moon."

The girl rewarded her with a tiny cautious grin. "I know where there's a hobbit hole."

Olivia left them to discuss Tolkien and turned back to Donna. "Shall we go rouse Dale?"

"Well—" Donna looked nervously at the hallway that led back to the den. Dale, theoretically on vacation, had been working at home for the last three weeks, doctor's orders, while he adapted to a new medication. But Edgerton, not the easiest of managing editors, continued to send him assignments. Not that Dale would want a real vacation.

"I'll go," Olivia told Donna. "I have something to say to him anyway." She marched through the hall to the last room, a den outfitted with file cabinets and an IBM typewriter that put the old machines in the *Sun-Dispatch* office to shame.

Dale was on the phone. "Of course I'll be discreet, Mrs. Resler. Thanks so much."

"Lying to sources again, Dale?" teased Olivia when he'd replaced the receiver.

He turned in his desk chair, not amused. He was a handsome man with shrewd hazel eyes and sandy hair, but small teeth made his smile seem miserly. "Hello, Olivia."

"How are you?"

"Rotten. As usual."

"It'll gradually improve, Jerry says."

"Yeah. Everyone who isn't going through it says that." He stood up, moving easily, Olivia saw, not the little hesitations and hurries that had characterized his last weeks in the *Sun-Dispatch* office. He'd be back to full-time soon.

Behind Olivia, Tina ran past into her own room across the hall. Little Sarah was right behind her. Dale winced.

"I've got a message for you from Nate," Olivia said.

"Oh?"

"Yeah. Leon Moffatt stopped by to complain to Edgerton about something you were doing."

"Moffatt?" Dale's eyes seemed to brighten.

"Yeah. Mrs. Resler came to complain too. But Moffatt really seemed furious. Edgy whisked him into the office out of earshot. But Nate thought you'd want to know."

"Moffatt! All right!" Dale hurried back to his chair. "Listen, Olivia, I won't be able to—"

"Sunshine on my shoulders," bellowed John Denver's recorded voice from across the hall.

"Goddamn it, Tina, turn that off!" roared Dale, charging to the door so vehemently that Olivia stepped back. In the sudden silence that followed he spotted his wife at the end of the hall. "Donna! Bring me one of those sandwiches you made!"

"A sandwich? But the picnic—"

"I can't go to the beach now! I still feel sick, and this story is getting interesting."

Olivia regarded Dale with amusement. A true reporter. Dale at work was a perfectionist, even rigid, with files that were actually orderly and a strict self-imposed schedule. she could never run her life that way. But she shared the insanity that relegated all things, even sickness and trips to the beach, to a lower order than the demands of a story. Still, she said, "Nate suggested that you go easy."

"Aw, come on, Olivia, you know better than that."

"Yeah. I do."

Donna came hurrying down the hall with a plate containing a wrapped sandwich, a little bag of potato chips, and a mug of coffee. "Dale, the children wanted to go to—"

"Right! Exactly!" He took the plate and plunked it onto the table. "Take them away!"

"You mean go without you?"

"Right."

"But honey, I was hoping you'd get some rest."

"Donna, honey." Dale took her by the shoulders. "I'll take my usual nap, I promise. And if you take my daughters away a few hours, I may even get some work done." He released Donna and rolled his eyes at Olivia. "Never, ever try to work in the same house with kids!"

"Yeah. My niece has already taught me that," Olivia agreed. "Come on, Donna, I guess he's serious."

Donna Colby was not only an immaculate housekeeper but a good organizer. The picnic basket she'd raided for Dale's lunch was packed, towels and toys ready. Nick and Jerry carried them out to the van and lifted Tina into the back seat. Olivia held open the door that led from kitchen to garage while Sarah jumped from the step with Maggie's help. Josie came running back in through the garage, coltish and stiff-legged, and bounded awkwardly past them and across the kitchen.

"What's the rush, honey?" asked Donna, who was picking up the last bag from the kitchen table.

"Tina forgot Ken and Barbie." Josie disappeared into the dining room and the hall beyond. Olivia heard her sandals slapping unevenly on the hardwood floor.

Dale's roar could be heard all the way to the garage. "Damn it, Josie, aren't you gone yet? I'm trying to make a call!" A whoosh, a slam, a click of bolts closing.

Josie, looking small and white, beelined from the bedroom to the garage, Ken and Barbie clutched in her fists. Donna looked after her despairingly, then stepped into the dining room. "We're leaving, honey. Bye."

There was no response. Donna waited a moment, steadying herself with a hand on the wall, then turned and came back into the kitchen with an apologetic smile. "He's really not feeling very well."

Olivia tried to think of something charitable to say. "It's tough to dig up stories even when you're healthy."

"Yes, and there's other pressure. He got a letter this morning from his first wife. I don't know what it said, but—" Donna shrugged. "It's hard for him these days."

"Hard on the kids too," Maggie observed. She and Sarah had negotiated the step and were watching Donna too.

"Yes. I wish the doctor had waited until they were in school before he started this new drug." Donna locked the door and followed them through the hot garage to the van. "They were in camp this summer, but it only lasted through July."

"Well, let's take them to the beach," Maggie said pragmatically, opening the van door. Jerry had turned on the air conditioner. They climbed into the coolness gratefully and headed for Bethany Beach.

▽

Thunderheads came boiling down from the northwest as they finished the picnic dinner. A cool gust of wind hit Olivia's damp back and sent goose bumps running along her skin. "God, that's great!" she exclaimed. "I haven't felt cold for months!" She joined Nick and Maggie, who had started to pick up toys and sandals from the water's edge. "Guess it's time to get back."

"Right," said Nick. "I think Donna will be just as glad."

It was true; they hardly arrived before Donna had sought out a phone to call Dale, though the line was busy so she soon gave up. She had been pleasant, had sat out the swim but had joined in the wild volleyball game that pitted the women—including little Sarah—against Nick and Jerry, who made up for their reduced numbers by shouting sexist comments such as "Here you go, doll babies," or "Hurry up, dainty Maggot!" It had been impossible to keep score, especially since the men insisted that points scored by women were more delicate and therefore smaller than their own robust variety.

Donna had smiled about it too. Afterwards, though, she had seemed restless, as though uncomfortable outside the well-ordered home she ran.

The wind grew stronger. The young children, excited by the looming black clouds, shrieked and ran around. Maggie didn't help by suggesting to Josie that it looked like the arrival of the evil Lord of the Nazgûl on his unholy winged steed. Josie had been quiet all day, refusing to put on her swimsuit and collecting shells and pebbles instead. But she enjoyed this idea and began to instruct Tina and Sarah about ways to save Barbie and Ken from doom. Sidestepping the darting children, the adults threw toys and towels into the van helter-skelter, no trace remaining of Donna's careful packing. Even so the first drops were falling as they finally rounded up Sarah, wriggly and sandy in her little red swimsuit, and closed the van door. The return trip, through heavy rain, was slow. At last they drove through the last of the storm into an oddly cool, cloudy twilight. The world seemed stunned by its sudden scrubbing.

The children were inspired all over again by the wet unfamiliarity of the yard. Tina ran to the side of the garage. "The little house is gone!" she squealed, pointing at the muddy remnants of some earthen creation. Josie renewed the doomsday chronicle of the beach, which required much running about and flapping of arms. Nick and Jerry joined in, to the delighted screams of the girls. Well, Olivia had to admit that the relative coolness was invigorating.

She helped Maggie carry some of the towels as far as the kitchen door. Donna, visible through the dining room door, was calling timidly, "Dale?" There was no answer. She turned back, hand trailing along the wall, then shrugged as she crossed to them. "Probably on the phone," she said with a quick apologetic smile.

"No danger he won't know we're back," observed Olivia as they sauntered back to the van. The excited squeals continued, punctuated by Nick and Jerry's hilarious versions of the doom-laden Nazgûl squawks.

Maggie pulled another towel from the van and shook

sand from it into a puddle. "Is anyone else hungry?" she asked.

"We just had a huge basket of sandwiches," Olivia objected. She grabbed a towel and hurled it at Jerry as he ran flapping by. He caught it and came over to help.

"Yeah, I'm hungry," he said, fishing a pink plastic swim ring from the van. "Pizza, right, Maggot?"

"With anchovies and extra cheese!" she agreed enthusiastically.

Tina galloped past her mother and there was a crash.

"Oh, dear!" Donna, her hand at her mouth, looked down at the picnic basket she'd just dropped onto the wet driveway.

Nick was already kneeling to pick up the scattered contents. "Nothing broken except the jar of pickles," he said, handing her a packet of paper plates. "But the napkins got wet."

They cleaned up, repacked the basket, and tucked all the toys and towels inside the kitchen door. Then Nick and Jerry took Tina with them to the mall to get pizza. The others wiped their shoes and went inside. It seemed stuffy after the rain-washed air outdoors.

"Dale!" Donna called. There was no response. She put a kettle on the range and pulled out a pitcher and some tea bags, her face troubled.

Olivia frowned. Damn it, Dale was acting like a total asshole today. No story could keep him *that* busy. "I'll go get him," she said.

The office door was closed. She banged on it. "Hey, Dale!"

No answer. She listened, but if he was on the phone the other person was doing a hundred percent of the talking. A paper napkin drifted across the polished floor of the hall in the soft air-conditioned breeze. Olivia stuck it in her pocket and hammered on the door again.

Still nothing.

The knob turned but she couldn't budge the door itself.

She went back to the kitchen. "No answer," she said. "I heard him say he was going to take a nap."

"Not many people could sleep through this homecoming," Maggie observed with a doubtful glance toward the bedroom hall. She was squatting on the vinyl floor, belly bulging, to help Sarah get into her little blue shirt and shorts again. "You tried the door?"

"I couldn't get it open. Will you come try, Donna?"

"Sometimes he bolts it." But Donna looked increasingly uneasy.

Maggie straightened. "Sarah and I will go have a peek in the window while you try the door."

Donna followed Olivia to the den door and pounded on it. "Dale? Open the door!"

They knocked and shouted. Josie, her hazel eyes curious, sidled along the wall behind them to watch.

After a moment Maggie came flying down the hall. "Move over!" she shouted. "Let's get that damn door open!"

She was carrying a crowbar. Olivia pulled Donna aside and watched, astonished, while Maggie rammed the bar between the door and the jamb. She braced a foot against the doorframe and then levered the bar violently back and forth until the door sprang open with a piercing, agonized creak.

Donna gasped.

Dale Colby lay prone, splayed on the plaid carpet, his half-turned face resting in a dark stain.

Olivia's mind refused to consider what that stain might be.